HOME RENOVATIONS

I pried and ripped, ripped and pried, glancing over at Tim, laughing. We weren't really racing, because he kept stopping to fill bags with debris and haul them out.

But . . . opposite me wasn't the storage area. I gazed into a dark space, with the lathe side of another antique wall so close I could almost touch it.

Huh? I kept prying, enlarging the space. I stared, frowning. I dropped the hammer and fumbled to rip off gloves, glasses, and mask. I shone the flashlight from my phone into the space. My breath rushed in.

"Tim!"

He hurried in. "What is it?"

I could only point. He leaned over my shoulder to look.

The light illuminated a skeleton seated on a wooden chair. What was left of her arms stretched behind the chair. *Why?* A cracked leather suitcase sat on the floor between her and the back wall.

"There's a skeleton in here." My voice wobbled. "A really old skeleton."

"I can't believe it."

"You're going to have to." I shook my head slowly, still staring at the bones . . .

Books by Maddie Day

Country Store Mysteries
FLIPPED FOR MURDER
GRILLED FOR MURDER
WHEN THE GRITS HIT THE FAN
BISCUITS AND SLASHED BROWNS
DEATH OVER EASY
STRANGLED EGGS AND HAM
NACHO AVERAGE MURDER
CANDY SLAIN MURDER
NO GRATER CRIME
BATTER OFF DEAD
CHRISTMAS COCOA MURDER
(with Carlene O'Connor and Alex Erickson)
CHRISTMAS SCARF MURDER
(with Carlene O'Connor and Peggy Ehrhart)

Cozy Capers Book Group Mysteries
MURDER ON CAPE COD
MURDER AT THE TAFFY SHOP
MURDER AT THE LOBSTAH SHACK
MURDER IN A CAPE COTTAGE

And writing as Edith Maxwell

A TINE TO LIVE, A TINE TO DIE
'TIL DIRT DO US PART
FARMED AND DANGEROUS
MURDER MOST FOWL
MULCH ADO ABOUT MURDER

Published by Kensington Publishing Corp.

Maddie Day

MURDER IN A CAPE COTTAGE

Kensington Publishing Corp.
www.kensingtonbooks.com

KENSINGTON BOOKS are published by

Kensington Publishing Corp.
119 West 40th Street
New York, NY 10018

All Kensington titles, imprints, and distributed lines are available at special quantity discounts for bulk purchases for sales promotion, premiums, fund-raising, educational, or institutional use.

Special book excerpts or customized printings can also be created to fit specific needs. For details, write or phone the office of the Kensington Sales Manager: Attn.: Sales Department. Kensington Publishing Corp., 119 West 40th Street, New York, NY 10018. Phone: 1-800-221-2647.

The K and Teapot logo is a trademark of Kensington Publishing Corp.

First Printing: October 2022
ISBN: 978-1-4967-3567-6

ISBN: 978-1-4967-3568-3 (ebook)

10 9 8 7 6 5 4 3 2 1

Printed in the United States of America

For Nancy Drew, the gateway detective to so many of us. She would have been a natural with a skeleton in the wall.

Acknowledgments

So many thanks to Professor Sean Tallman, forensic anthropologist at the Boston University School of Medicine. He generously advised me on the eighty-year-old skeleton-bride: how she would look, what would remain, and what wouldn't.

Once again, I called on Amesbury PD's Lieutenant Kevin Donovan for a couple of matters of Massachusetts police procedure. Thank you, sir! I need to thank retired Portland (Maine) Police Department Detective Sergeant Bruce Robert Coffin—a talented crime fiction author in his own right—for reviewing the crime scene details after the skeleton is discovered. You're the best, Bruce.

I stole the façade and front doors of the Westham Historical Society from my town's beautiful old public library building, built in 1900.

My local friend Pamela Fenner, also an author, was the top bidder at the Amesbury Carriage Museum fundraising auction for the right to name a character, and she chose her twin sister, Penelope Johnson. I had fun sliding Detective Sergeant Penelope into the story. Sadly, Penelope passed away before the publication date. I had given Pam an early copy of the book, and she was able to read Penelope's scenes to her, reporting back that her twin was delighted with her fictional self.

Thank you to my wonderful daughter-in-law, Alison Russell, for helping me with the Hanukkah procedure. She also filled me in on the matter of wearing contact lenses as well as eye makeup and which to apply first. And thanks to my talented and lovely hairdresser, Ashley, for inspiring this New Year's Eve wedding with her own a few years ago.

I enjoyed looking up clothing from the late thirties. The rayon dress in the suitcase is inspired by blogger Verity Vintage Studio. I loved coming across a story by Lucas Phillips in the *Boston Globe* about Jews and Cape Verdeans celebrating the Passover seder together—including the national dish, *cachupa*—and being able to mention the event in this book.

Always, blessings to the women of Wicked Authors: Jessie Crockett, Sherry Harris, Julie Hennrikus, Liz Mugavero, and Barbara Ross. Come join us at WickedAuthors.com! Sherry Harris—friend, blogmate, and author—gave this book a close read and straightened me (and Mac) out in all kinds of ways. If I've ignored some of your advice, Sherry, it's on my head.

I've loved featuring a different cozy mystery for the Cozy Capers members to read in each book, and it was fun to include one from Krista Davis's Pen & Ink mysteries in *Murder in a Cape Cottage*. Sorry the group never got to actually reading and discussing *The Coloring Crook*, Krista!

I'm ever grateful to John Scognamiglio, my editor at Kensington Publishing, and the expert team of publicists, artists, production staff, salespeople, and everybody else who makes the process of getting my books into the hands of readers appear nearly seamless. As always, I thank my agent, John Talbot, for making it all possible.

To my sons, John David and Allan, and my daughter-in-law, Alison; to my sisters, Janet and Barbara; and to Hugh: I'm deeply grateful for your support. Not all writers are as lucky as I am.

And I'm always thankful for my enthusiastic readers and fans. You guys rock.

CHAPTER 1

Starting a home renovation project five days before our wedding was possibly a risky move. I had my fingers crossed nothing would go wrong.

Outfitted with work gloves, construction mask, and safety glasses over my contact lenses, I lifted my sledgehammer as my soon-to-be-husband, Tim Brunelle, hefted his own larger one. He'd wanted to add a bathroom to the bedroom downstairs in his hundred-year-old Cape-style cottage. A bedroom suite did sound kind of nice. And this, the day after Christmas, was the first chance we'd both had to begin the demolition. On Christmas Eve afternoon, I'd closed Mac's Bikes, my Westham, Massachusetts shop, for three weeks. Tim had done the same with his bakery, the best one on Cape Cod. Sure, I had a lot to finish up for our Saturday night New Year's Eve wedding. But I could fit in a morning of demo with everything else on my list. Maybe.

"Ready, Mackenzie Almeida?" Tim asked, his big baby blues twinkling behind his safety glasses.

I nodded. We whacked opposite sides of the wall in unison. And again. We'd decided to sacrifice one of the two closets in the room for the bathroom. It backed up onto a utility room at the rear of the house. On the other side of the closet wall were awkwardly situated deep shelves that Tim had used only for storage. Combining the closet and the shelf area would yield enough space for a compact full bath, and we could replace the storage with a tall cabinet in the utility room. The other bathroom in the house already had a tub, so a shower stall would suffice for this one. It would have been nice to get the work finished before the wedding, but that wasn't going to happen. We were both busy people with bustling successful businesses. We did what we could.

We whacked away, the plaster crumbling and collapsing. It was fun to work together and felt like it was helping with my pre-wedding nerves. Our work revealed a framework of the thin, inch-wide lathe. Plaster had been spread over the lathe when automobiles still shared the roads with horses. When only risk takers flew in airplanes. When cell phones were a science-fiction fantasy.

"Why don't you use a regular hammer and start prying those off while I clean up the debris?" Tim handed me a hammer.

"Sure." This was only the second time I'd done something like this. When I'd moved back to my hometown and bought the building my bike shop was in, I'd helped demolish one wall to expand the back. It was a bit nerve-racking to destroy something well built, except I knew a new space would be the result, and it would end up orderly and clean. That was how I liked my life, when I was honest with myself.

"There's a pry bar here if you'd rather use that." Tim pulled down his mask and leaned in for a light kiss.

"Ooh, plaster. My favorite flavor." I smiled at him.

The nails squealed as I wedged the claw under them and pried. It was almost as satisfying to rip the boards off as it was to smash the plastered walls. I pried and ripped. I started off kneeling and worked my way up. At six-foot-one, Tim could easily finish off the top of the wall.

He came back from hauling a bag of plaster outside and picked up the pry bar. "Race you? I'll take down this side and you do that one."

"You're on. Loser buys lunch at the Rusty Anchor."

He gave me two work-gloved thumbs-up, with eyes smiling above his mask.

I had a head start on him. I pried and ripped, ripped and pried, glancing over at Tim, laughing. We weren't really racing, because he kept stopping to fill bags with debris and haul them out. I finally got to more or less my eye level. I'm five seven, so at about five and a half feet up.

But . . . opposite me wasn't the storage area. I gazed into a dark space, with the lathe side of another antique wall so close I could almost touch it.

Huh? I kept prying, enlarging the space. I stared, frowning. I dropped the hammer and fumbled to rip off gloves, glasses, and mask. I shined the flashlight from my phone into the space. My breath rushed in.

"Tim!"

He hurried in. "What is it?"

I could only point. He leaned over my shoulder to look.

The light illuminated a skeleton seated on a wooden chair. What was left of her arms stretched behind the chair. *Why?* A cracked leather suitcase sat on the floor between her and the back wall.

"There's a skeleton in here." My voice wobbled. "A really old skeleton."

"I can't believe it."

"You're going to have to." I shook my head slowly, still staring at the bones.

"Is she wearing a wedding dress?" he asked, his voice muffled by his mask.

I slid off my mask. "She is."

CHAPTER 2

I stared at Tim. At the skeleton. Back at Tim, who took off his own mask and frowned.

"How could I have missed that space?" He extended his arm and touched the opposite wall without leaning in. "I thought I'd measured it all out. I clearly missed two and a half feet by five."

"We have to report what we've found." But I didn't jab 911. I gazed at the remains, parts of which had been remarkably well preserved in a gruesome kind of way. Bits of skin remained, now brown and leathery. Her skull lolled back against the tall-backed chair. The jaw yawned open with upper teeth missing. The eye sockets were empty, dark holes. A gold chain encircled her neck, with a heart-shaped locket hanging against her sternum. A wide ribbon anchored a short lace veil to dark hair.

Her dress looked like it had been made of a fine white linen. It was now stained, with portions in shreds, but the long sleeves showed delicate pintuck pleats at the shoulders. The skirt of the dress reached nearly to the floor. She wore similarly stained light-colored low heels with an ankle strap, her forlorn toe bones visible in the peep-toe cutout. I peered at her lap, where several teeth lay, and shuddered.

I shifted my position a little, shining the light along her arm bones, and gasped at the sight of a metal chain bolted into the wall.

"Tim," I whispered. "I think she's handcuffed to the wall."

"Really?"

"I think so. See how her hands are behind her? The poor thing. Somebody seriously didn't want her to get married." My heart broke for her, but it was also starting to feel like a horror movie. And me with my own wedding only days away.

"Or go on her honeymoon." He focused on the suitcase. "Maybe she was planning to elope?"

"Could be. But then why is she wearing her wedding dress?" I stared at him. "Nobody elopes in their wedding finery."

"I'm clueless about that, obviously." Tim cocked his head, regarding me. "The authorities are going to need the whole wall open. Let's finish removing it and then we'll call."

"I don't think we should. We could contaminate the area with our DNA." I'd learned a few things during the previous murder investigations in Westham, and that was one. "This might be a big enough opening for them to get at her."

"I hadn't thought of that. I'm sure you're right.

No more working, then. Why don't you call? I'll keep hauling out the rubble."

"Hang on. I want to take a few pictures first." I held my phone up to the opening. I itched to see what was in the valise but restrained myself. It'd be my luck the leather would disintegrate in my hands and, anyway, I had no business mucking around in there. I made sure the flash was on and shot a couple of pictures without touching the bride or her traveling case, which I now saw was marked with the initials *DLR.*

I zoomed in behind her. Sure enough, each wrist had a metal band clamped around it, bands attached to a thick, short chain, which in turn was linked to a chain bolted into the wall. I checked the bones of her left hand. Neither a wedding band nor an engagement solitaire adorned the second-from-last digit, but a delicate gold bracelet encircled the wrist next to the metal that had imprisoned her. That, and the wall her jailer had constructed after she was in there, was called homicide.

I shook my head. What a terrible way to die. Alone, helpless, with no water and no comfort. My eyes welled up. I swiped at them. This was murder, plain and simple, and we needed to inform the authorities. Tim wrapped his arm around my shoulders, and I leaned into his warmth.

I'd somehow gotten myself involved in solving a few murders over the last year, with the help of the cozy mystery book group I was part of. My intrinsic need for order and having things tidy—which certain people in my life called an obsession and a compulsion—made me want to sort out the facts of this ancient murder, too, horrific as it was. A young bride had been chained to die in here. Alone, without her love, whoever he was—unless he had killed her himself, which was even more horrible to contemplate.

"I'm okay," I said to my own love. "It's just . . . unbelievable, isn't it? And so terribly sad."

He gave a slow nod. "Now call."

"Yeah." It was hardly an emergency, so I tapped the Westham Police Department's regular number, which I happened to already have in my contacts list. They used a regional dispatch for 911, but the office was answered by whichever officer got the short straw.

"Westham Police, Officer Kimuri speaking."

"Hi, Nikki." I'd met her in the fall after a body had been deposited in the Lobstah Shack's walk-in. "This is Mac Almeida. I need to report a human skeleton."

She went quiet for a moment. I could picture her pressing her eyes shut, trying to process my words.

I jumped into the auditory gap. "Tim Brunelle and I are doing demolition inside his—well, our—cottage on Blacksmith Shop Road. We opened up a wall and found a skeleton."

"All right. Please keep away from the scene. You and Mr. Brunelle. Have you disturbed the remains?"

"No. The thing is, the skeleton is chained to the wall."

Nikki's gasp was unmistakable.

"So it has to have been a homicide." My voice no longer wobbled.

Nikki cleared her throat. "I'll get a team over ASAP."

"Great."

"And, Mac?"

"Yeah?"

"How do you do it?"

I waited, pretty sure she meant how I kept encountering murder victims.

"Never mind," she said. "Leave the room, close the door. Both of you. That's all I ask."

"Yes, ma'am." I disconnected and turned to Tim. Except he was gone with the latest bag of plaster and lathe. Now that I thought about it, there might be evidence on the lathe. The bags hadn't gone anywhere except outside. I would alert the crime scene team to them.

I held out my left hand and gazed at my lovely, simple gold engagement ring, which featured a simple Victorian knot with a small diamond in the middle, then looked back into the formerly hidden compartment. "We'll figure this out, Bridey," I whispered to the bones. "I'll get you justice. I promise."

CHAPTER 3

Despite my wanting to linger in there, Tim and I behaved ourselves and shut the door to the room, as Nikki had ordered.

"You know what finding this skeleton means, don't you?" I asked him.

"We'll have to put the project on hold."

"Yeah. But if they're prompt with their crime scene team, maybe they'll be done with it today."

"Somehow that seems optimistic."

Of course it was, but a girl could dream. "Tim, what do you know about the history of this house?"

"I know it was built in 1925 by the Swift family. That's what the original deed says. By the time I bought the place five years ago, it had passed through several families. I purchased the cottage after the matriarch of the most recent family died, and none of her children wanted it. That family had lived here since 1971."

"Swift. I feel like I know that name." I'd grown up here in Westham, but I'd been essentially away since I'd left to attend Harvard College at eighteen until I'd returned to open my bike shop almost two years ago. An absence of seventeen years could do a number on memories of people I hadn't known well to begin with.

The doorbell rang. "I'll let them in." At the front door, I greeted Nikki and Officer August Jenkins, who did bicycle patrol during the warmer months. I peered behind them but didn't see my favorite state police detective, Lincoln Haskins.

I greeted them. "No Lincoln?"

"Hey, Mac," Nikki said. "No, he's out of town. So you and Mr. Brunelle happened across a skeleton in a closet."

"I'm afraid so."

"And you left everything alone?"

"After we spoke with you, we did, of course." They didn't need to know about the pictures I'd snapped or about the itchy fingers I'd managed to control. "But before that, we had opened half the wall. That's when I saw her."

"Her?" She squinted up at me. "How can you tell it's a female?"

"The wedding dress is kind of a giveaway."

August whistled.

"And what's left of the dress looks pretty old-fashioned." I stepped back from the open door. "Come on in. You can see for yourselves." They followed me down the hall.

Tim held up a hand in greeting from the kitchen as we passed. Nikki only nodded at him. He and August exchanged a dude-type fist and elbow bump. I opened the door to the bedroom and pointed at the gaping hole inside the closet. August pulled a flashlight off his duty belt, picking his way through the rubble still remaining on the floor.

He shone the light in and whistled again. "That's an old one, all right." He stepped back.

Nikki took the light. She spent a long moment shining it around the space. She examined the walls. It looked from where I stood that she made a careful study of the suitcase, too.

"The luggage has the initials *DLR* on it," Nikki murmured as she turned.

I hadn't thought of it earlier, but if those were the bride's initials, she wasn't a Swift, even though she'd been imprisoned within their cottage walls.

Tim appeared in the doorway to the room. "Should we assume we have to cease demolition for a while?" he asked her.

"Yes. I'll get the Cape & Islands SPDU crime scene team out here, and some kind of forensic historian." She frowned as she smoothed back a wisp of her black hair into the bun she wore at the nape of her neck.

"What's SPDU?" Tim asked.

"State Police Detective Unit," Nikki said. "I have to admit, this is a first for me."

"That's probably a good thing," I said. "I'd hate to think you found a lot of skeletons in walls around here."

She nodded. "Jenkins, we'll need crime scene tape up."

"Not on the whole house, I hope." I grabbed Tim's hand.

"We're both living here," Tim said in his deep, soft voice.

"And we're getting married on Saturday," I added.

Nikki waited a beat too long, but finally said, "Only this room should be fine. Show me the back wall, will you? We should block that off, too."

I followed Tim and her around through the kitchen to the utility room near the back door. A stacked washer and dryer sat next to a deep sink on the outer wall. Across from them were a deep set of now-empty old shelves where he'd kept odds and ends of extra laundry soap, a box of extension cords, a small toolbox, a few vases, and other miscellany. That was the area we'd decided to sacrifice to the new bathroom on the other side of the wall.

"I guess I never made careful measurements before we started," Tim said.

"You don't have an architect?" Nikki asked.

"No. I've done other renovation projects elsewhere, and I have good design software. Never had a problem before."

I'd seen his plans. They looked professional to my eyes and had been adequate to pull a building permit for the project. I was learning so much, including that one uses the verb "pull" for applying to the building department for permission to knock out walls and add plumbing and electricity. I had many skills, including high-end bicycle repair and maintenance. Home renovation had not been among them until now.

"You haven't broken through here yet." Nikki waved a hand at the wall.

"Clearly not."

"I guess we don't have to tape this off, then." She set her hands on her slim, uniformed hips. "You're both to stay out of the other room, though. Understand?" She addressed the two of us, but her gaze was firmly on me.

"Yes, ma'am." I restrained myself from saluting.

"Good. Someone will be around all day to let in the team?"

Tim and I exchanged a glance. "Sure," he said.

Since we'd both closed our businesses in part to be here doing demolition, one of us could easily be here.

"Thanks." She headed for the kitchen. "I'll be in touch."

Nikki knew I'd been involved in three murder investigations in the last year. The department's chief, who happened to be my high school nemesis, remained reluctant to accept that I had any contribution to offer. It was too bad Lincoln wouldn't be the lead on this one. He and I had come to a tentative agreement. Then again, with an old case like this one, maybe he wouldn't have worked on it, anyway.

CHAPTER 4

After Nikki and August left, I changed out of my work clothes upstairs in one of the two dormered bedrooms we were using until the downstairs was ready to move into. I wanted to wait around until the crime scene team came, but I also needed to walk downtown and check on wedding flowers at the florist. I pulled on skinny jeans and a green turtleneck sweater and ran a hand through my inch-long curls, which was basically the only styling they ever needed—or got.

I stepped into the other bedroom and unzipped the tall garment bag holding my wedding dress. My friend Gin, who was serving as my attendant and lead bride team member, had insisted I abide by the rule that Tim didn't get to see the dress until I was in it for the ceremony. The tradition seemed silly to me, but I'd agreed, and he'd promised not to peek into the bag.

With the high metabolism I'd inherited from my tiny dynamo of a grandmother, I still sported a slender figure at thirty-seven. When Gin and my mom and I had started looking for wedding dresses this fall, I'd been worried. I so wasn't the lace-and-ruffles type, and I also didn't want some strapless extravaganza. By some miracle we'd happened across a simple, body-hugging satin dress cut on the bias, and we'd found it right here in Westham at Cape Bridal, a new shop on the outskirts of town. The cream-colored dress—also comfortable, as it turned out—had a flattering scoop neck, pintucked short sleeves, and a short train that could be buttoned up and out of the way for dancing. It hadn't broken the bank, either. I still couldn't believe my luck.

I'd loved the vintage look of it, and my team had, too. The woman at the shop had eyed my short hair and produced a pretty hairpiece of the same satin, with pintucks like those on the sleeves. The hairpiece was shaped like a stretched-out oval, and I could pin it to the top of my head for a little bit of simple decoration.

Mom and Gin had convinced me to buy a pair of low heels to wear with the dress. Without their knowing, I'd also ordered some glittery purple Keds to change into. Comfort meant a lot to me.

But what about the poor, abandoned bride in the secret room? She'd had no luck at all. Had her groom known what had happened to her? Was her imprisonment the result of an angry father or a stern, disapproving mother? A jealous competitor

for the hand of the young beau? Also, had she struggled and tried to resist her fatal imprisonment? Or
did the villain press a cloth soaked in ether to her
face before he or she locked the young woman's
hands to the wall? Did she come to as the room was
being boarded up? Did anyone hear her cries for
help?

I had so many questions. Right now, not one had
an answer.

When I heard the doorbell, I zipped up the bag
and ran down the stairs. Tim showed three people in
police garb into the living room. Two carried black
equipment cases and another held a professional-
looking camera.

Tim introduced himself and me. The woman introduced the men. The tall one was Osborne and the
skinny older one with the camera was Fleming. They
both had Cape & Islands SPDU on their uniforms.

"And I'm Penelope Johnson, detective sergeant
with the Westham PD." She smiled and extended
her hand. Wearing a Westham PD jacket, she was
taller than me by a couple of inches and looked fit
in her uniform while still packing some padding on
her hips.

She must be new. I hadn't run into her before. I
brought up my Namaste hands, pressing my palms
together at my sternum. I'd gotten out of the habit of
shaking hands when the pandemic had ripped through
the world, and I wasn't eager to resume pressing the
flesh with people I didn't know.

"Nice to meet you, Penelope, gentlemen."

With a nod, the detective also briefly brought her
palms together in front of her chest.

"Penelope is an unusual name these days, Detective," I said.

"It is. I'm the only one I know. It was my grandma's name, and my mom always loved it."

"I hear you have a homicide victim in here." Osborne pointed to the yellow tape blocking the bedroom.

"Yes," I said. "A very old one."

"It's a skeleton, actually," Tim added after he'd shaken hands with all three of them.

Osborne set down his case. "Bones?"

"They didn't tell you?" Tim asked.

"Messages must have gotten crossed," he said. "Well, it doesn't matter. A body's a body."

Could they lift fingerprints or DNA from old, cracked leather? From the chains or the chair? Bridey herself, as I'd started thinking of her, had barely any skin left to take prints from, and what she had resembled the suitcase.

"What made you think this is a crime scene?" Penelope asked.

Tim bobbed his head at me, and I repeated a version of what I'd told Nikki. "It's a skeleton in a chair. She's wearing a white dress, or what's left of it, and her hands are chained to the wall. Seems like she was walled in the room alive and left to die."

Osborne whistled. Penelope blinked. Fleming, who now held a camera, swallowed.

I shook my head. How could Nikki not have communicated this? Messages crossed, definitely.

"I thought a forensic historical person was supposed to be here, too," I said.

"The kid will be along soon," Penelope said.

What the heck did "the kid" mean?

"The kid?" Tim asked what I'd been thinking.

"It's fine," she said. "She's smart. Our usual forensics guy is on vacation, like half the rest of the department. You do know it's the week between Christmas and New Year's, and Hanukkah starts tomorrow."

Duh. I nodded without speaking.

"Anyway," she went on. "Win is an intern both with us and the Westham Historical Society. She's a criminal justice major at U Mass Dartmouth. My statey buds here have a forensic anthropologist on call, too."

"That's fine," I said. *Whatever.*

"Shall we?" Penelope said to her team. She handed them each a pair of paper booties and slipped on her own.

She stepped forward to detach the tape at one side. They trooped into the room, with Tim following. I peered after them but stayed where I was.

"She's at the back of that closet," Tim said. "I hope you have lights."

"Thanks, we're good," Penelope said. "Please stay out of the room, both of you."

"Yes, ma'am." Tim joined me in the living room but didn't shut the bedroom door.

"Does it seem strange they've called an intern to do the history part?" I asked him, keeping my voice down.

"It sure does. But we don't know this person's expertise."

"No. Or when she's going to show up." I pulled my phone out of my back pocket.

The time was now after ten thirty. Voices of the

team filtered out from the closet. Tim lowered himself into an armchair that faced the bedroom. I was torn. I wanted to stick around to see and hear what they discovered. I was eager—or something—to meet this Win person. But I also had a day suddenly free of demolition obligations, and my wedding to-do list was burning a hole in my phone, as it were.

"I think I'll pop by for a chat with Forrest, if you don't mind staying here," I said. "I'm nervous about the flowers."

Tim reached for my hand and pulled me onto his lap. This being one of my favorite seats in the whole world, I did not resist.

"I thought we wanted to have a small, simple wedding." He laid his hand on my cheek. "What happened to that?"

I tossed my gaze at the ceiling. "Family happened, I guess. I don't know, darling. It's still going to be simple but a little more fraught than I'd hoped." I pointed at his chest. "Your family is coming, all from out of town." Including his troubled sister from Seattle and her kids, but we didn't need to go there right now. "My relatives will be here. Our local friends and coworkers. My local family."

"And we need food and music and pretty stuff. I get that."

"Yeah." I kissed him and stood. "And I do want it all to be nice."

"As do I. You go check on the flowers, then." He tilted his head, wearing one of those adoring looks that made me want to do nothing more than stay on his lap and make out as if we were teenagers.

He went on. "I think I'll meditate right here until

someone needs me." He pulled his feet up to sit cross-legged, set his hands on his knees, and closed his eyes.

"See you in a bit," I whispered to my favorite Buddha. I, the high-strung one of the couple, could no more meditate while a crime scene team was at work yards away than jump out of a plane without a parachute.

CHAPTER 5

At Beach Plum Florist, I waited while Forrest Ruhlen helped another customer. The humid fragrant air of the shop was a welcome balm after the icy winter wind blowing outside. I wasn't sure what all the scents were besides roses and maybe gardenias. I only knew it smelled tropical—and divine.

"Hey, Forrest," I said after he was free. "I want to check that you're all set for Saturday."

"I believe we are." He pulled a book out from below the counter and flipped through to the page where he'd written my order last month. He tapped the page with a pen and looked up at me with hazel eyes from under white ski-jump eyebrows that matched his full head of hair. "You want mostly purple, with yellow accents, correct?"

"That's right." I'd thought red and white would be nice for New Year's Eve until Gin pointed out that it would look like leftover Christmas. I shrugged out of my puffy jacket. "Any shade of purple is fine."

"Five boutonnieres, four wrist corsages, one flower girl wristlet, one maid of honor bouquet, and your bouquet. Plus table flowers, etcetera, etcetera."

I counted frantically as he reeled off the numbers. How many men needed a flower in their buttonhole? Tim; his dad; and my father—Pa—of course; plus my brother, Derrick; Tim's best man, Eli; and . . . were we leaving someone out? No. Then wrist corsages for Abo Reba, Mom, Tim's mom, Greta, and his sister, Jamie. Gin had her own bouquet, and Derrick's five-year-old daughter, Cokey, would have a floral bracelet and her basket. I hoped Jamie's older daughter, age six, wouldn't feel left out, but it had seemed too complicated to loop her in on flower girl plans from Seattle, find her a dress to match Cokey's, and so on.

We'd cleared it with Derrick and Jamie that they were both fine not being attendants. They each needed to be free to take care of their little ones, especially Jamie, with a young toddler in tow. Eli, a researcher at the Woods Hole Oceanic Institute, and Gin were already a couple, which made for a nice symmetry. Eli had moved in with Gin last month, in fact.

"I think that's the right count," I said. "Gin Malloy ordered all the table flowers, didn't she?" Counting the number of tables in the reception hall at the Westham Hotel had sent me over the top, and Gin had assured me she'd handle it. Mom and Reba were taking care of the place cards and guest book, and the caterer had all the food and drink under control, plus what to serve it on, right down to the table-cloths. Eli and Tim had assured me the music was

taken care of, too. We had a day-of wedding orga-
nizer lined up so none of us had to do any work during the actual event.

"Yes." Forrest glanced up. "Having a few bride jitters, are we?"

I blew out a breath. "I guess." I was a detail-
oriented person, and an event like this was completely
nerve-racking. A skeleton at home didn't help. Neither did a delay in our construction project.

"You'll be fine, Mac." He smiled, revealing a gap
behind his canine tooth on the left side. "It'll be a
lovely evening. Just try to relax and enjoy it."

"You must get this a lot. Crazy, nervous brides dou-
ble- and triple-checking."

"From time to time, yes. I'd rather have the brides
breathing down my neck than their mothers, I can
tell you."

"I bet. I assume my mom hasn't been in?" She was
totally not cut from mother-of-the-bridezilla cloth.

"She hasn't. That wouldn't be something Astra
would do." He glanced at an old black-and-white
photograph in an antique frame sitting on a shelf on
the wall. The picture showed a beautiful young
woman looking solemnly into the camera lens. "My
aunt was getting ready to be married long ago. She
never got the chance. That's why I'm always happy to
do flowers for weddings, because she didn't get to
have one."

I opened my mouth to ask why not when the store
phone emitted a ringtone from Beethoven's sixth
symphony. The "Pastoral" was my favorite of
Beethoven's works. A woman hurried in the front
door. A couple strolled in after her.

"I'll touch base on Friday." I gave him a little wave. That was two brides who hadn't had the chance to be married. I hoped "third time's the charm" would apply in my case.

He nodded. I squeezed past the newcomers and out the door, where I nearly collided with a tall man in a black overcoat peering in the shop's window.

"They do good work," I said.

He started, as if he hadn't seen me, then gave me a quick glance. "Thank you." His eyes, a shade of blue that was almost violet, had a strange look to them. His clothes looked well-made, but his graying hair needed a trim and was greasy.

I nodded and moved on, the "Pastoral" still playing in my mind. I had other errands I could do while I was out. I needed to pick up the marriage license at Town Hall. And it wouldn't hurt to stop by the Unitarian Universalist parsonage, otherwise known as my parents' home and the place where I grew up. Mom and Pa were keeping Belle, my African gray parrot, during the renovations to Tim's house. I knew Belle missed me. It was mutual.

But that poor, abandoned bride was calling me back home. Maybe the forensics intern had arrived. Maybe the crime scene team had discovered a clue to the skeleton's killer. Errands could wait.

CHAPTER 6

I was wicked hungry by the time I got home at noon. My morning granola and banana were a long-ago memory, at least according to my stomach. The state police van was still parked out front, so the crime scene team members were probably still in the house. Or not. As I drew closer, I spied Osborne and Fleming sitting in the front seats, both absorbed in their phones.

Halfway up the walk to the front door, I turned at the whir of a bicycle behind me. A young woman braked a Cannondale to a stop in the driveway, a black bag slung across her chest. She climbed off and leaned the cycle against the fence before unclipping her helmet. I didn't think I'd ever seen her before.

"Can I help you?" I asked.

She strode toward me with an easy gait, black leggings tucked into clunky black boots, her purple-streaked hair shaved up one side and falling to her chin on the other. A tiny silver ring in one nostril flashed in the sunlight. "Mackenzie Almeida?"

"That's me. I go by Mac."

"I'm Winslow Swift, Mac. Otherwise known as Win." A little shorter than me, she held out a hand bedecked with three silver rings.

"Nice to meet you." I used my Namaste hands again. I should feel solidarity. Here was another woman with a last name for a first name. Like me. But *Swift?* If she was related to the people who had built Tim's house, that would be too crazy of a coincidence. Except now wasn't the time to ask.

"Same here. The team called me." She dropped her hand and gestured with her chin toward the cottage. "You have remains and an artifact, I understand?"

"We do, and you're the intern."

"Yep." She bounced on her heels, holding the hefty-looking cross bag against her chest so it didn't bounce, too.

"Follow me, Win." I led her inside.

Tim no longer sat in the chair. I thought I heard noises from the kitchen, to which my stomach growled in response. Detective Johnson emerged from the bedroom.

"This is Win Swift," I began. "The intern."

"Penelope and I know each other," Win said.

"We do," Penelope said.

"Good. How's it going in there?" I asked.

"We're done for now, but we wanted to wait until Win arrived so she would get the whole picture. I assure you, Mac, we'll take the remains away before the end of the day."

"Where, um, do you take them?" I asked.

"Namath from the medical examiner's office is inside. I told you they have a forensic anthropologist on call, a professor at Boston University."

"Is it Professor Tallman?" Win removed her bag and pulled out a pair of latex gloves that matched her hair perfectly.

"You know him?" Penelope asked.

"Yes," Win said. "Sean's a great guy."

Penelope handed her a pair of paper booties, which Win slipped on.

Without asking permission, I followed them and stood in the doorway to the bedroom. I sniffed the scent of coconut, maybe from Win's shampoo. A burly man in latex gloves and a pullover sweater stood near the closet, no doubt Namath, the medical examiner. He nodded to me.

Penelope glanced behind her. "No farther, Ms. Almeida."

"Yes, ma'am."

"Mr. Namath, this is Mac Almeida. She called in the remains."

He nodded again.

"Good to meet you, sir." I'd never run into a medical examiner before.

When Win reached the hacked-out opening at the back of the closet, she sucked in a breath.

"Wow."

Penelope ticked off everything the team had sampled and checked. "We can easily extract the bolt holding the chains to the wall."

"Don't cut it, though," Win said.

"We won't. If it doesn't pull or turn, we'll chisel

into the wood." Penelope faced me. "That's okay, right, Mac?"

"Whatever you need to do," I said.

"I want to get a look at that bag," Win said.

You and me both, honey. But I kept my mouth shut.

"You have pictures of everything in situ, I assume?" Win asked Penelope.

"We do. Go ahead and have at it. Later we'll seal the space and fume it with cyanoacrylate to develop latent fingerprints. In a closed, finite room like this, there's no reason prints won't still be there, even after decades. But the bones and the artifact should be out before we do that."

Win eased past me and retrieved a sheet of metal from her bag. She edged back into the space, avoiding Bridey's knees, and eased the metal under the suitcase, lifting it all carefully up and over the skeleton.

"Do you want to put that on a table?" I asked from the doorway.

She gazed at me. "Sure."

"We have a coffee table through there." I led her to the front room. Penelope followed.

Win set her precious load on its metal base on a magazine, then turned to Penelope. "I came on my bike. Can you transport this to the Westham Historical Society when you leave? I can meet you there."

"We'll transport it," Penelope said. "It's evidence, and we need to check it in first. You work for us, remember, Ms. Swift." Her voice held a hint of chiding.

"You're not going to open it here?" I tried to keep the plaintive note from my voice but didn't quite succeed.

"Not at all," Win said. "It needs to be protected."

I swore, but silently. "I'd love to know what you find when you open it. I mean, since it was found in our house and all." At least the historical society building wasn't far.

"Not a problem," Win said. "You can stop by later today if you want, maybe around three."

"Perhaps," Penelope said. "We'll see."

Win spoke to Penelope. "I'd like to take a closer look at the remains, but you know I'm an artifact person, right? I don't have the expertise to assess bones."

"I know," Penelope said. "Go ahead in and look at the remains. But don't touch. Osborne and I will bag her up and take her away when you're done."

Win turned away, but not before I spied her eye roll.

Namath came out of the room.

"Did you get what you needed?" Penelope asked him.

"I did. You have a good day, now."

I watched a few minutes later as Penelope and Osborne carefully transported a light-looking body bag through the house to the vehicle out front. What a sad thing, that a murdered bride should be reduced to a skeleton in a zipped-up black bag.

Win followed them carrying the suitcase, now enveloped in a big paper bag, out to the SUV while Fleming came for the chair and the chains. Penelope came back in, closed the door to the bedroom, and fastened the crime scene tape across it again.

"This is still off-limits for the time being, you understand," she said, stripping off her gloves.

"Any idea how long it will be before we can re-sume work?" I wanted to keep the bathroom project moving forward as soon as we could. I knew Tim hoped for the same.

"No, ma'am." She smiled as if to soften her words. "That would be above my pay grade. Here's my card." She handed me an official WPD card. "Do contact me if you find any artifacts elsewhere in the house."

"We will." Heaven help us if we did. We might have to move out entirely.

She gave me a mock salute before heading out.

Tim appeared in the doorway from the kitchen. "Lunch?"

CHAPTER 7

"Yes, Belle's a very good girl." I stroked my parrot's head at two that afternoon. After a relaxed lunch with Tim, I'd stopped by my parents' place to say hello to Belle and found my grandma, Reba Almeida, hanging out with the bird. My parents were keeping Belle for the duration of the construction project. I didn't want to risk her inhaling plaster dust or any kind of fumes.

The parsonage was fully decorated for Christmas, with garlands and colored lights strung above the kitchen cabinets and the still-fresh scent of the tree wafting in from the living room. Tim and I hadn't bothered decorating at home because of the wedding and the demolition. And we knew we'd be spending the holiday here, where my mom always went all out on seasonal décor.

I sat across the kitchen table from Reba, Belle

perched on my shoulder, as my *abo* peered and poked a gnarled finger at her extra-large cell phone.

"Abo Ree, what are you doing?" I asked, using the Kriolu word for "grandmother," even though it had been her husband, my father's father, who'd immigrated from the Cape Verdean islands, not Reba herself. Her family was a hundred percent Boston, part of the Black educated class.

"Abo Ree, Abo Ree." Belle cocked her head. "Belle wants a treat. Belle's a good girl. Treats, Mac?"

"You just had some grapes, Belle," I said. "You're fine."

Belle hopped down to the floor and waddled into the next room.

Abo Reba glanced up. "You found a skeleton in a closet at Tim's?"

Why was I not surprised that she already knew? Nothing slipped past this old lady.

"Yes, we did. It was quite the shock to open up the back wall of a closet and find a set of bones."

"Why, I should think so, honey. How are your nerves?" She tucked a stray white curl back into her signature rainbow-streaked Rasta beret. "I know you don't like things out of order."

No kidding. "I'm okay. More curious than anything, really."

"My friend says they were old bones. What did you see?"

"It was sad. The skeleton wore shreds of a wedding dress. She sat on a chair, and her hands were chained to the wall behind. Completely awful."

"A wedding dress?" Reba stared at me.

"Yes, the poor thing."

"How old was she? I mean her bones, of course."

"I don't know."

"What sort of style was the dress?" my grandma pressed. "Could you tell what kind of fabric it was made from? That can tell you a great deal."

"I never thought of that. Let's see." As an accomplished seamstress, of course she would ask. I thought back to our discovery. "It wasn't a high-necked dress, but it had long sleeves, with pintucks at the shoulders. And maybe not made out of cotton. It might have been linen."

"Long?" She cocked her head. "Floor-length?"

"Yes." I pulled out my own phone. "I took pictures." I found the pictures and showed her.

"Looks like linen. If I had to guess, I'd say the style of that dress was from the late thirties or forties."

I blinked, listening. In the next room, Belle was muttering, "No. No. No."

"Uh-oh. That means Belle is doing something she knows she shouldn't." I hurried in to find my bird trying to eat the popcorn strings on the Christmas tree. She pulled at the string so hard the tree wobbled. I picked her up and brought her back to the kitchen, where I could keep an eye on her. I shut the door between the rooms to be sure.

"Was somebody being a bad parrot?" Reba asked.

"She knows the word 'no,' and she can obviously say it. If I tell her 'no' when she's doing something she shouldn't, she'll stop. But she'll never stop doing it in the future even though she tells herself not to while she's in the act. Right, birdbrain?" I petted her head.

"No. No. No," Belle said. "Birdbrain. Birdbrain."

"*Birdbrain* is an entirely accurate name for her." My grandma laughed as she rose and headed to the liquor cupboard. "I think we need a drop of sherry to talk about your ancient bride." She stared up at the cabinet way over her head, which topped out at just under five feet. "Instead of me hauling over the stool, you're going to have to do the honors, Mackenzie."

"I'm happy to."

Belle waddled up to Abo Reba. "Do the honors, Mackenzie. Do the honors, Abo Ree. Belle wants a snack. Snacks, Mac?"

On my way to the ever-present bottle of sherry, I grabbed a few chunks of frozen carrots from the bag I'd stashed in the freezer and set the bowl on the floor for the bird. Back at the table, Reba and I clinked glasses.

"Where's Tucker, by the way?" I asked. My parents, Astra and Joseph, had gotten the puppy last summer, for themselves, but also for my niece, Cokey.

"Your father has taken him on his pastoral visits. The shut-ins apparently love that pooch." She sipped her drink. "You know, I've only lived in Westham for twenty years, since I retired, and your father convinced me to give up my house in Roxbury. But I know a lot. And I've heard of a planned wedding gone terribly wrong quite some years ago." She did know a lot, and she also knew everyone in town, it seemed.

I swallowed a sip. "You have?" Was she talking about Forrest's aunt?

"You don't think it's bad luck to talk about such a thing on a week like this one?"

I gave that one second of thought. "No. I don't believe in that kind of luck, or non-luck."

"And you are right. You and that man of yours are

going to have a lovely ceremony. I'm blessed to be alive for it."

I patted the thin, soft skin of her hand. "We're the ones who are blessed, Abo Ree."

"Did your mother tell you about my dress?" Her faded, chestnut-colored eyes sparkled.

"No. Did you find one?"

"Of course. I'm sure Astra thought I'd show up in my pink tracksuit." She grinned.

"You do wear it, or one of them, every day," I pointed out.

"Sure, but that's because it's comfy. But for the ceremony, I found the prettiest violet number, with lace on top and a swirly skirt. Plus sequined sneakers to match!"

"I found glittery purple Keds, too." I laughed. "Not for the wedding itself, but for after. We'll be twinsies in footwear on the dance floor."

"I like that idea." She drained half her glass and set it on the table. "Well, then. Let's get back to your skeleton. My friend at aqua aerobics told me about her cousin's sister-in-law's grandmother."

I sat back. This was going to be a long tale. My grandmother was nothing if not the queen of story-tellers.

"Here's what happened." She folded her hands on the table. "A young lady from a nice family fell in love with an Azorean fisherman."

I was surprised she hadn't begun with, "Once upon a time . . ." "And her 'nice' family wasn't happy about it." My finger quotes said what I thought about the adjective.

"They were not."

"What were their names, the couple?"

"Let me think. He was Vinnie somebody?" She frowned. "No, that wasn't it. I think Carvallo was the last name. Or maybe Cabral. One of the two." She tapped the table. "Vinnie? Manny? Johnny? I can't remember."

Belle perked up from where she'd been dozing on the floor. "Vinnie? Manny? Johnny? Vinnie?"

"Go back to sleep, Belle. We don't know his name." To my grandmother, I said, "Or her name either, I guess."

"No, but it's on the tip of my tongue. Delilah, perhaps. Delia? Maybe it was Darlene."

The suitcase in the closet bore the initials DLR. If the valise had been the skeleton's, as it had appeared to be, we were getting closer.

"Did they ever get married?" Not if it had been our Bridey, they didn't, at least judging from her lack of a ring. But this story might be about another couple entirely.

"No. And they'd had to hide their engagement, too." She took a sip of her drink. "I'm sorry about my silly senior memory gaps, sweetie. It'll all come back to me at about three o'clock in the morning." She guffawed her surprisingly deep laugh. "I'll send you a text when it does."

"You do that."

"Somebody whose memory is better than mine is my friend Ursula. You know, Flo's mama. She lives at Westham Village, the assisted living joint. She remembers every little bit about the past."

"Thanks, Abo. I'll go see her."

"Tell her I sent you."

I finished my glass. I wanted to get over to watch

Win open that suitcase. "Is your toast for the dinner all set? I know you wanted to offer one."

"I expect I'll be the oldest family member there. I most certainly do want to speak. I'll be ready, *querida.* Don't you worry about a thing."

Who me, worry? Sometimes I felt like it was my middle name.

CHAPTER 8

I trotted up the front steps of the Westham Historical Society building at a few minutes before three. The stone edifice, constructed in 1900, had been the town's public library for over a hundred years until a much-needed modern library was constructed next to the town hall down Main Street. The new, light-filled library had temperature control, community meeting rooms, digital capacity, handicapped access, and room to expand, none of which this lovely building could offer.

I paused to admire the fitted stone arch over the heavy front doors, which also were topped by a decorated wooden arch. All the wood had recently been refinished, and it gleamed like golden maple syrup in the afternoon light. A lion's head was carved into the frame on each side and under the beveled glass inserts in both doors. I'd visited the New York Public

Library once, the entrance of which was guarded by big stone lions. Those regal felines must be the universal keepers of books.

Inside, the walls were lined with framed black-and-white photographs of the town's long history. One wall held maps dating from the 1600s up to about when this building was completed. There were a couple of long tables in the main room, but nobody sat at the reception desk, which held a leather cylinder full of pencils and a squat, heavy-looking black phone from the 1950s, cord and all. I was eager to see the opening of the suitcase. Why was no one around?

"Hello," I called. "Win?" A dehumidifier hummed in the corner. It must be working, because the place didn't smell musty. If it had, I would have had to clear out. Mold is one of my worst allergens. But the air was chilly. I kept my coat on.

I wandered around, peering at the pictures while I waited. One showed a parade of early automobiles decorated with flowers and American flags. Westham still held a classic small-town Independence Day parade every year. The vehicle in the lead in the photo was a cream-colored Packard convertible with whitewalls, a long nose, and a showy vertical radiator at the front. A young woman in gown and tiara sat up high at the back waving a gloved hand. I bent over to read the caption. "Quahog Queen Miss Katherine Swift, 1939." The year about fit the style of the parade watchers' clothing. The word *quahog*, meaning "clam," came from the Narragansett language and was mostly used only on the Cape and islands and in Rhode Island.

Which was all well and good, except I was here to

learn more about the bride in the hiding place, not about the history of the Quahog Queen.

"Win?" I called again.

Footsteps clattered up from somewhere, accompanied by a voice. I hadn't spent much time in here. The building must have a basement the society used. Win came around a corner, her phone to her ear. She signaled she'd seen me but kept talking.

"All right," she said. "But don't you want to know more about her?"

All I could hear was the tinny drone of a voice on the other end.

"Of course I know she's been dead for a long time!" She tossed her head, her exasperated gaze accompanying the movement. "But the sooner I can examine the contents of the suitcase, the sooner you'll have more to work with."

She listened some more. "If it has to be tomorrow, then, whatever."

Rats. I wouldn't be learning about Bridey today, apparently.

An additional tinny response emanated.

"Yes, ma'am. I do understand chain of evidence." Win jabbed at her cell to disconnect. "Hi, Mac. Sorry about that." She stroked the landline on the desk. "I've seen old movies where they slam down the receiver at the end of an argument. That had to have been a lot more satisfying than merely poking a button."

"It must have been," I agreed. "I guess you don't have the suitcase."

"I do not." She blew out a breath. "In their infinite stupidity—I mean, wisdom—the state police decided to hang on to it until tomorrow. I would have let you know, but . . ." She tossed her hands to the side. "As you heard, I just found out."

"It's okay." And actually, Win should know that they needed to keep a piece of evidence in custody except in special circumstances. It wasn't stupid at all. But I kept my opinion to myself. "I'm interested in who the skeleton was and how she ended up in our wall. But she's been dead for a long time. What's one more day, right?"

"I guess. I only hope they're careful with the valise."

"You don't think they will be?" I asked.

"Not everybody in the police has specialized training."

I narrowed my eyes. "They must have somebody they call on." Or maybe not. Penelope had said the expert was on vacation. Something like that.

The little ring in Win's nose moved as she flared her nostrils. "That someone would be me. Except they think I'm too young to know what I'm doing. I've already apprenticed at the Boston Athenaeum and the Massachusetts Historical Society. I even did a winter break behind the scenes at the Louvre."

Someone had been pulling strings for this girl. Unless she simply had a drive to learn about history.

"I know historical preservation, conservation, and provenance, Mac. I know how to take care of old things."

Taking care of old things and preserving evidence to find DNA were two very different things.

Win sank into the chair at the desk, swiveling to face me. "Have a seat if you want."

"Thanks." I turned around one of the chairs at the nearest table and sat.

"So, have you, like, been in here before?" she asked.

"Only a couple of times."

"It's pretty awesome, isn't it?"

"The building is gorgeous," I said. "I'm glad the historical society got it after the library moved. But tell me, Win, you're young, what twenty or so?"

"I just turned twenty-one."

That seemed about right. "Why are you so interested in history? In old stuff?"

She jumped up and strode to the parade photo. "See this sweetheart in the tiara? That was my great-grandmother, Gran Kit, otherwise known as Katherine Swift." She blew a kiss at the glass.

"I saw that photograph earlier. The Quahog Queen. Did you know her?"

"I did."

"Lucky you."

"I'll say." Her voice softened. "She only died a few years ago at a ninety-eight. She was awesome, Mac. A total pistol. She always told me never to abandon the past but to learn from it."

"So your family has been in the area for a long time?"

She faced me. "The Swifts are one of Westham's First Families." The pride in her voice was unmistakable as she raised her chin. "It's my heritage."

"My fiancé says our house was built by the Swift family. Do you know if that was your ancestors?"

"It pretty much has to be." Again the pride in her voice. "Gran Kit's father founded Westham First Bank and developed quite a lot of real estate in town."

"I'm sure." I stood. I had a list of errands to accomplish that weren't going to run themselves. With no antique bridal suitcase to explore, I didn't have the leisure to sit here and chat with a young woman who seemed a bit too full of her so-called status as a founding daughter. I didn't think anyone cared about that kind of thing anymore, especially not college students.

"I need to get going," I said. "Please text me when I can come back and see what our poor skeleton planned to take along on her trip."

"I will. Hopefully tomorrow."

"Thanks. See you tomorrow, I hope." I let myself out. The lions now guarded a young woman gazing with reverence at the image of her father's grandmother. I wondered if Win ever went clubbing or got high with her peers. Did she participate in student protests or have marathon study sessions with her classmates? She was an unusual college student, that was for sure. Still, variety was good. We were all unusual in our own ways, me included.

CHAPTER 9

I popped into the library to see if head librarian Flo Wolanski was at her desk. She was a Cozy Capers book group member. More important, she was a friend with deep research skills and special search software at her disposal. Except they told me she was in a meeting. Out I trudged.

Clouds had blown in, darkening the sky, while I'd been inside talking with Win. Now in the four o'clock gloaming, with the weak winter sun officially setting in twenty minutes, it was the most depressing part of the day. When I'd first read the word "gloaming," I'd thought it was just about a perfect description for the gloomy hour of gradual dimming, especially in this season.

I couldn't remember if I'd had seasonal affective disorder when I was younger. I knew SAD affected me now—and had anything ever had a more fitting acronym? Short, dark days made me feel, well, dark. And inexplicably morose.

Even the town's Christmas decorations felt sad. They'd been up since before Thanksgiving. I never liked dragging out holidays after the fact. Once the festivities were over, things should be cleaned up and put away. And Christmas stuff should definitely go away before New Year's Day. It was time to go forward, in my view. Unfortunately, I was in the minority.

At least now we were past the solstice. The length of time the sun was up was imperceptibly getting longer. Right now that felt like a logical construct, not something to actually lift my mood. Scheduling a wedding at the darkest time of year now seemed supremely stupid. Except it was a done deal. Of course, I was excited about marrying Tim. Maybe part of what was dragging me down was discovering a body this morning. I was aware that what I needed was to go home, get cozy under a blanket with the natural-spectrum light Tim had given me for Christmas, sip a hot toddy, and watch a funny movie. But my feet were clumps of lead.

Poor Bridey hadn't had the chance to snuggle with her almost-husband. She'd died alone, imprisoned in a rudimentary room. How terrified she must have been. Had she called for help until she had no more strength to cry out? Had the skin of her hands grown bloody trying to escape her bonds? It was awful to imagine her. And I didn't even know her name. I'd really hoped for information from her suitcase. Or . . . I froze. What if the cottage was the house they were to live in and her fiancé decided he didn't want to marry her? He could have walled her in and found a different bride. That was too horrific to contemplate.

Brr. The wind blowing in the clouds slid a chilly blade along my neck. I pulled up my infinity scarf, tugged down my black beret, and shoved my hands in my pockets as I passed the Book Nook, Westham's independent bookstore. It looked like they'd acted fast in removing their Christmas display. In the window was an array of coloring books for children and adults.

Our Cozy Capers book group was scheduled to be reading *The Coloring Crook* by Krista Davis, the latest in a series featuring adult coloring books—and murder, of course. Normally we read and discussed a cozy mystery every week. With the holidays plus a wedding, we'd agreed to postpone the discussion until later in January. I hadn't even cracked the spine of the book. Still, the premise of coloring was its calming, meditative effect.

I pulled open the Book Nook's door. As with the windows, all traces of Christmas were gone inside. I approved. The only holiday display was a narrow bookshelf facing the door that held books for all ages about Hanukkah and Kwanzaa. I pivoted in a circle but didn't spy the coloring books.

"Let me know if I can help you with something," a man's voice said.

I looked around, finally seeing him where he sat on a stool behind the counter on the other side of the store, half glasses perched on his nose, a full head of salt-and-pepper hair. I headed over there.

"Thanks. I'm looking for coloring books. For myself."

He arched his hand over the counter and pointed down. "Like these?"

"Oh!" I laughed at the sight of what I sought displayed right in front of me. Several dozen coloring books were arrayed in a magazine-type rack at my waist level and below. "Thank you." I squatted to examine the selection. Intricate animals. International capitals. Spring flowers. I perked up at a Ruth Bader Ginsburg coloring book. A snarky marriage book? No thanks.

I finally settled on the world capitals, mostly because Bangkok was on the cover, where I'd served in the Peace Corps for two years. I picked up the RBG book, too, because she was one of the most awesome women ever. I had my mouth open to ask about art supplies when he beat me to it.

"Colored pencils and markers are there." His voice was low and comforting, his smile nearly beatific.

"Thank you." I selected a package of each, laying them on the counter. I knew I hadn't brought any to Tim's, and I might as well start with fresh coloring implements.

He peered at the prices and tapped them into a laptop, then told me the sum.

I handed him a credit card.

"Thanks." He peered at it. "I'm Barlow Swift, Mackenzie. Proprietor."

Swift? He was the second member of the family I'd encountered today. "Nice to meet you." I smiled but kept my hands at my sides. "Mac Almeida."

"Of Mac's Bikes, I think." He handed me the slip to sign.

"That would be me." I pulled out my own pen, another only slightly obsessive habit I'd developed in the last couple of years, and scribbled my signature. "I haven't seen you in here before. Have you owned the store a long time?" Flo's daughter had been managing the bookstore. Maybe she'd moved on.

"No. I was in the bond-trading business. I, ah, decided to move on." A tic beat in his upper lip, and his gaze was over my shoulder, even though I knew no one else was in the store. "Anyway, I'm in the process of hiring. If you know anyone who loves books and is good at retail, send them over."

"I promise." I had a thought. The store hadn't stocked cozy mysteries up to now. Maybe I could put a bug in his ear. "I'm part of a book group that only reads cozy mysteries. We're called the Cozy Capers, and we'd love it if you stocked more cozies. Your previous manager didn't seem to think the cozy genre had enough 'literary' appeal." I put the word in finger quotes. Our group was in agreement that most of the cozy tales we read were well written, well told, and had loads of literary value, whatever the heck that meant.

"I'd be happy to," he said.

"We buy a lot of books." I smiled. "Just saying."

He typed on his laptop. "Kensington, St. Martin's, Berkeley. I can order books from all those publishers." He looked up. "It's a deal. Stop back next week and see if you notice anything different."

"I appreciate that." I accepted the paper bag he handed me. "Would you be related to Win?"

"She's my niece. Smart girl."

"I met her earlier today."

He gave a little laugh. "When she was small, I heard her tell a friend once that her uncle traded bombs."

"Kids." I held up my bag. "Thank you, Barlow."

I was quite sure spending time coloring inside the lines would not solve all my problems. But it might help.

CHAPTER 10

Stepping out onto the sidewalk into the darkening afternoon, suddenly I didn't feel a bit better, my conversation with Barlow notwithstanding. Of course not, I chided myself. I had to actually do the coloring to feel an effect. Head down, I pointed my feet toward home and nearly collided with someone.

"Excuse me." I glanced up as I apologized to see Astra MacKenzie. My mother, in other words. I mustered a smile. "Hi, Mom."

"Sweetheart, what a treat." She held out her arms, even though one hand held a cloth shopping bag, and the strap of her purse was slipping off the other shoulder.

The warmth of her hug and a whiff of the incense she loved made me blink sudden tears. I sniffed. She stepped back, peering with her light green eyes into my face. Eyes exactly like mine.

"What's wrong, honey?" A turquoise and purple ear warmer didn't keep her wispy graying blond curls from flying everywhere.

"I'm okay." I gestured vaguely in the air. "But I'm not feeling very, you know, cheerful."

"I can see that." She tucked her free hand through my arm. "And I know exactly what you need." She steered me firmly, briskly, down the sidewalk, her skirt swirling around her leggings, her turquoise hiking boots marching along. Mom always wore exactly what she wanted, saying being over sixty was only a state of mind. She pulled me to a stop in front of the Rusty Anchor, the town's funkiest watering hole. An actual rusty anchor hung at a rakish angle above the door, and neon beer signs lit the windows. Inside she scooted us into a booth near the fireplace.

An orange-haired waitperson of indeterminate gender appeared almost immediately.

"Hi, Kim," Mom said. "We'll take two hot buttered rums. Yes, Mackenzie?"

I opened my mouth to object. Then again, why not? I shut it and nodded. *Yes.*

"And a big plate of fries, hon," Mom added.

"You got it, Ms. Mackenzie." The server smiled and bustled off.

"I didn't know you were such a regular at the pub, Mom."

"Why not? Sometimes my clients feel more comfortable learning about their charts over a drink here than in my office."

Mom, aka Astra, was a professional astrologer. Some years ago she'd gotten tired of being a minister's wife named Edna. She changed her first name, hung out her shingle—almost literally—and now made a pretty good living analyzing people's natal charts and current situations according to the stars and planets. To his credit, Pa hadn't minded her new career or her name change. He still didn't, and they continued to have a strong marriage. My brother and I weren't believers in the basis of her practice, but we only made fun of her astrological analysis when we were alone.

Big mugs of fragrant toddies were in front of us two minutes later, and with a few sips in the belly, I let out a long breath. I was warming up, inside and out. My psyche was, too.

"This is nice." I sat back. "Thank you for rescuing me."

"I'm your mom." Her tone was matter-of-fact, as if that was what moms did. "Now, what's bothering you? Is it the wedding?"

I thought. She deserved an honest answer. "No. I'm fine with that. I mean, there are lots of details that need to fall into place, but we're in good shape. I think. Thanks to you and Gin and everybody else."

"That's logistics. What I meant was, you're not having cold feet? You've lived independently a lot longer than many brides." She cocked her head. "I wouldn't blame you if you were. Your Venus is having several negative influences for the next couple of days. But they will have moved on before the big day."

"No cold feet. I love Tim. I'm happy about marrying him."

"Good. Is it the body you found?" Her pale eyebrows went up. "Was it terribly hard?"

"Yes." Of course she also knew. "It's very sad, and these short, dark days don't help my mood. How much have you heard about our discovery?"

"You found an old skeleton." Mom kept her voice to a murmur. "That's all I heard."

Kim set down a platter of golden fries that could feed a family of six. "Enjoy."

I inhaled the aroma, suddenly starving. "Thank you." I salted my half.

Mom poured a little pile of ketchup on her side. I savored several spikes of hot, salty crispness, skins and all. These had not come out of a freezer bag.

"The fries really hit the spot. So, here's the story, Mom." I filled her in on Bridey and on not knowing who she was. "But Abo Reba said she almost remembers something about that story."

"And the suitcase?" Mom asked.

I shook my head. "The intern didn't have it when I stopped by the historical society. Maybe I'll get to see the contents tomorrow."

"Is the intern the Swift girl?"

"You know her?"

"Purple hair?"

I bobbed my head, my mouth full of fries.

"Winslow and her mom got their charts read together about a year ago." Mom sipped her toddy. "Two Scorpios. They have a rich and fraught relationship, those ladies."

"Win talked about her great-grandmother, Katherine. She called her Kit."

Mom nodded, but her gaze was fixed across the room. She raised a hand. "Al," she called.

I glanced over to see a snowy-haired man approach with a jaunty walk. He beamed when he reached us.

"Al, this is my daughter, Mackenzie Almeida. Mac, this is Al Cabral."

"It's a pleasure to meet you, Mac." His caterpillar eyebrows were still dark, his bushy mustache was a salt-and-pepper blend, and his white hair was thick and combed straight back from his brow.

"And you, sir." I smiled up at him.

"Al runs Westham Village," Mom added.

Where Reba's friend Ursula lived. "Out on Old Port Road," I said.

"Yes," he said. "Visitors are always welcome, especially young folks like you."

Thirty-seven didn't feel that young to me. Compared to ninety-two, I supposed it was. The muted sound of a bell rang out.

"Excuse me." He pulled out a phone from his jacket pocket. After he glanced at it, he frowned. "I'll catch you ladies later." He pressed it to his ear and hurried toward the door.

"Now, where were we, honey?" Mom asked.

I should have answered her. Except my mind was on the man who'd left the pub a minute ago. *Cabral* was a common last name in these parts, where a good percentage of residents bore names of some kind of Portuguese extraction, including my own. But *Cabral* was one of the names my grandmother had tossed around when she tried to remember that long-ago couple. I wouldn't mind a chance to talk with Al Cabral again. I wouldn't mind that at all.

CHAPTER 11

I wore my full cold-weather wind gear the next morning at seven thirty as Gin and I swung our arms striding on the Shining Sea rail trail. I'd pulled down the earflaps of my fleece cap, and silk long johns kept my legs warm under double-layer exercise pants. My friend was similarly attired. Her breath formed wispy puffs as she walked. The clouds had kept on going overnight, and now it was twenty degrees, clear, and just plain cold, with the sun barely peeking over the marshes. Still, the prospect of a bright, clear day cheered me.

"Are you going to Zane and Stephen's tonight?" she asked.

"To the Hanukkah party? Of course. Aren't you?"

"Yes. It'll be fun." She wrinkled her nose. "It's funny, somehow I didn't know Stephen was Jewish."

Stephen Duke was Westham's town clerk and husband to Zane King. Zane owned and ran the local distillery and liquor store, stocking all the best alcohol. Both belonged to the Cozy Capers Book Group and had invited all of us to celebrate the first night of the festival of lights.

"Are you bringing Eli?" I asked.

"No. It's a book group party, isn't it? Anyway, he has a paper to present next month at a conference that he's working on."

"Tonight will be a welcome distraction for me," I said.

"From the wedding jitters?"

"That and . . ." I let my voice trail off. Did I really want to get back into the whole situation with Bridey and feeling frustrated at my lack of information? After I'd left the pub yesterday, I'd done exactly what the doctor prescribed. A bowl of soup with my man and a few belly laughs at an old Marx Brothers movie had taken my mind off everything. I'd worried I wouldn't be able to sleep, knowing a skeleton had been downstairs, but I had conked out and slept soundly.

Broad, dark wings soared overhead, wings with a majestic white head leading them. I pointed so Gin could see the mature bald eagle, too. Winter was their nesting season around here. I didn't know where they spent their summers, but it was somewhere farther north.

"Majestic is the only way to describe eagles," I said.

"I agree. Tonight will be a distraction from finding some bones in a closet, too, am I right?" Gin kept her voice gentle.

I guess we were going to get into it. And truly, she was my best friend. We talked about everything on our daily walks, including past murders we'd come up against. Last summer she'd even been the prime suspect for a while. While she was as sweet as her candy store, Salty Taffy's, Gin was also an astute business-woman in her forties and a loyal BFF.

"You heard," I murmured.

"The news is all over the place."

"I guess it would be." I frowned. "Do you mean like on the TV news?"

"Yes. But they didn't identify the house or its own-ers."

"Good. As far as I know, there haven't been any television trucks or reporters at Tim's." I slowed, star-ing at her. "Wait. So how did you know Tim and I were the ones who found the skeleton?"

"Flo started a group text thread last night." Gin glanced over at me. "You didn't see it?"

Gah. "No. I mean, I saw a thread this morning, but I thought it was about the party tonight. I was going to check it later." I pulled out my phone. Yep, there it was.

"Let's pick up the pace, Mac." Gin smiled to soften her words. "Some of us have to work later."

"Right." I stashed my phone and we resumed our brisk clip. I swung my arms again, my thoughts rac-ing almost as fast as my feet. "So, yeah. Tim and I were doing demolition for a new bathroom, and we broke through the back wall of a closet to a narrow space he hadn't realized was there. It was like, two and half, three feet wide. And we found poor Bridey sitting on a plain wooden chair. In her wedding dress, with her hands chained to the wall behind her, her suitcase on the floor."

"The poor thing. You know her name?"

"No. I wish I did. I'm only calling her that because of her dress." And it seemed better than thinking of her as a pile of bones. "Gin, the thought of her dying there alone is horrible."

She reached out and squeezed my hand for a second. "Of course it is."

I filled her in on the crime scene team, on Win, on the suitcase. "I hope I get a chance to see the contents today."

"Do you have any idea how long your Bridey has been in there?"

"Not really. The house was built in 1925, so under a hundred years. I feel like her dress and her shoes looked kind of thirties-ish, but I don't know for sure."

"That's a really cold case."

"Exactly. I don't know how hard they're going to work to solve it, either. Will anyone but me care who killed her?" I shook my head. "Lincoln is on vacation. He would pay attention to the case if he were here." *Huh.* I hadn't even asked who would be working on solving it. Maybe Penelope Johnson. I would add finding that out to my list for later today.

"Winslow Swift," Gin said. "I might know her mom. There's an Emily Swift who is a regular in my shop. She looks about my age."

"In her forties. That could work to have a daughter who turned twenty-one recently."

"Right. The woman has a major sweet tooth. She's in there all the time."

"For your candy? I don't blame her." I smiled. "I do have some good news. I went into the Book Nook yesterday. Have you ever met the owner?"

"No, I don't think so."

"Actually, I guess he's the new owner. His name is Barlow Swift. He turns out to be Win's uncle."

"Barlow Swift." Gin furrowed her brow. "I feel like I read about him in the news last year sometime."

"When he bought the store?"

"No. There was some kind of crime involved."

"Really?" I asked. "He said he had been a bond trader."

She snapped her fingers. "That's it. He lost his license because of questionable practices or something vague. I think he avoided prosecution by agreeing to leave the industry."

"Wow." That would explain how he hadn't met my gaze and had seemed a little nervous when he'd talked about changing his career. "Well, he owns the bookstore now, and he said he's hiring. I told him about the book group, and he's going to start stocking cozy mysteries. For our group, for anyone."

Gin made a sound in her throat. "It's about time, don't you think?"

"Of course." How strange, though, that we were benefiting in a convoluted way from Barlow's wrong-doings. We strode along. The sunshine and brisk air, combined with the exercise, was helping my mood considerably.

"I bought a couple of coloring books at the book-store, too," I said.

"For yourself?"

"Yes."

"Like in the Krista Davis book. Which I have not even started yet." Gin gave me a mock frown. "Some-how coloring doesn't seem like you, Mac."

"I know, right? Except it's supposed to be medita-tive, and I could use some calming down right now.

Or distraction. Or cheering up." I hadn't even opened the Book Nook bag last night.

"This time of year is tough for you," Gin said in a gentle tone. "Despite the joy of it, any wedding is stressful, and a really old murder victim can't be helping."

"Understatement of the decade, my friend. How I let Mom and Abo Reba talk me into a New Year's Eve ceremony is anybody's guess."

"But it's going to happen, and it's going to be fabulous. I checked in with the caterer yesterday."

We spent the rest of the walk going over last details about food, logistics, music, and all the other details of the celebration happening in five days. Bridey didn't leave the back of my mind, though. I knew she wouldn't until I had an answer to the question of what had happened to her.

CHAPTER 12

I sat across the table from Win in the historical society building at around ten. She'd texted an hour earlier that she had the suitcase and invited me to examine its contents with her. Of course, I'd said I'd be right over. Our demolition site was still off-limits, so the day stretched unscheduled in front of me. If anything, it was colder in here today. I didn't even unzip my jacket.

Officer Osborne from the crime scene team was there, too, standing behind Win. He'd nodded to me when I came in. I supposed I was lucky to be allowed to be present at all.

Win, wearing a thick sweater, spread a white cloth on a bare table and pulled on purple gloves. She brought over a big paper bag from another table, holding it horizontally, the bag she'd used to carry away the suitcase yesterday.

"This is their evidence bag," she murmured as she set it to the side. "We have an hour, right, Officer?"

"Yes, Ms. Winslow." He apparently was a man of few words, who took the chain of evidence seriously.

On the side of the bag was printed a list of blank lines, with column headings of date, location, and name. The top three were filled in. Winslow Swift filled that slot on the third line along with today's date and WHS. Win lifted out the monogrammed suitcase, laying it flat on the cloth.

My heart thudded in anticipation. Would we learn Bridey's name? Who her enemy was, her murderer? The piece of luggage wasn't large, maybe twenty-four inches by fifteen, and four or five inches deep. Had she packed for a honeymoon or for the rest of her life? I needed to pack for my own honeymoon some-time before Saturday. Tim and I were traveling to his mother's house in the Virgin Islands on St. John. Greta was staying here on the continent to visit with friends and with Tim's sister and her kids until we got back.

I leaned closer.

Win glanced sharply at me. "No touching, right?"

Yes, Mom. "I understand." I sat back and shoved my hands in my jacket pockets, not that I could reach across the table anyway. Something looked familiar about Win's eyes. They were the oddest shade of blue. Maybe it was the influence of her purple hair, but her irises looked almost violet. And I'd seen eyes like that recently. Where? I thought back. Nope, it wasn't coming to me. Like my grandma, I would probably remember at three in the morning. Or maybe Win was wearing tinted contact lenses.

She pushed both latches of the suitcase to the side and slowly lifted the lid. Shreds of dark leather flaked off from the hinged side, scattering onto the white cloth. Win gently folded back the lid until it lay on the table. The top was lined with a taffeta-like fabric in a faded gold. It smelled old but not musty with mold, a testament to Tim's dry basement.

Inside were neatly folded clothes secured by two ribbons tied in bows.

"So the police didn't already go through the suitcase?" I asked Osborne.

"No, ma'am."

"I'm going to take a few photos, if that's all right." I pulled out my phone.

"It's fine," Osborne said.

"Good idea," Win said. "You'll send me copies?"

I nodded.

"If the society ultimately gets to hang on to this stuff," Win added, "we could use photographs for our archives."

I watched as she untied the ribbons and carefully lifted out garments, laying them on the cloth next to the suitcase. A sage-green rayon dress with figure-eight appliques at the shoulders. A belted dress in white cotton printed with yellow flowers. A blue-and-white striped one-piece bathing suit with legs that would hit the top of the wearer's thighs. A light-weight navy-blue sweater. A pair of high-waisted linen trousers and a navy silk blouse. Near the bottom, wrapped in cream-colored paper, were a pair of red espadrilles.

"This girl packed for warm weather," Win said.

I had to agree. No thick scarves were in the suitcase, no warm hat or socks, nothing of wool. A coat
hadn't been thrown over her wedding dress, either.
It was the kind of clothing I would be packing for my
own honeymoon.

Next to the shoes was a silky, sleeveless nightgown,
or maybe it was a slip. Win uncovered a filmy yellow
headscarf, several pairs of silk stockings, and two
well-armored bras and girdles. I glanced up at Osborne. His neck had turned red, but his face remained expressionless.

Next Win took out a few pairs of white anklets and
four pairs of high-waisted underwear. A small black
book labeled *Holy Bible* lay among the undergarments.
The Bible looked new, with gold coating the edges of
the pages. The body of the case sat empty.

"Open the Bible," I suggested. "Maybe she wrote
her name inside."

Win flipped it open to the frontispiece, which was
blank. Nothing was handwritten on the first few
pages, either.

"Oh, well," I said, disappointed. "It was worth a
try."

"Interesting that we haven't found any cosmetics,"
Win said. "Face cream, lipstick, powder, soap. None
of that."

"She might have had a separate smaller case for
that." A makeup case hadn't been with her. But neither had a handbag, come to think of it.

A gathered pocket that was divided into three sec-
tions ran along the back. Win slipped her hand into
the first section and extracted a deck of Aviator play-

ing cards in its box. From the next she pulled out a
black-and-white snapshot of a handsome, dark-haired
young man standing on a dock. Bridey's intended?
Fishing boats and calm water filled the background.

When Win flipped the picture to the back, I
peered across the table. She held it up for me to see.
The photograph was signed, "Love always, Manny."
This was definitely Bridey's groom. Manny was also one
of the names my grandmother had tossed around.

"Let me get a picture of the front and the back," I
said.

Win held up each side while I snapped. We still
didn't know who the corpse was, or Manny's last
name, and we'd exhausted the contents of the suitcase. Or had we? I held my breath. Win felt around
in the last pocket and withdrew a folded booklet.

"Aha." She held up the object with a triumphant
look. The stiff red cover was labeled, *Passport. United
States of America*, and it had a narrow, rounded window in it revealing the passport number.

I sucked in a breath.

Win flipped it over, and then back.

"Aren't you going to open it?" I asked.

She turned a serious face toward me. "Do you
think I should?"

Seriously? "Yes, Win." It was all I could do not to rip
the passport out of her hand. Instead, I took a picture of the cover.

A mischievous smile split her face. "I'm just pulling your chain, Mac." She opened the document.

If I'd blinked, I would have missed her eyes narrowing for a split second. *Huh.* Did she recognize the
name?

She read out loud. "This passport granted to Della Louise Ruhlen on December eighteenth, nineteen thirty-nine."

Bridey's name was Della. Della Louise Ruhlen. DLR. Not Delilah or Delia, as Abe Reba had mused, but close. And Ruhlen. As in Forrest, the florist?

Win's nostrils flared. "Della Ruhlen," she whispered, almost to herself.

"Does that name mean something to you?" I asked.

"Never mind."

Win was lying about the name. She'd obviously recognized it.

She kept reading. "Birth date April twelfth, nineteen-twenty."

I did some quick math. "So she was nineteen when she got the passport. I wonder if eighteen was the age of consent then?"

"We can check." Win flipped through the rest of the passport pages. "She hadn't traveled outside the country yet. At least not on this passport." She showed me. "The rest is blank."

"No country stamps, no visas. So the document was new." Although just because she'd gotten the passport in 1939 didn't mean that was when she was walled off and left to die. "I wonder where they'd planned to go on their honeymoon."

"Any time after the middle of May would mean warm weather in North America and Europe," Win said. "And it's always warm in the tropics. Kind of hard to pin down."

I wrinkled my nose. "It must have cost a lot to travel outside the country back then. Our Della didn't pack for a transatlantic ship. She would have filled a trunk. Maybe the passport was a just-in-case scenario. They could have planned a week in Boston or Maine, or the Jersey Shore."

"Or Montreal."

"Yes, of course. A day's drive." Or not. Travel by automobile took a lot longer back then. Maybe they were going to take the train to California and start over. I sank onto the nearest chair. "Wherever it was, she didn't get to go."

Win stripped off her gloves and pulled out her phone.

Osborne cleared his throat. "Hour's almost up, miss."

"Yes, sir," Win said. "I'll just be a minute."

I started to reach for research on my own phone but stilled my hand. I could start digging into the murdered Della later. Instead I gazed at the stacks of what she'd deemed essential to take with her as she traveled with her beloved Manny, now husband. Hopefully she'd also been his beloved. The silky nightgown she'd never gotten to wear on her wedding night broke my heart the worst. And now I wondered, what in the world had happened to her groom? Had he been left to die somewhere else? His skeleton had better not be behind another of Tim's walls.

Win glanced up from her phone wearing an odd expression. With her head tilted and her eyes narrowed, it looked like she'd read something disturbing. Thought-provoking. Or maybe something she didn't want me to know.

"Did you find her?" I asked. "Della?"

"It's nothing." She batted the air. "Something else."

Whatever. Me? I was going find justice for those two long-ago lovers. And I'd better find it before Saturday. If I didn't, I knew I'd feel their ghosts casting a shadow over my own wedding.

CHAPTER 13

"I thought you'd never stop by," Flo said from be-hind her desk in her head librarian's office on the second floor. A big window to her right looked out onto the town green, with our carefully preserved and restored Town Hall beyond, a building constructed at about the time Della Ruhlen was born.

"I've been busy." I'd texted her when I left the his-torical society to make sure she was free, and she'd said she was. Earlier I'd read the Cozy Capers thread, but nobody knew anything. On the contrary, mem-bers had primarily been asking me for the story.

"Sit." Flo now pointed at the visitor's chair. "Tell all."

I sat. I told all, ending with the suitcase. "Flo, it was so sad to see her carefully folded clothes. Her stock-ings, her nightgown. Della packed for a short trip in warm weather. A honeymoon she never got to take."

"Was there ID?"

"Yes. Her passport was the last thing Win found." I relayed the information on the first page.

Flo typed, her keyboard emitting a comforting, soft tapping. "Della Louise Ruhlen, born in nineteen twenty?"

"That's her. And I'm pretty sure the Manny in the photo was the man she was planning to marry."

"No last name for the dude?" Flo asked.

"Unfortunately, no."

Flo's fingers began to fly. I scooted the chair around to sit next to her so I could see her large dual screens. Except I couldn't even begin to track where she went. She whizzed through what looked like photographs of old newspaper articles on one monitor. The other seemed to be a genealogy site.

I sat back to wait. I wasn't about to start quizzing the expert on sources only she could navigate. Her office was loaded with bookshelves and file cabinets. A framed picture of Flo and the late, great Sue Grafton had a place of honor on the wall. Flo had said she'd met Grafton at an American Library Association meeting, and the author was gracious enough to agree to a photograph. Next to it hung a commendation from five years ago from the governor of the Commonwealth of Massachusetts for thirty years of service. Flo was barely sixty and had found her calling early.

She relaxed in her chair, too, and pointed at the monitor closest to me. "His name was Manuel Cabral."

"The Manny in her photograph."

"I expect so. They both disappeared at the same

time. The *Westham Times* quotes anonymous sources saying Della and Manny eloped. Their families were scandalized. The couple was never heard from again. The parents were devastated. And so on and so forth."

"Anonymous sources?" I asked.

She shrugged. "A jealous girlfriend? An irate father? I don't know."

"What's the date of the story?"

"March twelfth, nineteen forty."

I thought. "Interesting. Early March is still plenty cold in New England. With the clothes she packed, they had to have been headed somewhere south or southwest." Definitely not Montreal or Maine, or even Boston. I thought some more. "I wonder if she was related to Forrest Ruhlen."

Flo tilted her head. "The flower guy."

"Right. It's not a very common name."

"I can call him." She reached for the landline on her desk.

"No, don't. I'll stop by his shop. It's the kind of question best asked in person."

"You're right."

My brain flashed on the photograph on Forrest's shelf. "Wait. When I was in there Monday checking on the wedding flowers, I saw an old photograph of a young woman, in black and white, of course. He said his favorite aunt was to be married long ago but never got the chance."

"Our Della?"

"It could be. He said that was one reason he loves doing flowers for weddings, because she didn't get to have one."

Flo bobbed her head. "Now, tell me. How did

young Winslow Swift get to be the first to examine the suitcase?"

"Good question," I said. "She's studying criminal justice and forensics, and she's apparently an intern with both the police and the historical society. Their actual experts are all on vacation. She seemed to know how to handle the suitcase and its contents, at least."

"Win's a smart kid. Grew up in this library. She'll go far."

"Can we return to your searches, Flo?" I asked. "There aren't any later stories about the couple? Or about Manny or Della separately?"

"Give me a minute." Her fingers flew again. "Not a one."

"What about this? Your mom lives at Westham Village. Yesterday my mother introduced me to—"

"Al Cabral," Flo said. "The director. I can certainly find out if he's related to Manny. You must be aware of how many Cabrals live on the Cape and in New Bedford, though."

"Whatever. He'll either be a relative or not."

"And he'll either know something or not."

"I might run over there later. Do you mind if I visit your mom?"

"Are you kidding? She'd love it."

"You know, Tim said our house was built by the Swifts in nineteen twenty-five." How quickly I'd slipped into thinking of the house as ours, not solely his. "Fifteen years later, somebody boarded poor Della into that space. It had to have been the owners, right?"

"I would assume so," Flo said. "Or it was done with their knowledge, anyway."

"It would help narrow the search if we knew who owned the house in nineteen forty." I gestured toward her monitors. "Can you access deeds from there?"

"I should be able to, if Barnstable County has digitized them that far back. Gimme a sec." Flo smiled as she glanced at her wall clock. Her smile switched to an alarmed expression. "Jiminy Cricket, I'm late for a meeting."

I smiled to myself at her disguised swearing.

She stood in a hurry. "Out we go. Sorry, have to lock the door."

"No worries, Flo. See you tonight?"

"Yep. Got my dreidel all warmed up."

"You what, now?" I scrunched up my nose, following her out.

"You should see the look on your face, Mac." Flo snorted, locking the door. "Yes, I'm Polish, and no, I'm not Jewish, or particularly religious at all except to worship at an altar loaded with books. But I know what a dreidel is."

CHAPTER 14

At Beach Plum Florist, I again inhaled the swoon-worthy, humid fragrant air. I wandered back to the counter, which was empty. What would it be like to work in a place like this every day? I supposed one would get accustomed to the scents and no longer smell them. It would certainly rehydrate the skin, especially during these dry months of winter. This was the time of year when skin like mine started resembling parchment paper, when I got cracks in the tips of my fingers that didn't heal until April no matter how much lotion I applied. Gin had the same problem.

When Forrest didn't make an appearance after a minute or two, I tapped the little dome-shaped bell on the counter.

A woman about my age hurried in from the back. "What can I do for you?"

"I'm looking for Forrest."

"I'm sorry, he's out."

"Do you know when he'll be back?" I asked.

"I don't. If you want flowers, I can certainly help you."

Darn. "No, thanks. I'm all set for flowers. I'll stop back tomorrow." I was disappointed not to find out today if Forrest's ancestor was, in fact, Della Louise, but that was life. Joys and disappointments all blended up in one big smoothie. With some chunks remaining.

As the noon bells chimed out from Our Lady of the Sea, Westham's Catholic church, I began walking home had but paused and pulled out my phone. I must have something else that needed doing on my pre-wedding to-do list. "Pick up license" was the second item. I was nearly in front of Town Hall, so that was an easy one to knock off. I was pretty sure the town officials didn't close for lunch, at least not the public-facing ones. The noon hour was when lots of people liked to run errands.

A text came in from Tim before I could move along.

Crime scene team was here all morning, just left, said we can resume work. XXOO

That was good news. I could get back and help for a couple of hours this afternoon. I tapped out a response.

Am doing errands, home soon. OOXX

Proceeding with the project meant we would wipe out all traces of Della Ruhlen from our home. Sadness washed over me again. I didn't want to open a ghoulish museum or anything, but couldn't we find some way to memorialize her terrible penultimate resting place? I would talk to Tim about it when I got home. Between us we could come up with something to leave in the wall. At the least it could be a written document of what we had found and when. Maybe a print of the photograph I'd taken when I'd only known her as Bridey, as a memorial to be found by the next person who renovated the space.

A minute later, I stood in the lobby of the lovely old stone Town Hall, which was on the National Register of Historic Places. The town had renovated and modernized the inside, but they'd kept the beautiful wooden trim, tall windows, and high ceilings. I headed into the Clerk and Records area.

Tim and I had come in together to apply for the license, but the person had said either one of us could pick it up this week. Today a different person sat on a high stool behind the counter.

"Can I help you?" she asked without looking away from her monitor. She had ear-length graying hair and wore a blue cardigan over a white shirt.

"Hi, uh . . ." A metal nameplate sat on the counter read *Hope Ruhlen*. I nodded to myself. Could she be a relative of Della? "Hello, Ms. Ruhlen. My name is Mackenzie Almeida, and I'm here to pick up my marriage license."

She tapped away. "What's the other party's name?"

"Timothy Brunelle."

"It's ready. I'll be back in a minute." She lowered her reading glasses to hang from the cord around her neck, slipped off the stool, and headed away, her black sneakers quiet on the carpet. She walked with a slight hitch, as if her hip bothered her.

I called out my thanks as she went. I gazed around the room, which held several cubicles along the walls. Stephen's office was at the back, but the door labeled *Clerk* was shut, and no light shone through the glass in it. He might have taken the day off to prepare for tonight's party.

Hope returned with a manila envelope and slid it onto the counter. "The officiant needs to sign it, and it must be returned here within two weeks of the ceremony. Congratulations, Ms. Almeida." No smile accompanied her words.

Up close I saw that she'd earned her silver hairs. She had to be at least seventy, judging from the lines in her face and the age spots on her hands.

"Thank you so much." I stuck the envelope into my cross bag. "Forrest is doing our flowers. Are you related to him?"

Hope finally looked me in the eye. "He's my brother." Her eyes were also hazel, like Forrest's, although her eyebrows were neatly plucked.

"He does beautiful floral work."

"Yes." She boosted herself back onto her chair and focused on her monitor, resettling her readers on her nose.

I didn't move. Should I just jump in and ask?

"Is there something else you need?" she asked.

No time like the present. "I wondered if you'd had an older relative named Della. Della Louise?"

She faced me with a sharp move and peered over the top of her glasses, blinking. "How do you know about Della?"

Now what? Did I tell her the whole story? I suddenly wasn't sure I should. The police must not have contacted her yet. There had barely been time for them to pick up the suitcase from Win. I scrambled.

"I was flipping through old newspaper stories at the library and came across her name." At least that much was true.

"She was my aunt, my father's sister." Hope blew out a soft breath. She tapped a knobby index finger on the counter. "The family story was that Della eloped with her lover. I've never thought that was true, but I can't explain why."

I opened my mouth to tell her exactly why when a man hurried up behind me, and a couple behind them. I stepped out of the way. I held up the envelope holding my license to legally marry in the Commonwealth of Massachusetts. "Thank you."

Hope squared her shoulders and faced the newcomer. "Can I help you, sir?"

She would find out what happened to Della soon enough. But from the authorities, not from me. I supposed it would be Hope's decision, and Forrest's, what should be done with their great-aunt's suitcase and its contents, and with the sad, abandoned skeleton of a bride.

CHAPTER 15

I really wanted to know what the police were doing about Della's remains—and how she'd become the skeleton in the wall. Maybe Nikki would talk to me, or Penelope Johnson. I hadn't learned much at all from Hope.

I ran up the antique granite steps to the police station. The facility was also accessible by way of a ramp that met at the same landing. By some stroke of luck, Penelope pushed open the door before I could put my hand on it. She was alone, with a watch cap pulled over her head and a zipped-up WPD winter jacket.

"Good morning, Detective." I took a step back. "Or I guess it's afternoon already."

"Hi, Mac. Have you found something else relating to the remains?"

"No. I mean, Win let me sit with her as she opened

the suitcase this morning, so I know the skeleton was named Della Ruhlen."

"Yes."

"With a passport and lightweight, summer clothes. And a picture of a young man signed, 'Manny.'"

"Yes, I know. We have the suitcase in custody. We have examined the contents."

"Well, a little while ago Florence Wolanski over at the library found a newspaper article suggesting Della and Manny Cabral eloped."

"Oh, she did?" Penelope folded her arms. "She apparently hasn't found it necessary to inform us of that discovery."

"She had to run off to a meeting. She's the director. Very busy. I'm sure she'll convey that information when she gets back." She would if I texted her that she'd better.

"That would be very helpful."

An aged pickup truck passing by thumped over one of the ubiquitous potholes, hazards that would only grow worse over the course of the winter. The lobster traps piled in the back clattered, startling me and scattering my thoughts.

I swallowed. "So, uh, where is Della now? I mean, her remains."

"She's in the county morgue in Barnstable, of course."

"Of course. I assume that forensics guy is coming down from Boston to check her out."

"I'm not at liberty to say."

Penelope had seemed a lot friendlier yesterday. Maybe she didn't like being questioned by a civilian. I probably wouldn't either, if I were in her position. Except I still had questions. And didn't I, as one of the two people who had discovered Della's skeleton, deserve a few answers?

"Was her disappearance listed as a cold case?" I tried to keep my voice casual.

"It is now." She unfolded her arms. "If you'll excuse me, I have a couple of much warmer cases I need to investigate. We've had crimes all over town this week." She stepped around me and trotted down the stairs.

I watched her go. Della's disappearance in 1940 hadn't been considered a case of wrongdoing. Of malice domestic. Of homicide. Nor had Manny's, apparently. Which made me feel unspeakably despondent.

Standing here, morose and no wiser, however, was not going to move this case forward. I could go home and search for the deed to our cottage on my laptop. It didn't seem like something that would be very easy to see on a tiny phone screen. If deeds weren't digitized from eighty-whatever years ago, I could fire up Miss M, my convertible Miata—red, of course—and drive to our county seat of Barnstable.

Except Flo would probably do the search once she got out of her meeting. Knowing who owned the house when the secret compartment was constructed seemed like an important piece of information. One might expect it would be those who built the home— that is, the Swift family—but they could have sold it by then. Win herself might know. I hadn't thought to ask her.

And I should probably be helping Tim with the demolition. The sooner we had the space ready, the sooner our builder guy could start creating the bathroom. Him, along with the plumber guy and the electrician guy and the tile guy. My head hurt a little thinking about the project. When my stomach rumbled, I laughed. Hunger could account for the headache part, although it didn't reduce the size of the bathroom to-do list. I was a big fan of lists.

Maybe I should pop by the parsonage and hang with Belle a little. My parents never minded if I raided their refrigerator. Except I should probably go home to eat, then change and start helping tear down walls built before the Second World War.

CHAPTER 16

"Titi Mac," a high voice called before I could go anywhere.

I smiled to see my niece and her daddy, my half-brother Derrick, holding hands and crossing Main Street toward me. With his other hand, Derrick held Tucker on a leash, keeping him close to his side. I trotted down the police department stairs to the sidewalk.

"How's my favorite Cokester?" I crouched, opening my arms.

Cokey flung herself at me at full-tilt. If there's anything better than a whole-body hug from a five-year-old girl who adores you, I don't know what it is. She planted a loud kiss on my cheek, then stepped back, holding out her arm.

"Look, Daddy buyed me a brathelet for the wedding." She pushed up her purple parka sleeve, rotating her wrist this way and that to show off a silver bracelet with different-colored inset stones, or bits of glass, more likely.

"That's so pretty." I assumed the whole thing was all costume jewelry. Derr wasn't exactly rolling in cash. But Cokey wouldn't care. "I love all the colors. Which is your favorite?"

"Blue." She always pronounced it with an extra vowel between the consonants.

Tucker yipped, so I stroked his silky black head. "Daddy's very sweet." I wrapped an arm around my teddy bear of a brother. "Hey, bro."

"How's it shaking, sis?" He lowered his voice. "You know, with your find? Also, what's up with the police station?"

"I'm working on figuring out how she got in there," I murmured back, then gestured behind me with my thumb. "They weren't particularly forthcoming, but Flo's been helping."

"I'm very good at helping, Titi Mac." Cokey gazed up at me, now all serious, her curly blond angel hair backlit in the sunshine. "My teacher told me so. Do you want me to help you?"

"You're already going to help by being our flower girl, right?"

"Yes, I am," she lisped. "I'm going to wear my new dress and my new bracelet, and I'm going to carry a basket and scatter the petals along the, the . . . what's it called, Daddy?" She frowned.

"The aisle, honey."

"Along the aisle," she pronounced. "Maybe I'll skip, too. Want to see?" She skipped away along the sidewalk.

Tucker strained at the leash. At a command from

Derrick, the pooch sat again, watching her. He was a
Portuguese water dog, a breed my parents had gotten in a nod to my allergies. It was one of the few
kinds of dogs I didn't react to. He was nearly full
grown at seven months, his head coming almost to
my waist. Not a puppy any longer, at least not in size.
Behavior was a different matter.

"That's great, *querida*," I called. "Come back now."
To Derrick, I said, "The skeleton was named Della
Ruhlen. We found her passport. I picked up our wedding license a few minutes ago, and Hope Ruhlen in
the clerk's office said Della was her aunt. Forrest's,
too."

"Wow," Derrick said. "Hyper-local."

"I know. What happened to Manny Cabral—her
betrothed—is anybody's guess. Do you know any
Cabrals?"

"Besides Al?"

"Yes. Mom introduced me to him yesterday."

Derrick shook his head. "No, I don't think I do
know anyone else by that name. But if I think of
someone, I'll let you know."

"I'm going to head over to Westham Village later
and see if Al will talk with me."

"I'm back," Cokey announced.

"I can see that." My stomach growled again.

Derrick snickered.

"It's not funny," I protested.

"Titi Mac, you need to have a snack," Cokey said,
concern written all over her little face.

"I know, sweetheart. I'm going home right now to
have lunch with Tim." I gazed down at her. "Did you
know you have Grandma's hair?"

"Abo Astra's?" she lisped.

"Yes, exactly," I said. "Hers has some white in it now, but otherwise yours is so much like hers."

"We have a very mixed-up family," Cokey declared. "I'm part French, and BisAbo Reba has brown skin, and Abo Astra is Scottish, and Abo Joseph talks Kriolu, and you lived in Thailand, and Daddy has light hair. We're all mixed up and all the same, too."

"And isn't that the best, really? What a great family we have." I knelt to hug her again. "I'm going to go feed my mixed-up stomach now. I love you."

"See you around, donut." Cokey beamed.

"See you soon, spoon," I returned. I'd taught her a bunch of these phrases, and now we had to go through the whole routine.

"See you later, alligator."

"See you in a while, crocodile."

"See you in a jiff, Biff." She'd made that one up and always followed it up with peals of laughter because I never had one to come back with.

I stood, ruffling her hair. "Are you going to Zane and Stephen's?" I asked Derrick.

"Probably not, unless I stop in with Cokey at the beginning. I know it starts early, but she's pretty wound up this week, what with Christmas, your wedding, and no school. She needs her sleep—and I need a little downtime at night."

"I hear you. We'll talk soon."

Cokey took Derrick's hand. "Let's skip together, Daddy."

I watched the tall and short of them skip away, my heart full. Derrick had had some rough years, but he was doing so well now, with his own life as well as being a doting and responsible dad.

Tim was eager to be a father. I wasn't quite as

eager to become a mother—talk about a messy, un-controllable process—but the thought of him skipping with a mini-version of himself—or of me—filled my heart. Family meant the world to me, and I couldn't think of anyone I'd rather create one with than Tim.

Della had to have felt that way about her Manny. She'd been robbed of her chance, and I was deter-mined to find out who had been the thief.

CHAPTER 17

Once again, I was about to start home when a text came in from Sand Dollar Gifts saying my special order was in. Instead of heading left, I pointed myself to the right toward the popular gift shop nestled between the liquor store and Yoshinoya, Westham's Japanese restaurant. I had ordered insulated wine tumblers as thank-you gifts for Gin and my mom—otherwise known as Team Bride—and was having a special inscription painted on the side.

Inside, I strolled past shelves of jewelry, mugs, and glassware. A tall rack held pairs of socks with pictures and puns woven into them. Stacks of alpaca shawls on a table were in gorgeous jewel hues of turquoise, purple, maroon, and green. Sea-themed pieces of stained glass hung from the ceiling next to mobiles made from sand dollars. A round mirror featured ceramic mermaids and seahorses around the edges.

A man in a long wool coat was studying a glass case holding silver and gold pendants and bracelets. He was blocking access to the counter in the back where I needed to pick up my order.

"Excuse me, sir," I murmured.

He whirled, glaring at me. *Whoa.* I hadn't bumped into him or anything. I took a step back and mustered a smile in the face of the ire in those eyes, now nearly concealed by heavy brows. The same eyes I'd seen outside the florist yesterday. And actually, the same eye color as Win's.

"I need to get by you." I pointed toward the counter beyond. "If you'll excuse me?"

"Oh." He gave his head a quick shake. "Sure." He pressed himself against the glass so I could pass.

"Thank you." I waited at the main counter until the older woman finished with a prior customer. She wasn't the owner, whom I had placed the order with last week. "I'm Mac Almeida, here to pick up a special order." On the periphery of my vision, I could swear the man shot me a glance. Did he know my name? I certainly didn't know his. When I looked his way, he again studied the jewelry.

"They came out real nice." The woman set three boxes on the counter and lifted a cup out of one. In a shimmering frosted lavender, it was the shape of a stemless wineglass. "It comes with a lid you can sip out of, but of course you don't need to use that."

I inspected the inscription. "Perfect. Thank you so much. Can you gift wrap two of them separately?"

"You got it." She drew turquoise tissue paper off a roll. "Are you the bride?"

"I am." I smiled. "The wedding is Saturday, and my

team—my best friend and my mom—has made it all happen."

"Many congratulations." She added three paper bags stamped with turquoise sand dollars to a larger bag. She'd stuffed the tissue paper into all three and tied ribbons through the handles. "Looks like you paid when you ordered, so you're all set."

"Thank you. They're going to love these." I turned to go.

The man with the odd eyes now stood, fists on hips, in front of a large, framed piece of art near the door. When I approached, I saw it was a black-and-white photograph of a building labeled *Winslow Granite* with some people standing in front.

"What's this doing here?" The man, irate again, didn't quite shout, but almost. He caught sight of me, his gaze burning.

I shook my finger. "I don't work here."

The woman hurried up. "Is there a problem, sir?"

"You better believe there is. You're selling a stolen picture of my family's company. My grandfather took that photograph." He loomed over the woman. "How dare you?"

How could he know his grandfather took that particular picture? It looked like a building that existed in public. Anyone could have photographed it. As far as I could tell, it wasn't signed.

"Those are my relatives," he continued, pointing at the figures in the foreground.

The woman cleared her throat and squared her shoulders. "You'll have to come back and ask the owner, sir. We sell the work of quite a few local artists and artisans. I can assure you, no theft was involved."

"We'll see about that." He stormed toward the door, letting cold air rush in after him.

"Angry much?" I asked, shaking my head.

"He was in yesterday, too," the woman said. "He hasn't bought anything, but both times he was checking out our most expensive merchandise."

I blinked. "Really?" Like he was assessing what to come back later for, maybe? That didn't sound good.

"Yes. Unfortunately, the boss is out of town this week." She headed back to the counter, still talking. "Good thing we have an alarm system and security cams outdoors and in."

"Glad to hear it." They might need them.

I studied the photograph more closely. I hadn't paid it any attention when I'd been in before. It was a big enlargement, maybe twenty-four by eighteen inches, showing an Art Deco–style building with *Winslow Granite* prominent on a sign. An older man stood with a younger man and a woman about the same age. Judging from the clothes, the shot was taken in the thirties or forties. I took out my phone and snapped a picture of it.

Was this Winslow connected to Win Swift? The man had said his grandfather took the photo. If the intern's name was a family name, he might be a relative. A relative with an anger problem. I knew one thing. I didn't need to run into him again.

CHAPTER 18

I never did get to my plan of helping Tim. I drove toward Westham Village at three after telling Tim I would go straight on to the Hanukkah party since he wasn't attending. He wanted to stay home and keep doing demolition and said he didn't need my assistance. Plus, it would be only book group members at the holiday gathering.

The senior residence was a smaller establishment than I'd expected. I'd seen those big assisted-living places run by corporate chains, cookie-cutter copies of each other. This looked like someone's antique house, with a modern addition on the back.

I locked Miss M. Owning a red Miata sports car was a big indulgence. But I'd been a prudent and savvy investor back when I'd worked in finance in Boston, and after I returned from my years traveling, I'd treated myself to her.

A ramp on the side of the addition led to a wide door. I hit the fat button with my elbow to automatically open the door, still opting for hands-free in public whenever I could. Inside on a desk were three binders labeled *Guests, Residents,* and *Care Providers* in front of a sign reading, "Please sign in and out." I dutifully wrote my name on the first open line in the Guests book, adding the time and *Ursula Wolanski* as the person I was here to visit.

Except, how was I going to find her? Nobody sat behind the desk. I glanced around for someone to ask. A man in navy-blue scrubs with a stethoscope around his neck hurried away in the distance. This entryway appeared to open up into a common room. Then I spied an office with glass in the wall and the word *Director* on the door.

I poked my head in and found Al Cabral sitting behind a desk talking on the phone. After he saw me, he gestured for me to sit in one of the visitor's chairs. I sat.

The walls showed photographs of happy senior citizens. Several held sheet music and sang as a woman played piano. Two residents gardened in a flower-filled box built at waist level. A foursome played bridge at a round table. Walkers and wheelchairs were in evidence, but everyone looked alert and engaged. A framed certificate stated that Westham Village had won an award for the Best Family-Run Senior Residence in New England. *Family-run.* The Cabral family, or was Al an employee?

Al hung up the desk phone. "Good afternoon, Mac. How can I help you?"

I greeted him. "I came to visit Ursula Wolanski.

Her daughter, Flo, said it was fine, but I don't know where Ursula's room is."

"Of course, you're welcome to visit." He stood. "I'll help you locate her. She's often in the sunroom in the afternoons."

"So you are family-run here." I pointed to the certificate. "I had expected to find one of those great big assisted-living residences."

"No, the management likes to keep it small so we can provide better care. Personalized care, if you will. Come with me." He motioned for me to precede him out of the office.

I stayed put. "Is it your family who owns the business?"

He frowned. "Not anymore." He stepped into the hall.

I followed. He had not looked happy about my question. Or maybe he wasn't happy about the "anymore" part.

He led me through the big, open common room, where residents read, played cards, or snoozed in their wheelchairs. He pulled open the door to a light-filled space beyond it, with walls of windows and skylights overhead. Potted and flowering plants were everywhere. Outside was a garden, or it would be when the weather warmed up.

On the other side of the room, a man slouched in a wheelchair, apparently snoozing. A woman with white hair in a bun atop her head sat in an armchair gazing out the closest window. A book lay open on her lap.

"Ursula, you have a visitor," Al said to the woman.

I came around to face her. "Ursula, I'm Mac Al-

meida, Reba's granddaughter and a friend of Flo's."
I spoke clearly in case she was hard of hearing.

"Hello, dear." She held out a long-fingered hand.
"Sit with me for a bit, will you?" Her face was full
of fine-textured wrinkles that deepened as she smiled
at me.

"I'd love to." I pulled up a chair and perched on it,
then glanced up. "Thank you, Al."

"You ladies have a good visit." He hurried away.

"Al takes good care of us," Ursula said. "Now, Reba
has told me all about you, Mackenzie, and so has Florence. You run that bike shop, and you're getting
married soon."

"All true. The wedding is Saturday, in fact." I slipped
out of my jacket. It was nearly tropical in here, what
with all the plants and light.

"Florence has let slip that you and that mystery
book group have figured out a few murder villains recently. Real ones, I mean." Her laugh was a carillon
of tiny bells.

"That's true, too." Outside, a brisk breeze ruffled
the silky tan tops of tall decorative grasses.

"And I expect you're here to ask about the skeleton." The blue of her eyes was faded, but her gaze
was intense.

I bobbed my head. "I would like to, if you don't
mind. Have you heard who it was?"

"No, and the news hasn't said where the remains
were found, or by whom."

"It's a little bit personal. My fiancé and I found it.
Her. And she was wearing a wedding dress."

"Oh, my." Ursula brought her hand to her mouth.
"Was this an old skeleton?"

"Yes, with a suitcase. Her name was—"

"Della," she whispered. "Della Ruhlen." She gave her head a quick turn toward the napping man, then looked at me.

"You knew her."

"I did. She was ten years older than I, but we were neighbors. She let me come over and look at her pretty dresses, her jewelry. She was kind to me, unlike Richard, her mean SOB of a younger brother." Again Ursula glanced at the man. "I saw Della and Manny canoodling behind the shed once."

"My grandmother said Della's family didn't approve of her dating Manny."

"Gracious sakes alive, Mac. They most certainly did not." She shook her head, making a *tsk*ing sound. "The Ruhlens fancied themselves one of the better families in town, along with the Swifts and the Winslows."

Winslow Granite. That family might bear further investigation.

"But Manny?" Ursula went on. "Not only was he not a Yankee, he was also a lowly fisherman. Lowly in their eyes, at least."

"And Della was sweet on Manny."

"I'll tell you, it was entirely mutual. He was a hardworking young man and always polite, but her family couldn't see past the Portuguese name. He was good-looking, too." She gazed out at the waving grasses.

Reba had been right. Ursula certainly did have a keen memory.

"So when they disappeared, everyone simply assumed they'd eloped and found a place to live where people wouldn't judge them." She gave a little laugh. "Of course, I was nine and had to pester my mother to tell me what the word 'elope' meant." Her eyes drifted shut.

Maybe I should slip out. Keen mental faculties or not, she might be accustomed to an afternoon snooze. Before I could stand, her eyes flew open again.

"I need to know more about how you came to find poor Della," she said.

"Well, Tim Brunelle, the man I am going to marry on Saturday, owns a cottage on Blacksmith Shop Road, which I am moving into. We want to add a bathroom downstairs. On Monday morning, we were breaking through a wall at the back of a closet. But we encountered a narrow space he hadn't realized was there. That's where we found her, on a chair."

"With a suitcase, you said?"

"Yes. I think she must have been about to elope, judging from the dress and the contents of the suit-case. But somebody really didn't want her to. Ursula, her hands were chained to the wall behind her."

"Poor Della." The corners of her mouth turned down. "Wait a minute, now. What's the address of that cottage?"

"Eighty-five Blacksmith Shop Road."

"Why, that was the Swift guesthouse. It used to be on the Swift estate. Their big house was around the corner." She stared at me. "Kit used to throw parties at the guesthouse."

"Katherine Swift?" Miss Quahog 1938?

"The same. She fancied herself Della's rival. They ran in the same circles, but Della was much prettier than Kit, who had a horsey face. Della could have had any of the boys. All she wanted was her fisher-man. Her Manny."

CHAPTER 19

I sat in Miss M for a moment in front of Zane and Stephen's home. It was a little ways outside town on a bluff overlooking the broad bay to the west of town. The sun was a cold orange orb about to sink into the water. And I needed to get inside if I didn't want to miss the lighting of the menorah, which Zane had said would begin right after sunset.

Except my thoughts were on what I'd learned about Della and Manny. And Kit. And the Swift guest cottage, now my new home, where a teenage Kit had thrown parties. According to Ursula, Kit had been jealous of Della for no reason except her looks. Jealous enough to kill her? The thought made a shudder ripple through me. Surely she would have had to have help to abduct Della, chain her to the wall, and build a new wall as she sat there. Alive? Maybe. Or maybe they waited until she was dead and then built the interior wall. Either way, it was far too much like a Poe horror story. Who could be that evil?

A small truck pulled up behind me. Norland Gifford climbed out, holding a covered plate. Our now-retired chief of police and a widower, he was an enthusiastic member of our group. I'd better go in with him. I climbed out and locked my scarlet ride.

"Hey, Mac." He gestured with his chin toward the sun, now a flattened sphere. "We're almost late."

"I know." I glanced at his plate. I hadn't brought anything to contribute. *Oh, well.* They all knew I didn't cook, and thank goodness for men who did, including the one I was about to marry. Contributing a bottle of wine to the party was kind of coals to Newcastle, since I would have bought it from Zane. "What did you bring?"

"I made some dreidel cookies." He smiled. "My grandson helped me decorate them, so don't expect a professional icing job."

"I won't—I promise."

Inside, we were clearly the last of the group to arrive. The others—Gin and Flo, since Derrick wasn't coming—stood with Zane, holding drinks in front of a dining room table laden with food. Tall, slim Zane looked snappy as always, tonight wearing a light blue bow tie and a striped shirt tucked into very skinny jeans. Stocky Stephen, about my height, wore a maroon brocade blazer and an open-collared black silk shirt, more fashion flair than I'd ever seen him sport in his role as Westham town clerk. I felt distinctly underdressed in the same leggings and long green sweater I'd worn all day. On the other hand, these were my best friends. They didn't care what I wore, how I looked.

Stephen stood behind the table with a menorah on a silver tray in front of him. Blue and white dreidels were scattered on the table in front of the tray along with disks wrapped in gold foil that looked a lot like the chocolate money I used to get in my Christmas stocking. He was about to strike a match.

"Come in, you two," Stephen called to us.

I shed my coat. Norland set his cookies on the table.

"Ready?" Stephen asked.

We all nodded.

He lit the candle in the middle, whose holder stood higher than those on either side, and began to sing in Hebrew. He then removed the lit candle and used it to light a candle in the far-right slot of the menorah. He replaced the one he had used back in the middle, still chanting in a musical way for another minute.

Stephen spoke softly. "That last one is a prayer thanking God for keeping us alive, for sustaining us, and for bringing us to this season."

The room fell quiet. We all gazed at the flickering lights.

"That was beautiful, Stephen, thank you," I said. "I've never witnessed the lighting of a menorah before."

He smiled. "I'm glad you could be here."

"Norland, and Mac, grab yourselves a drink before Stephen starts storytelling." Zane gestured toward the bottles and glasses on the sideboard. "I can fix you a Menorah Martini if you want."

"What's in that?" I asked.

"Vodka, sweet vermouth, blue curaçao, with a blueberry garnish."

"It sounds wonderful," I said, "but I think I'll stick with wine." The last thing I needed was to down a couple of sweet vodka martinis and get arrested for an OUI on my way home a few days before my wedding.

I poured a glass of pinot noir, while Norland cracked open an oatmeal stout from the Cape's best brewery.

"Here's why we celebrate the light for eight days," Stephen began. He told the story of the Maccabees and the Temple and the one-night's supply of oil that burned for eight nights.

"Did you know there's a long history of Jews and Cape Verdeans in the Boston area celebrating Passover together?" I asked him.

"I didn't."

"We share a history of enslavement, liberation, and diaspora. Plus, a number of Jews escaped persecution in Portugal around the fifteenth century and settled in the Cape Verde islands." I'd attended one of the joint seders while I was at Harvard, even though I had no idea whether Pa's family had Jewish ancestry in its past.

"Nice to know we're related, after a fashion." Stephen smiled. "Now, everybody, load up a plate and let's go in the other room to talk about skeletons."

A skeleton who had been forcibly detained behind a wall. By putting our heads together, maybe we could learn something more about who did that to her.

CHAPTER 20

Twenty minutes later, I sat next to Flo with the remnants of some amazing appetizers on my cobalt-blue plate. Brisket-filled turnovers. Swedish-style meatballs on toothpicks. Greek dolmades, rice and meat wrapped in grape leaves. For a bit of crunch, Thai fresh rolls, translucent wrappers holding bits of carrot, cabbage, basil, and chopped shrimp, with a delicious peanut dipping sauce. Bite-sized latkes. Little round jelly donuts dusted with powdered sugar. And more, all finger food. Not vegetarian or even kosher, not with the shrimp. But every morsel delicious.

"I just realized Tulia isn't here," I said to Flo, who sat next to me. The owner of the Lobstah Shack was an integral member of the Cozy Capers.

"She's out of town. On vacation in Puerto Rico, if you can believe it. Her brother's running the shop."

"I hope she'll be back by Saturday. I thought she said she'd be at the wedding."

"She will."

"I visited your mom this afternoon," I added in a murmur.

"Oh? What did she know?"

I opened my mouth to answer when Gin raised her almost-empty glass.

"Here's to the chefs," she said. "Have you been cooking for a week?"

Stephen laughed. "Thank you, but no. I made a few things, including the brisket for the turnovers, and Z called a caterer for the rest."

Zane grinned and shrugged in a "what can you do?" gesture. "I brought the alcohol. Speaking of which . . ." He jumped up and brought back bottles of red and white, offering refills all around.

"Now, Mac," Flo began. "Tell us everything."

"Yes, every little bit," Gin added.

"Please," Norland said as he sat back.

"About the wedding?" I played dumb.

Flo gave me a Look over the top of her glasses.

"Okay, okay. You all know Tim and I found the skeleton in a wall of his—I mean, our—house." I glanced around. I'd checked the thread before I'd headed out to visit Ursula. Flo had added Della's name and what she'd found online, plus what I'd seen in the suitcase. "Perhaps most interesting is what I learned from Flo's mom, Ursula, a little while ago."

I gazed around at the group. Among us, could we solve this cold case? We never had before. We'd only attempted to help the police with the current-time cases that had sprung up in town. I forged on.

"Ursula said Tim's house was the Swift guest cottage, that at the time it was on the Swift estate, with the big house, as she put it, around the corner. Does anybody know about that place?" I must have walked down that side street, but maybe not. It led away from town. Whenever I left Tim's, I was always going into town. "Is it still there?"

"I believe a large antique home is still at that location, but I don't think the Swifts own it anymore," Norland said. "When I was a child, we thought it was haunted."

"Really?" Gin said. "By Della's ghost, maybe."

Norland looked over his glasses at her. "We thought it was haunted because it was a derelict with unkempt grounds. The house was in dire need of repair."

"If any house would be haunted, it should be Tim's, right?" Zane's eyes sparkled at the thought. "With Della herself right there in the wall."

"Stop it, Zane," I said. "You'll give me nightmares." I'd been able to sleep last night, but that was no guarantee I wouldn't be freaked out tonight by the thought of Della in the walls.

"I can check the deeds tomorrow," Stephen offered. "I imagine the property was subdivided after they sold both structures and the land, but I can get the details."

"Thanks, Stephen." I went on. "Anyway, Ursula said Kit—Katherine—Swift threw parties in the cottage when she was a teenager. That she and Della had the same group of friends, but Kit was jealous of Della because she was pretty."

"Typical teenage-girl stuff," Flo said.

"Yes," I said. "Except Della didn't want any of the boys Kit was sweet on. She only wanted Manny."

"This Kit wouldn't have known how to build a new wall, would she?" Zane tilted his head. "I mean, of course girls can do that kind of thing, but in that era? A society girl would have been unlikely to be that handy, I'd say."

"I don't know about that," I said. "I think we underestimate women of the past. But she would have needed help, in any case."

"I knew Kit a little," Flo said. "She was a benefactor of the library and helped fund our new building. She pretty much demanded we name it the Swift Family Public Library. Yeah, no. That wasn't going to happen."

Stephen rolled his eyes.

"She had a family." Gin frowned. "Who did she marry? How was her last name still Swift?"

"That's a good question," I said.

"She married Simon Adams," Flo said. "But he died when she was pregnant with her first child. She went back to using Swift and gave her son that last name, too."

"That's remarkable for that era," Gin said.

"I wonder if she remarried, had other children," Zane mused.

"Win, her great-granddaughter, said Kit was a pistol, or something to that effect," I said. "Reverting to her maiden name probably wasn't out of character. She might have kept the Swift name even if she did remarry."

"Who knows?" Norland lifted a shoulder. "Maybe she was handy with a hammer and knew how to put up an interior wall, too." He stood. "Anybody want a cookie?"

CHAPTER 21

I came downstairs the next morning to the irresistible aromas of coffee, something fresh-baked, scrambled eggs, and bacon. An aproned Tim turned from the sink, where he was washing the mixing bowl.

"Good morning, sunshine," he said. "I was about to go up and wake you."

"What time is it?" In fact, I hadn't slept well at all. It had taken me hours of restless tossing to put the thought of Della's skeleton out of my mind. I pushed up my glasses and yawned as I plopped into a chair at the kitchen table. The place mats were already set with silverware, and an empty mug sat at my place.

"Eight thirty." He dried his hands and slipped the apron over his head.

"Shoot! I missed my walk with Gin."

"Last night you said you canceled it." Coffee

carafe in hand, Tim leaned down to kiss me, then filled my mug.

I blinked. "Oh, yeah." Gin and I had decided, at the end of the Hanukkah party, that we would suspend walking by default this week. If one of us wanted to, we would arrange it explicitly. "I guess I needed the sleep. I'll see her at lunchtime for my Team Bride meeting with her and Mom." I added a splash of whole milk to my mug and took a sip of a drink sent straight from heaven.

"To hammer out all the last-minute details?"

"Yes. Which I hope we don't have any surprises with."

He dished up plates for both of us and sat down kitty-corner from me.

"This looks so good." I picked up a scone and examined it. "Blueberry?"

"Yes. You're my guinea pig for a recipe I want to make Saturday morning."

"For our pre-wedding breakfast?"

"Ours and for whoever in either family wants some." He tossed off the remark casually.

My scone-holding hand froze halfway to my mouth. "You're making breakfast Saturday morning for, like, everybody in our families?" My voice ended on a squeak as I stared. "Have we talked about that?"

He chewed the bite of bacon already in his mouth and swallowed. "No, but why not? You've been doing most of the arranging. We're going to have a boatload of folks in from out of town, and they're going to want breakfast." He threw open his hands and smiled. "Why not?"

Mentally, I poked my finger at my forehead and

told myself—silently—to calm the heck down. I took a deep breath and let it out. I looked at my adored betrothed, who loved cooking for others. I exhaled again.

"Why not, indeed?" I asked. "Breakfast here?" I raised my eyebrows as I smiled, hoping beyond hope he would say he'd arranged to cook and serve elsewhere.

"Sure. We agreed we're not putting anyone up here, but they're all going to want to see the house." He reached for my hand. "Our home."

"Of course." I squeezed his hand and let it go. I would tame my morning-of jitters and cope with a dozen or two family members crowding my peaceful—and still new—home.

Or . . . maybe not. My tiny house, which had had its first location behind my bike shop, had been moved to the backyard here. It was built on a trailer base and, like any tiny house, was always meant to be portable if it needed to be. I could see it through the window from where I sat. I had put a lot of thought into the design, since space was at a premium. It was like living on a boat without the gentle rocking. The outside was sweet, with a little attached porch, window boxes, and the stained-glass clerestory window, wider than it was tall, in the loft that rose above the main roofline.

For now, an extension cord and a hose ran out there, but one of these days soon it would have water and electrical hookups. It didn't need sewer because of the composting toilet, and it was already connected to a propane tank for the stove and hot water. Even if my former home wasn't fully hooked up by

Saturday, I could still slip out there and shut the door to my refuge if I got overwhelmed. I took a bite of scone.

"You seemed tired last night," Tim said.

"I was," I mumbled around the bite, then swallowed. I had been exhausted, from the day as well as from the wine. I'd stopped after a second half glass, but the party hadn't wound down until eight, and by the time I'd arrived home and filled Tim in on the group's ideas about Della, I'd been ready for an early night, not that going to bed had done me much good.

"I wanted to tell you what I uncovered as I was continuing the demolition," Tim continued. "I'll show you after we've eaten."

"What? Tell me you didn't find more human remains."

"Nothing like that. Keep eating, Mac."

"Yes, sir. By the way, this scone is delicious. Is it a little tangy?"

His face brightened. "Great. Yes, I used sour cream instead of heavy cream. I thought it would brighten the flavor."

"It does. Did you use frozen blueberries?"

"Yep."

We ate, talking about nothing else that was difficult. I wasn't even sure he'd registered my alarm about Saturday morning. Abo Reba had once cautioned me, "Pick your battles, honey, and make sure they're worth fighting." Blueberry scones for the family on the morning of our wedding was definitely not worth fighting over.

When my plate was empty, Tim stood. "Come. You'll want to see this."

I followed him, not into the bedroom leading to the hidden space, but into the laundry room. The wall now had a three-foot-wide gap in it, with a straight-shot view into the bedroom on the other side.

"I thought we were going to leave this side intact," I ventured.

"We were. But with the surprise of the body, I wanted to make sure that was the only unexpected discovery." He picked up a piece of wall leaning against the washing machine. Covered with overlapping wood shingles, it was about two feet by three feet.

"Shingles?" I asked.

"Yes. It must have been the outer wall at the time. I bet where we're standing was an open porch that somebody later closed in to add more space to the house."

"That makes sense."

"And this was inside the wall." He handed me a brittle piece of newspaper. "Isn't that cool?"

"Wow." The front page of the *Westham Times*, dated February 27, 1940, was absolutely cool. But it also chilled me. Della's killer might have left this newspaper when she was abandoned to die.

CHAPTER 22

I walked out the front door of the cottage an hour before my lunch meeting because I wanted to do a couple things on my way to the parsonage. One of them was to see if Barlow Swift would talk with me about Kit. He had seemed congenial and approachable. And Kit had to be his great-aunt or his grandmother or something. I hoped he would know something about her and could help shed light on what had gone down in 1940 among that group of friends.

I had perused the newspaper page after Tim showed it to me earlier. But it wasn't the edition Flo had uncovered where Della and Manny's elopement was speculated about. That paper had been dated the second of March. This one included news about Europe. A short piece about the first televised hockey game. A teaser about Richard Wright publishing *Na-*

tive Son. But there was no mention of any Swifts, Ruhlens, or Cabrals, not on the front page anyway.

Still, it might be evidence Penelope Johnson would want to see, and when I turned it in, I might be scolded for touching it at all. *Tough.* Tim had touched it first. And anyway, I hadn't heard a word from her. Was she even working on this old, cold case?

A text came in on the thread as I stood on the landing. It was from Stephen.

Orrin and Emily Swift bought the big house on Salt Marsh Lane twenty years ago. Big house built 1906.

So one branch of the Swifts was back in the ancestral family home. I wondered if that meant anything. All the more reason for me to see what Barlow had to say. But my plan to visit him was interrupted when the electrician arrived as I hurried down the front walk. And Tim had gone out for a run.

"Connection to an outbuilding?" the man asked after he identified himself.

"I thought you were coming tomorrow."

"I had an opening, and your husband had said the job was urgent."

I smiled for several reasons. "It's fine. Thank you for fitting us in." I took him around back to the tiny house and told him what it needed.

"Shouldn't be a problem."

"Let me go in and open the bulkhead so I can show you the electrical box in the basement. I'll be right back."

I emerged from the basement a minute later through the flat, slanted bulkhead doors. One friend had called them "Dorothy doors," which always made me giggle, imagining Auntie Em locking them against the cyclone.

"Okay if I switch off the power to the main house?" he asked.

"Not a problem."

He thanked me and went to work. Tim knew I would be needing my refuge, thus the "urgent" designation. I hadn't bothered correcting the dude on my relationship to Tim. He'd be my husband soon enough.

I paced the first floor, waiting for that soon-to-be spouse to return. I didn't want to leave the electrician alone in the house. I knew I should sit down and crack open the coloring book I'd bought from Barlow. Maybe coloring would calm me down. Except I was too antsy even to occupy a chair. Pacing indoors made me hot with my coat on, so I headed back out and paced the front walk as I waited.

When I reached the sidewalk for the fourth time, I stopped and faced the house, picturing the cottage being home to teenage parties in 1940. What would they have looked like? That was before the United States entered the war. The girls would be in ankle socks, saddle shoes, and skirts falling a little below their knees. The boys in high-waisted pleated trousers and open collars. Would alcohol have flowed? Would they have danced to songs on the radio or on the RCA Victrola record player housed in a piece of furniture? People would have been smoking, for sure. In the summer, had they piled into someone's Chevrolet convertible and driven to the beach, sans seat belts?

When Della Ruhlen had gone missing that late February, her family must have missed her. But did her friends? Surely she had been to parties here, Kit's animosity toward her notwithstanding. I swore out loud. There was so much I didn't know. Who were the other friends? Were there older Ruhlens around I could talk to? I wouldn't get that information from Hope Ruhlen, but maybe Forrest would tell me. Other grandmothers or great-grandfathers, town old-timers, might still be alive who could remember a crucial clue about what happened to Della and Manny.

Tim must've been out on a really long run. It was now eleven twenty. I let out a sigh and trudged up to sit on the front step, pulling out my phone. It was brisk out here, but the bright sun offset the air temperature. What could I learn from everyone's best friend, Mr. Google? Or better yet, from Ms. Knows-Everybody, my grandma? Except Reba Almeida did not answer her phone. *Shoot.*

A text dinged in on the Cozy Capers thread. My eyes flew all the way open when I saw it was from Stephen.

Found more. Swift family divided two acres, sold large house and cottage separately in 1946. Col. Owen Swift, Katherine's father, killed in WWII.

Huh. So Kit's father had been a colonel, and she was twenty-six when the property was sold. Was she already married in 1946? Or maybe she was even widowed by then. Her husband—Simon Adams—had died, so he could have also perished in the war. Whatever the details, the Swifts still owned this cottage in 1940.

I tapped out my thanks.

What I didn't know about the history of the Ruhlen family was getting on my nerves. If they were that unhappy about Della marrying Manny, would one or more of them go to the extreme of killing her? I instantly added Forrest to my list of people to pop in on after the lunch meeting. I wasn't going to have time to make any detours on the way there.

To be fair to Tim, I hadn't told him I'd planned to leave at eleven for a noon meeting, and neither of us had known the electrician would arrive at exactly the wrong time. Wrong for my plans, but right for being able to use the tiny house, which had electrical heat. I returned to pondering the mystery of the skeleton behind the wall and the possible involvement of the Ruhlen family.

Wait. What had Ursula said? That Della's younger brother, Richard, was "mean." As in murderously mean? I did a quick search on his name. No, not the high school teacher in San Diego or the salt-and-pepper-haired man in Tennessee whose profile was on Facebook. I slowed at an Ancestry mention of a Richard Ruhlen born in 1918, but he lived in Ohio and, as of the 1940 census, was twenty-two and married.

I added a message to the thread.

Anyone have any info on Richard Ruhlen, Della's younger brother? Ursula told me he was mean.

I remembered I hadn't mentioned Winslow Granite or the man with the odd eyes.

Anybody know about the Winslow family? Their granite company, or the man with the odd-colored eyes who has been lurking around town this week? The dude got really angry at the Sand Dollar yesterday when he saw an old framed photo of the company for sale.

I added the picture of the photograph I'd taken and sent the message. I zoomed in on the people in it and on the cool Art Deco building. The man in the gift shop had said these were his relatives. He had the same strange eye color as Win. If I ran into her again, I could ask if he was her relative or if Winslow Granite had been in her family.

The electrician came around the side of the house at the same time as Tim jogged up, sweaty and red-cheeked. Five minutes later I was on my way. My lips tasted deliciously salty from Tim's kiss, and my brain was full of questions I aimed to get answered before I returned to the cottage with the corpse. The skeleton between the studs. The body in the bedroom. I didn't mean to make light of her death, but I couldn't help thinking that the situation with our Della was starting to sound like the title of a Nancy Drew mystery.

CHAPTER 23

On my way into town, I paused at the corner of Salt Marsh Lane. I wanted to take a look at the former and once-again Swift mansion. I checked my phone. I still had a little time before my lunch meeting with Team Bride, and the house shouldn't be too far down the street, because at one time it had sat on the same property as Tim's house.

The third house on the right had to be the one. It was a lot bigger than any of the other homes. Silvered shingles covered the outside of the large structure. Chimneys with fancy brickwork at the top rose up from each end, and two peaked roofs facing the front were connected by a lower roof running parallel to the street. Several windows at the top level featured small diamond-shaped panes. The entry to the front door was covered by a flat white roof held up by white pillars. The entryway roof had a white railing around it like a balcony—except no door or window on the second floor led to the balcony.

A dumpster sat in the driveway next to a new-looking black Prius. Maybe Win's parents were doing renovations, too.

It was a fancy, roomy home. But when I looked closely, the paint was chipping on the fake balcony. Some of the shingles on the walls were cracked and curling. The slate shingles on the roof didn't look in very good repair, either. It made me wonder what Win's mother and father did for work. Property taxes on a place this big had to be pretty steep.

A man in faded jeans and an even more faded green Dartmouth College sweatshirt came around from the back and tossed a broken wooden chair into the dumpster. He spied me and approached before I could walk away.

"Can I help you with something?" In his fifties, he had a full head of salt-and-pepper hair that was receding only at his temples.

"I was admiring your home." I smiled. "I'm Mac Almeida. I've moved in around the corner."

"Orrin Swift." He removed a work glove and extended his hand.

I shook it with my leather-gloved hand. "Good to meet you. Are you Barlow's brother?"

"Yes, I'm his older brother." His smile was warm, kindly. "By five minutes."

Twins. I thought he'd looked familiar, but it wasn't a resemblance with Win that I'd noticed.

"You were saying you moved in around the corner." He cocked his head.

"I did, into a cottage that apparently had been a guesthouse on the same property as this house."

He narrowed his eyes. "Were you the one who found the skeleton?"

"I was, on Monday. I met your daughter that day." I gazed up at the mansion. "Was this your ancestor's home?"

"Yes, back in the days when the Swifts were a family to be reckoned with." He pivoted to look at the house. "Fortunes rise and fall, though, don't they?"

I wasn't touching that one. "Has the house always been in the family?" Even though Stephen had sent an account, I was curious as to what Orrin would say.

"No, it was sold. Fully furnished, if you can believe it. My wife and I bought it back twenty years ago, around the time Winslow was born. We wanted to raise her here."

"It looks like you're doing some renovation." I pointed my chin at the dumpster.

"Clearing out the attic, at long last. I can't believe the interim owners never did, but that's the reality. I'm eager to use the space." He gave me an abashed smile. "I've done quite well trading stocks. But what I really want to do is teach yoga."

"Good for you." I gazed at the top floor of the house. "It looks like you'll have plenty of room up there."

"I will. The back stairs go straight up there from a side door. The maids' stairs, I guess they were called. So I can open a studio with direct access for the public from the outside when I'm ready."

"Are you finding any family treasures in the attic?" Like a clue to who killed Della, with any luck.

"Not many. Lots of old, broken furniture. Ruined mirrors. Dusty old portraits. But I am going through all of it carefully. You never know when you'll find something valuable from the past."

"My fiancé and I certainly found something valuable—and tragic—when we opened that wall."

"You did, didn't you?" He folded his arms, looking thoughtful.

"Did you ever hear any family lore about what happened to Della Ruhlen?"

"Only that she and her lover eloped. At least, that was what Grandmother Kit said."

"You knew her?"

"Yes, of course. Talk about a force of nature. What Katherine Swift wanted, Katherine Swift got."

Huh. "I'd better get going," I said. "It was lovely meeting you, Orrin."

"Likewise, Mac."

"If you find anything up there relating to Della, will you let me know? Or rather, let the police know."

"I could do both, and yes, I will."

I smiled and strolled back toward town. A man in his fifties following his dream to teach yoga. I liked that. I usually pictured women my age and younger in their stretchy outfits hurrying to yoga class carrying their rolled-up mats. Maybe after Orrin opened for business, I'd sign up for a class. It couldn't get any closer to home.

But that was a distraction from what I'd heard. Kit Smith always got what she wanted. Fingers crossed I could learn how she accomplished it.

CHAPTER 24

O n my way to the parsonage, my step slowed in front of my bike shop. This was the first time I'd closed it for more than a couple of days since I'd returned to town and opened it almost two years ago. I loved this place and had made a go of it. We'd been running in the black for most of that time. With the winters warming, I'd had rental customers last January—and last week. We'd also sold a hefty number of retail items before Christmas, including stocking stuffers, as well as new bicycles. The bottom line was happy, and so was I.

The red window boxes on both sides of the front door were tidy with evergreen arrangements. Inside all the bikes for sale and rent were stored in neat rows, and the cash drawer was empty and open. My mechanic and Derrick and I had scrambled a little on Christmas Eve to get everything stowed and ship-shape, as it were, before we shut down for three weeks, but it was worth it. We all needed a good long break.

I continued on, passing the Lobstah Shack, the Paws and Claws pet supply store, and the big white UU church where my father ministered. Inside the parsonage kitchen, Mom and Gin had already arrived.

"It's takeout instead of homemade lunch, but I had clients this morning. And it's my treat." Mom drew paper-wrapped lobster rolls out of the paper bag stamped with the Lobstah Shack's logo. She set them on the parsonage kitchen table, followed by two containers of sides. "Plus coleslaw and potato salad."

Right. Tulia's brother was minding the small but popular restaurant in her absence.

"Lunch from Tulia's? Thank you, Astra." Gin brandished a white Salty Taffy's box labeled *Peppermint Dark Chocolate Fudge.* "I have dessert covered."

"Christmas leftovers?" I smiled at her.

"Sorry." She rolled her eyes. "Fudge doesn't go stale, but nobody wants to think Noel once it's over."

"Think Noel, Mac, think Noel," Belle said from her cage in the other room.

I'd greeted her when I came in and given her a frozen snack. Now I closed the door to the living room so we could get our business done without her vocal contributions. I would hang out with her after the meeting was over.

"And I brought the booze." I pulled out a bottle of chilled pinot gris. I'd had enough time to dash into

Zane's shop on my way here. I knew if I was a few minutes late, my team wouldn't mind, especially if it meant a delicious bottle of wine for our meeting.

"I always said you were a smart girl." Mom beamed. "And it's a screw top, no less." She grabbed three jelly jars from the cupboard.

Gin laid her iPad on the table as she sat. She was the keeper of the master to-do list, even though it was a shared spreadsheet. I poured wine all around, then counted.

"Mom, four sandwiches?" I asked.

"Yes, your father wanted one, too."

Pa appeared in the doorway. "I certainly did. Hello, ladies." He kissed Mom's cheek, ruffled my hair, and held out his hand to Gin. "I won't stay, but I am hungry." His deep voice was as calming as ever, his smile as broad.

"Want a splash of wine, Pa?" I asked.

He chuckled. "I can't, *querida*. I'm on the Lord's clock, or at least the UU version of it. But if there's any left over, I'd be happy for a glass at the end of the day."

"Joseph, are you all set for Friday night?" Gin looked up from the tablet.

"Yes. I'll start the *cachupa* on Thursday, so the flavors have time to meld, and I'll be off work by noon on Friday. You girls don't have to worry about a thing for the welcoming dinner. Derrick and I have it under control, with an assist from Tim."

A welcome dinner the night before the wedding had apparently taken the place of the traditional rehearsal dinner. Pa had volunteered to make a massive pot of the Cape Verdean national dish to feed everyone. It was a delectable stew with meats and vegetables. A welcome dinner was fine, particularly one I didn't have to do anything about.

"But are we going to actually rehearse?" I scrunched up my nose. How did I not already know that? "I mean, Cokey has to know what's going on." And I did, too.

"Five p.m. sharp on Friday, Mackenzie." Pa pointed both index fingers at me, then blew me a kiss.

Whew. "I will be ready."

He picked up his lobster roll. "Thanks, hon," he said to my mom, then headed back to his office next door.

We ladies dug into our lunch, postponing wedding talk until after we ate. Except I didn't want to postpone my thoughts about Della and Manny.

"Mom, do you know of a Richard Ruhlen? He would be old by now. Or any other clear-minded town old-timers I could talk to about the past?"

"You're working on the mystery of the skeleton." She sipped from her little jar of wine.

"I am, and it remains a mystery. I don't know if the police are digging as hard as they can. It has to be one of their coldest cold cases. But the bride was a Ruhlen. Della Ruhlen."

Gin gave a single nod. "Who apparently had a younger brother named Richard."

"I'll think on it, sweetheart." Mom smiled. "Your grandmother, of course, would be the best source of information."

"I called her about an hour ago, but she didn't answer." I popped in the last bite of my sandwich. It was the pinnacle of delicious, with big, luscious chunks of lobster, just the right amount of mayonnaise, tiny bits of celery, and a dash of lemon. The lobster rolls were pricey and worth every penny.

"I met Orrin Swift on my way over here," I said. "Win's father. That's quite a house they have."

"On Salt Marsh Lane," Gin said. "They certainly don't keep it up very well. It's a shame."

"I noticed." I took a sip of wine. "I also want to find out what happened to Manny Cabral, the man Della loved. Is his skeleton sitting in some other hidden space?"

"Not in your house, I hope." Mom lifted one eyebrow.

A shiver rippled through me. "I hope not, too."

"Have we, and by 'we' I mean 'Flo,' run a search on his name?" Gin asked.

"I don't think so." I helped myself to a small portion of coleslaw. Not that I was still hungry, but Tulia's was better than any I'd ever tasted. She'd said a bit of horseradish was the secret ingredient. "We did find that article claiming the two of them eloped, but I think that was it."

Mom checked the clock, which read twelve forty. "This is fun, girls, but I have a client at one thirty. Are we ready to check the wedding list?"

"Sure." Gin brought out her phone. "The caterer is all set. I think that lobster pasta dish is going to be fabulous, Mac."

"It was delicious when we had the tasting," I agreed.

As we talked about place cards and cocktails, music and pictures, guest book signing and cake cutting, not to mention the all-important vows, I realized everything was falling into place for this happy event. I found my excitement rising. I was going to link my life with Tim's. That was pretty much the definition of *happy*.

"Your action items, Mac, are to write—and practice—your vows and to go for your last dress fitting," Gin said.

"I'm on it." Between Mom and Gin, it seemed everything else was set for Saturday. "Thank you both. I can't tell you what a relief it is to know we'll be ready."

"It's going to be glorious, Mac, darling." Mom stood and kissed my forehead.

"Glorious," Gin agreed.

As I walked out into the winter chill, my brain returned to handsome fisherman Manny. Had he been abducted and killed at the same time as his beloved? Could someone have asked him to take them out fishing but murdered him in deep water and dumped him overboard? Or maybe Manny had escaped, relocated, changed his name. Neither of the two had gotten their glorious wedding, or a marriage at all.

One thing I did know. I needed to go back to Westham Village and talk with Manny's nephew, Al, again. This time without distraction.

CHAPTER 25

"Hello, Barlow." I smiled at the Book Nook owner. I'd made the bookstore my first stop after my wedding team had disbanded a few minutes ago. Having everything all set for the ceremony freed me up to get back to the skeleton in the wall and her lost fiancé. I knew myself. If Della's killer hadn't been discovered by Saturday evening, the unanswered questions had the potential to bug me even during my own blessed nuptials.

Barlow smiled back from in front of the counter. "How'd that coloring book work out, Mac?" He kept on with what he was doing, restocking a display case with new hardcover biographies.

"I actually haven't had time to use it yet." I gave a little laugh. "I'm getting married on Saturday, so it's kind of a busy week."

"Let me offer my congratulations. All the more

reason to carve out time for some meditative coloring, I'd say."

"Thank you. It'll all be fine."

"What can I help you with today?" he asked.

"I'm only browsing, thanks." I wandered off to the mystery section, but he didn't seem to have gotten any cozies in yet. It had been only two days since our conversation about them, after all. I found the local history section. Which included nothing about coastal cottage architecture from the early twentieth century, not that I expected it to. Were all homes in the era built with a hidden space? I shook my head at my mind's flight of fancy and made my way back to the proprietor. I still had questions. Lots of them.

I mustered my nerve. "You grew up here, didn't you?"

"I did. I've spent my whole life—so far—in this lovely corner of the earth, and I wouldn't have it any other way. I can't think of a better place to live than Westham, can you?"

"Actually, no. I met your brother this morning when I was out walking."

He laughed. "Orrin never lets me forget he's my big brother."

I ran a finger down the spine of a book on women painters, a big work some would call a coffee table book. "Have you ever run into a Richard Ruhlen? He would be quite old by now." If he was even still alive. Somehow, I hadn't considered the possibility he might be deceased.

He didn't answer for a moment, then spoke, gazing over my shoulder. "I've heard the name. I believe he was a friend of my grandmother's. But Forrest over at the florist shop would be a better person to ask, being part of that family. His shop is down Main Street a couple of blocks."

"Thanks. I know Forrest, and I plan to ask him. He's doing our wedding flowers."

"He does excellent work," Barlow said.

I picked up a set of coasters featuring authors and set them down again. "So you must be related to the late Katherine Swift."

"Of course. She was my grandmother Kit, and a fine, civic-minded lady. I knew her well, but only in her older years, of course." He peered over his half glasses. "Why do you ask?"

"Just curious, I guess. I've learned that my house was the Swift family guest house. And that Katherine used to host gatherings of her friends there, back in, like, nineteen forty."

Barlow's hand froze. He blinked. Did he know about Della? I was pretty sure the address still hadn't appeared in any news stories. On the other hand, he was Orrin's brother and Win's uncle. Word traveled fast within some families.

He cleared his throat. "Yes, that cottage was part of the Swift estate. It was all sold after my great-grandfather lost his life in the service of his country."

"Did Kit ever talk about those days? About her friends?" *Ack.* I was totally asking too many questions. The last thing I wanted was for this kindly man to get suspicious. I mustered a laugh. "I'm trying to picture life in those days, now that I'm living in a hundred-year-old cottage. I love local history."

"That's funny, Mac." Win stood in the doorway behind the counter, her arms full of books, her lips pursed.

Whoa. Where had she come from? That must've been a storage room back there, or an office. Maybe she was working for Barlow.

"I'd never seen you in the Historical Society building before yesterday." Win's nostrils flared as she nearly glared at me, piercing and all.

"Hi, Win." Why was she wearing that expression? I smiled, trying to counter her response. "I haven't seen you there before, either."

Barlow looked from Win to me. "That's right, Mac. You said you had met my niece. She's helping me in the store this week when she has time."

Maybe Win told him about Della's remains in my wall. That must be it.

"I'm done, Uncle Barlow," she said to him. "See you tomorrow?"

"That'll be great." He beamed at her.

"See you, Win," I said.

She didn't answer before she pulled open the door.

"To answer your question, Mac, no. Grandmother Kit didn't talk about those days, at least not to me."

"Thanks. Nice seeing you, Barlow. I'm off to check on my wedding bouquet." I gave a little wave. It was time for me to make myself scarce. To skedaddle, as Abo Reba liked to say. I mostly wanted to see where Win was off to.

"Don't be a stranger now, Mac," Barlow said.

"I'm looking forward to the new cozy mystery display." I stepped outside, but Win was already gone.

She hadn't liked my asking about Kit. Or maybe she'd overheard my asking about Richard Ruhlen. Or both.

CHAPTER 26

Forrest was alone in the florist shop. *Good.*

"Hey, Mac." Forrest gave me a friendly look but didn't smile. "I heard you were looking for me recently."

"I was. Do you have time for a little chat?"

He frowned.

"I can come back if you're busy," I hurried to add.

He tapped the counter, frowning. He flipped over his wrist to glance at his watch, then looked up at me. "Want to grab a beer?"

I looked back. That was not what I'd expected him to say, but why not? "I'd love to."

He grabbed a laminated sign that read, *Closed Due to Circumstances Beyond Our Control.* He attached it to the door in place of the *Open* sign.

Several minutes later we were ensconced at a small table along the side of the Rusty Anchor with full pint glasses in front of us, his an Imperial Stout, mine a Devil's Purse IPA. The pub was quiet mid-afternoon, with a handful of patrons perched at the bar and a few other tables and booths occupied.

"Cheers." He held up his glass.

I clinked it with mine. I'd thought of ordering fries, too, but I was still full from my lobster roll.

He sipped, then set it down. "Pardon me if I jump right in, but the police said you found Aunt Della's remains in your house."

"We did. I'm sorry, Forrest."

He took in a quavering breath and let it out. "You wouldn't think it would be this emotional, learning of her death. She went missing so long ago."

I looked at him. I thought he was probably over seventy, but he had to be under eighty. I didn't think there was any way he had actually met Della.

"You're too young to have known her, aren't you?" I took a first sip of my cool, nicely hopped ale. The Rusty Anchor excelled at keeping IPA at the right temperature, unlike plenty of other bars, who served it way too cold. "You can't have been born before 1940."

"I wasn't born until six years later. But she and my mom, while sisters-in-law, were also close friends. Mother was devastated when Della left without saying goodbye. She used to talk about her all the time." He sipped his stout, savoring it. "I can't say the same about my dad—Della's younger brother."

I blinked. "Richard is your father?" Richard, whom Ursula had described as "mean."

"He sure is."

That was interesting. "Your dad didn't miss his sister?"

"He bought into the family elitism. My grandfather claimed Manny Cabral wasn't good enough for his girl." He scoffed. "Mother told me how much Della loved Manny. He was hardworking, self-supporting. My mom always hoped they'd found somewhere to be happy together. I'm glad she didn't live to hear about Della being murdered."

"Is your father still alive?"

He grimaced. "After a fashion. He has a blossoming dementia. I had to move him over to Westham Village a couple of years ago."

"I'm so sorry," I murmured. "Do they have a memory unit there?"

He lifted a shoulder and dropped it. "Not really. But because they are small, they can manage him."

Maybe I could talk with him. "Do you know we found a suitcase next to Della?"

"I heard."

"The police brought in their young intern, Win Swift."

At the name, his lip curled, but he didn't speak.

"She also works at the Historical Society and was able to look through the valise, with the permission of the police," I continued. "She let me be there yesterday when she unpacked it. Nobody knew who Della was until then."

"You found her ID."

"Yes, her passport. And it looked to me like she'd packed for a honeymoon somewhere warm."

He set his elbow on the table and his forehead in his palm for a moment. He gave himself a shake and focused on me again.

"I've heard you've been involved in more than

one homicide case here in Westham, Mac. How can I help you solve this one?"

I thought. "Do you have any letters Della might have written to your mother, or the reverse?"

"I don't think so. They lived in the same town. Why write letters?"

"I guess you're right."

"But I'll look when I get home," he said. "I have an old diary of Mother's. Perhaps that will contain a clue."

I liked the sound of that. "How about this? What do you know about Katherine Swift, who went by Kit?"

He stared at me, then glanced left and right before lowering his voice. "The Swift family was more influential than mine in Westham. So were the Winslows. I'd say they both still are."

"Do you mean Barlow, or Emily and Orrin?"

"All of them."

Interesting. I hadn't heard any of those names associated with local government or being active at the town meeting in the fall. Maybe there were other Swifts and Winslows I didn't know about.

"Did your mom know Kit?" I asked.

"Of course. Who didn't?"

"I've heard Kit and Della were rivals." I traced a finger through the condensation on my glass. "Or at least Kit thought they were."

"She held that view needlessly. Della was a sweet girl, from what I've heard. She wasn't interested in rivalries. She was prettier than Kit, certainly. Why, you saw that photograph in the shop. Wasn't my aunt lovely?"

"She was." I picked up my glass. "Tell me more about your father. Does he still recognize you?"

"Yes, and he remembers other things. He's increasingly not so sharp on what happened an hour ago, though. It's hard."

"So his dementia is still developing."

"Exactly." He turned his half-empty glass around and around.

"Are you married, Forrest?" I realized I didn't know.

"I was. My wife died some years ago."

"I'm sorry." Another family tragedy.

"It's okay. I have a son who lives near Boston." When the pub's outer door opened, his eyes lit up. "And there's my grandgirl right now. The light of my life." He lifted a hand in greeting. "And Kim is a whiz with anything technical. Phones, internet, all of it."

Waitperson Kim smiled and came over to greet him, leaning down to give Forrest a kiss. "Hey, Granddad."

"Kimmie, have you met Mac Almeida?" he asked. "She owns the bike shop down the street."

"Hi, Kim," I said. "I was in with my mom a couple of days ago. Astra? She seemed to know you."

"Good to see you again, Mac." She smiled. "Astra's great. If you'll both excuse me, I'm almost late for my shift. Love you, Granddad."

"Don't be a stranger, now." Forrest smiled as Kim sauntered away. "Nothing like a young person to cheer up an old guy."

"I have a five-year-old niece who has the same effect on me." At a booth near the door to the kitchen, I spied Win's unmistakable head popping up as she stood. Win must eat fast if she was now done with lunch. A middle-aged woman rose, too. Her mom, perhaps? Kim slowed. I couldn't hear what the two young people said, but it didn't look particularly friendly. Kim, with a shake of the head, disappeared into the kitchen.

Win and the woman were on a trajectory to pass our table. Forrest sat with his back to them.

I raised a hand and smiled. "Hi, Win."

She slowed, appearing only marginally more friendly than in the bookstore. She tapped the woman on the arm, alerting her to stop. "Mac, this is my mother, Emily Winslow Swift. Where I got my name, obviously. Mom, Mac Almeida."

I hadn't asked Win why she was named Winslow. So Emily was a Winslow. Of the Winslow Granite company? Emily was tall like Win, with tasteful make-up and a designer handbag over her designer coat-clad arm.

Forrest glanced up, and half stood. "Ladies." He gave a faint smile, then sat again.

"Nice to meet you, Emily," I said. "My first name is my mom's maiden name, too." Actually, Mom had never changed her last name when she married Pa. But should I mention I'd met Orrin that morning? I'd better. He would surely tell them. "I happened to speak with your husband this morning."

Emily tilted her head. "You did? Why?"

"I was out for a walk and was admiring your beau-tiful home. He came out to put something in the dumpster, so I introduced myself. We didn't talk long."

"Dad's got this thing going on about clearing out the attic." Win shook her head.

"Do you both know Forrest Ruhlen?" I asked.

"Emily and I are acquainted, of course," Forrest said.

Emily murmured a few polite niceties, then excused herself and Win.

Despite being the same age, Win and Kim sure hadn't looked like they were friendly. As the mother and daughter headed out, I thought maybe a little more digging on the Winslow family might be a good idea. Emily wasn't a Swift by blood, but she acted like one.

"That acorn didn't fall far from the tree," Forrest muttered, staring after them.

I didn't know a thing about the Winslow family. Could one of Emily's parents or aunts or uncles have been involved in the long-ago homicide—or homicides? "Do you mean Emily or Win?"

As if startled I was still there, he gave his head a little shake. "Both, actually."

CHAPTER 27

I didn't leave the bar until nearly five. I walked home deep in thought about Forrest; his father, Richard; even his grandfather. About families like the Ruhlens—with the exception of Forrest—and Winslows and Swifts thinking they were better than others because of their upbringing and their wealth. Wondering if Barlow also had that mindset, although he hadn't seemed to in the two times I'd seen him.

I was also trying to figure out how I could learn more about Kim Ruhlen and Win Swift. Their interchange could have meant nothing. Or it could relate to the long-ago crime in some way I didn't know yet. I'd wanted to ask Kim to talk to me about Win, but the server had always seemed too busy. I'd been about to ask Forrest when he'd started going into way more detail than I'd ever wanted to learn about the florist business.

Now it was dark out, and cold. I hurried the last quarter mile after I rounded the corner off Main Street. Blacksmith Shop Road wasn't particularly well lit. When a car door slammed, I jumped. I whirled at a creak, but it was only a big tree limb rubbing against another. Why was I so spooked? I didn't think I was in danger, except I'd thought that in the past and had been wrong. I was probably just haunted by the thought of Della's bones in the wall and the questions about what had happened to her.

The minute I walked in the door, Tim insisted I shut and cover my eyes.

"I have a surprise for you," he said, his voice excited.

My first thought was, *Let this not be another skeleton.* But Tim wouldn't sound so happy if it was, and anyway, he wouldn't pull something like that on me. I sniffed freshly cut wood as he led me through the first-floor bedroom to our new bathroom space, also known as Della's tomb for eighty years. I had to quit thinking of it like that or I'd never be at peace living here.

"Open your eyes," he said.

I obeyed—and gasped.

"Voilà!" he announced, wearing a big grin.

"Tim, oh my gosh."

I was met, not with a skeleton, but with a totally gutted and cleaned-up future bathroom, complete with metal receptacles in the walls. Wires, neatly stapled to the studs, led from the boxes into the floor.

"You got so much done," I said.

"I convinced the electrician to stay on."

"Well, I'm impressed." I tried not to think about the wall Della had been chained to. I couldn't help but look.

Tim noticed where my gaze had gone. "I filled the hole where the bolt was," he murmured as he slung his arm around my shoulders and squeezed. "Do you want to leave anything inside the wall before we close up? Like her name or something?"

Something to memorialize Della Louise Ruhlen. To bring more positive juju to the erstwhile Della Cabral's temporary grave.

"I love that idea. I'll have to think about what would be right." Forrest's photograph of the young Della popped into my mind. Maybe I could convince him to remove it from the frame so the glass wouldn't reflect back and let me take a picture of it. I could have it printed and write a tiny history of her on the back.

"It's no rush," Tim went on. "The plumber can't come until next week."

"But we'll be gone then." I heard my voice rise. "We'll be honeymooning on St. John!"

"Don't worry, sweetheart." He stroked my arm. "Derrick said he'd oversee the work here. And it's not like we won't have phone coverage down there, Mac. Mom is well set up at her place with both wifi and cell access."

"Okay." I took in a deep breath and let it out. This project was proceeding along, skeleton or no skeleton. Tim had it under control. I needed to let it go. "All right. Sounds good."

He pulled me in for an embrace. I stood there, accepting his warm, strong self, just being there. I didn't know why it was so hard for me to simply be present in the moment. But it was. Especially this week.

When my stomach rumbled, I pulled back, smiling. My metabolism had finally burned through both the lobster roll and the beer.

"How about I handle dinner?" I asked.

"Sounds good. Let me guess. Takeout?"

He knew me too well. "I was thinking a couple of Westham Flatbreads would hit the spot."

"Pizza? I'm in." He went off to wash up.

I sat in the living room. I called in an Equilibrium—roasted tomato sauce, artichoke hearts, goat cheese, fresh basil, and caramelized onions—and a WFB. The Westham Flatbreads Basic was your basic pizza, with sauce, mozzarella, pepperoni, and mushrooms. I said no to salad and yes please to delivery. We were such regular customers they had both Tim's and my cell numbers on file.

When they said it would be forty-five minutes, I stayed right there on the couch. If I was going to leave a memorial to Della in the wall, shouldn't there be one for Manny, too? Should it be with Della's or where he died?

I dug into the internet, searching for Manuel Cabral. Manny Cabral. 1940. Azorean American. Westham. Elopement. And all combinations thereof.

The article about Manny and Della's supposed elopement popped up, but that wasn't new. I kept digging, falling into rabbit holes, resurfacing.

Wait. I hit the Back arrow. I had flown by the name of his fishing boat. Actually, the vessel he apparently had co-owned with his father, Fernando. It was named *Boa Sorte*. Which meant "Good Luck." Now I had something to pair with Manny other than Della. I dove back into the rabbit hole.

I froze as I stared at the screen. It was a digitized article from the *Cape Cod Standard-Times* dated March 15, 1940, with a headline of, "Man's Corpse Washes Up on Beach. Identity Unknown." I kept reading. The article said the body must have been in the water for some time because the facial features were unrecognizable. The authorities asked for anyone missing a family member or friend to please contact them.

Digging more, I couldn't find anything else about this mysterious body. But what about the boat? Had it returned to shore? Been scuttled? I kept poking, following links until I found something. A lobsterman checking his traps off Woods Hole in April 1941, had found one of his traps snagged on something. His brother was a diver, who went down and located several pieces of a fishing boat, including the name painted on the side of the bow. The boat's name? *Boa Sorte*.

I sat back. The body had to be Manny's. That was the boat he'd owned with his father. Had his father become alarmed? Had anyone looked for Manny? Most important, had he met with a mishap himself? The boat sank, and Manny drowned? I couldn't believe he wouldn't have searched everywhere for Della when she disappeared. The couple's vanishing had to have been from two malicious acts. Somebody walled in the bride. And somebody took Manny out on the water under false pretenses, pushed him overboard, and sank his boat. The same somebodies, or different ones?

A loud knock at the door made me jump. Tim hurried in, his hair damp, his person smelling of soap and rainwater shampoo.

"Mac?" He set his hand on the doorknob. "Flatbreads texted you twice. The pizza is here."

CHAPTER 28

After dinner and a couple of *Great British Baking Show* episodes with Tim, he begged off, saying he was beat and needed to hit the sack. I kissed him and sent him upstairs, then switched off the show.

I wished tonight was an actual book group meeting so I could hash through what I'd learned with my fellow non-sleuths. Instead, I settled for tapping out a text to the group thread.

Found article in *Cape Cod Standard-Times* about male body washing up on a beach in March 1940. Face unrecognizable. Manny? Also found report of pieces of a fishing boat called *Boa Sorte* discovered the next month. Manny's boat name. Thoughts about who did away with him? Had to be two people—or not?

I sent it. Thinking back over my day, I realized I hadn't shared the little bit I'd learned from Forrest.

Forrest Ruhlen said his mom was good friends with

Della. He's going to look for possible letters they exchanged and has a diary, too.

While I was staring at my phone, I checked the weather for tomorrow. *Ugh.* Boston was going to get snow, but all we were due for was sleet and freezing rain. This was the worst part of living on the Cape. Often it was cooler than farther north and west in the summertime, but the temperature was a few degrees warmer than the rest of the state in the winter, which made all the difference in our weather. Precipitation that would be pretty, dry, and shovel-able farther north transformed into liquid down here. Cold, slippery liquid. *Double ugh.* With certain other storms, the fluffy stuff became heavy, water-laden snow, what some called heart-attack snow.

Was nine p.m. too late to call Gin? *Nah.* I was about to press her number when she called me first.

"Good thing we agreed not to walk," she said.

"I'll say. Tomorrow sounds miserable. I hate that kind of weather."

"I do, too. Hey, I saw the thread. Good digging."

"Thanks," I said. "I still don't have actual answers about who killed Manny and sank his boat. If that was even him."

"We'll get there."

"It had to have been two people. I mean, one might have gone out with him under some guise. Figured out how to kill him and shove him overboard. And was met by another person with a different boat."

"And together they sank the *Boa Sorte*?" Gin asked. "I wonder how you sink a boat? Fishing boats aren't very small."

"You'd have to put a hole in the hull to let water in, right?"

"Maybe they shot Manny and used the same gun to make holes."

"Could be, although the article didn't mention bullet holes in him." I thought. "Or they lit a piece of dynamite and threw it on board."

She laughed. "I don't dare go researching this on the internet. 'How to sink a boat from another boat.' If the NSA is watching, we're both sunk."

I groaned.

"Pun intended," Gin added.

"Gin," I began, my brain veering onto a tangent of sorts. "In 1940, do you think two women would have pulled off an attack like that?"

"Interesting question. They could have, and I'm sure there are other ways of sinking a boat. Like pulling some kind of drain plug, although I'm sure there's a nautical term for whatever it is. If the women knew boats or were good with guns or dynamite, why not? But would they have? I don't know. Who did you have in mind?"

"Information is kind of spotty. Kit Swift is the only woman I've heard of with a grudge against Della. An unfounded grudge, by all reports. I met Emily Swift today. Win's mom. I'm pretty sure the Winslows were another elite family here. Yesterday I saw a photograph in the Sand Dollar of the Winslow Granite company."

"Yes, the Winslows were a big name for a while," Gin agreed.

"I didn't know any Winslows in school, but I'm probably between their generations."

"You should hear Emily crow about them when she comes into my shop. You'd think they were bloody royalty."

"Does she mention anyone in particular?" I asked.

"Her great-aunt Sarah is on some kind of pedestal, I'll tell you."

The sound of ice cubes came over the phone.

"Are you having an adult beverage?" I asked.

"And why not? I am, in case you haven't noticed, an adult in my forties in her own home."

"Hang on a minute, okay? Now I want one, too." I set down the phone and poured myself a little glass of a twenty-year-old port. "I'm back. You were talking about Sarah Winslow."

"She apparently was tight with Kit Swift," Gin said. "They founded the Westham Ladies' Cycling Club, according to Emily."

"The club sounds cool. Do you know if Sarah had a brother?"

"A brother who could have helped her drive a boat out to sea, perhaps with an explosive aboard? I like how you think, Mac."

"Thanks. But did she?" I asked.

"I don't know. Emily put in a special chocolate order yesterday, and it'll be ready tomorrow. You can be sure I'll steer the conversation around to her aunt. If she had a great-uncle, I'll find out."

"Or Sarah could have done it with a sister or a father, even."

"Right."

"I tried to ask some questions at the police station," I said. "I didn't get very far."

"Too bad Lincoln is away."

"I know. How's Eli?"

"Good. He's in the other room working on a research paper."

I stifled a yawn. "Sorry, it's been a long day."

"For me too. Let's touch base tomorrow."

I agreed and disconnected. I heard a tapping on the window that faced east and looked up in alarm. Was someone out there in the night trying to get my attention? Here I was, sitting in a pool of lamplight, feet on the coffee table, alone. Had we even locked the doors? I hadn't lived in this house long enough to know Tim's habits. How easy it was to grow complacent in the usually safe atmosphere of a small town.

I reached up and switched off the light. The sound continued, almost a scratching. My thudding heart nearly drowned it out. My phone glowed in the dark. I wanted to shut off the screen, but I also thought I should keep it live in case I needed to hit 9-1-1. I strained my ears even as my hands grew clammy.

Then I laughed out loud. The noise on the window was freezing rain. Or maybe sleet. I had trouble keeping them apart. The frozen precipitation had simply started earlier than forecast. Hey, better today and tomorrow than Saturday. An ice-pocalypse was the last thing my wedding needed.

CHAPTER 29

After spending a bit of quality time with my parrot in the parsonage the next morning, my mood was only a little lifted. The clouds that had brought the dangerous precipitation still lingered. The dark way I felt matched the day. Still, I'd gotten myself up and washed and was determined to make headway on whatever I could learn about Della and Manny.

I drove Miss M—very carefully—over to Westham Village again at around ten. The world was encased in ice. The Westham road crews had been out salting, sanding, and scraping all night, from the looks of it, bless their hardworking and sleep-deprived hearts.

Sirens wailed, but I didn't encounter whatever emergency vehicles they came from. I hoped someone hadn't slid into a ditch or, worse, into another car. I had to be extra careful that didn't happen to me.

My mission here was to corner Al and ask more questions about his uncle Manny. I'd poked around a little more this morning online but hadn't really found anything additional about either the male corpse or the *Boa Sorte*. On the thread, Flo had said she'd mount a search once she got into work. I'd added a request to look into the cycling club founded a hundred years earlier by Sarah Winslow, and to find out if she had a brother.

Inside the facility, I identified myself to a young woman at the front desk and asked to speak with Al.

"I'm afraid he's out," she said. "Can I help you with anything else?"

Rats. Pivot, Mac, I told myself. "Um, sure. I wondered if I could have a chat with Richard Ruhlen. His son"—I crossed my fingers behind my back—"said it would be fine."

"Of course. You know he goes in and out of being present, mentally."

"Yes."

"That's fine, then. He's back in the solarium. He loves it there. Do you need me to show you where to go?"

"Thank you, but I can find it. I was there a couple of days ago." I made my way to the plant-filled room. The clouds from last night's storm hadn't cleared. If anything, the brooding, slate-colored sky looked like it was about to dump more wintry mix on us. So the solarium wasn't as light as it had been, but it was still a lovely, peaceful space.

The only person in it was the same man I'd seen when I was here with Ursula. He again sat in a wheelchair near the side, but today he was awake, wearing a narrow knit tie under a V-necked sweater.

I flashed back to my conversation with Flo's mom. Twice she'd glanced at this man, once when she'd spoken of Richard, but I hadn't made the connection.

He raised a quavering hand. "Hello, young lady," he called to me. "I expect you're here for my history lesson. Or were you going to sing today?" He beckoned.

I smiled and sat across from him. "Mr. Ruhlen, my name is Mackenzie—"

"It is not." He scowled. "What kind of a name is that for a girl? No, I know you're my darling Sarah. Miss Sarah Winslow, the belle of the ball. The talk of the town." Up close I could see Forrest's resemblance to Richard. They had the same hazel eyes and impressive eyebrows, except Richard's face was deeply lined, and he was thin and bent into himself.

I didn't know what to say, so I kept my mouth shut.

He peered at me. "But you look different today."

"This is a lovely room, isn't it?"

"Oh, yes. My gardener takes excellent care of it."

"Would that be Manny Cabral?" I kept my voice casual.

"Manny." Richard frowned and squinted into the distance as he rubbed his thumb and fingers together. "Manny Cabral. He wasn't a gardener. He caught fish. Yes, that's it."

"He had his own boat, I think."

"Why, yes, he did. My father warned him to stay away from Della." He nearly spat the name.

"Your sister, Della?"

"That's right, dear. Manny's boat didn't bring him very good luck after all." His smile was thin, tight. Satisfied.

The *Boa Sorte*. "You and Kit must have been good friends."

"Kit. She was a smart one, but it was a devilish kind of smart, don't you know." He shook his head. "No, I wouldn't say we were friends, per se. She was cordial only when it suited her purposes." He seemed to catch sight of something behind me, and his face lit up. "There's my lovely Sarah now. Hello, dear."

I twisted to see Win standing close behind my chair. *Odd.* How long had she been there, and how had she come in so quietly? This made twice now.

"Mac, I didn't realize you knew Mr. Ruhlen." She reached for Richard's hand and squeezed it. "Hello, Mr. Ruhlen. You're looking dapper today."

"Of course, my dear. I knew you were coming. You're looking lovely, as always."

"Thank you. Were you and Mac having a nice chat?" Win, in a skirt over leggings with chunky boots, spoke to Richard but gave me the side-eye.

I stood. "We were. And now I'll let you two catch up. Nice to see you, Mr. Ruhlen."

"You come back any time, young lady. We old men need all the pretty faces we can get."

CHAPTER 30

Al was back. When I knocked on the doorjamb of his office on my way out, he glanced up from his desk.

"Mac, come in. I heard you were looking for me."

"I was. Do you have a minute?"

He checked the wall clock, which read ten thirty. "I have fifteen of them. Please sit down."

"Thanks." Before I sat, I closed the door behind me. I didn't want anyone—that is, Win—sneaking up on this conversation. "You probably know by now that my fiancé and I found Della Ruhlen's remains in the wall of our cottage on Monday."

"I do." He inclined his head. "It's very sad news."

"I have learned that she was engaged to a Manny Cabral. Was he a relative of yours?"

"Manny was my uncle." Al stroked one end of his bushy mustache. "But I never knew him."

"He and Della both went missing at the same time."

"Yes. My father, Manny's younger brother, always said he was glad they'd eloped. That they must have found a place where they could be happy together."

"Last night I found an old newspaper article saying Manny's boat had been discovered a year later. The *Boa Sorte.*"

"That was part of the family lore, that he'd found a way to sink the boat before he left with Della. It didn't make sense to me, that he would trash such an expensive vessel. Why not sell it, or give it to my dad?" He straightened a pen on the desk and ran his finger around the rim of his black Westham Village coffee mug. "Except now we know Manny didn't leave with his bride."

"He didn't." I swallowed, hoping what I was going to say next wouldn't be too hard on him. "I also found a *Cape Cod Standard-Times* article from April 1940 that reported a body washing up on a beach."

He sat up straight and stared at me. "You what, now?"

"I'm so sorry, Al. It said they couldn't identify the remains." I didn't want to go into details of how the body's face was gone. He could read it on his own. "Do you want me to send you a link?"

"Please." He jotted down his email address on a slip of paper and passed it over to me.

I found the article again on my phone and sent him the link to it. "There." The town or county must have buried the remains somewhere. If Al could locate the grave and use DNA to determine if those remains were his uncle's, he could at least have a marker made, or maybe the Cabrals had a family plot in the cemetery here.

"Why are you looking into this, Mac?" Al tilted his head.

Could I trust him? I didn't see why not. "Della's death was obviously a homicide. From all reports, she and Manny were smitten with each other. I doubt he killed her. I haven't heard that the police have made any progress solving a cold case from eighty years ago. Two cold cases. And I don't know. She was wearing her wedding dress. I'm getting married in two days." My eyes filled unexpectedly.

"And you want to see justice done for her," he murmured.

"For both of them." I sniffed away the tears.

He pushed a tissue box toward me. "What can I do to help?"

"I'm not sure." I swiped at my eyes and shoved the tissue into my bag. "It's possible Richard Ruhlen was involved."

"Our resident?" His dark eyes widened.

"Yes. I was just talking to him, or trying to."

"He goes in and out a lot. Mostly out, lately."

"He said something about Manny's boat not bringing him good luck."

"But Richard was Della's brother," Al said. "He wouldn't have harmed her."

"One would hope not. But Ursula told me Richard was a mean young man. He might have had a hand in Manny's death."

Al rubbed his forehead. "I'm glad Dad isn't alive to hear about this."

"I can understand that. Do you have any brothers or sisters, Al?"

"Alas, I don't. Dad went through years of grieving, never hearing from his brother again. I think he didn't want me to have the chance to endure the same level of pain. My ex-wife was an only child, too."

Ex-wife. That explained the unadorned ring finger I had noticed. I thought for a moment. "When I was visiting with Richard, he thought I was Sarah Winslow."

"Richard's past and present are quite muddled."

"And then Win Swift came in. Do you know her?"

"I do," Al said. "She's quite the history buff and likes to visit the residents, try to pick their brains about the past."

"After she showed up, Richard called her 'Sarah'."

He lifted one eyebrow, a trick I had never been able to master. "Well, she is a Winslow as well as a Swift."

His fifteen minutes were almost up. I stood and thanked him, then opened the door.

"Do let me know if I can help," he said. "It would be unethical of me to try to grill Richard to find out if he has a nefarious past. But I promise to keep my ears open."

"I appreciate that. And you have my email address now." I picked up one of his cards from the desk. "I'll text you my phone number."

"Please." He sat, picking up his desk phone.

I turned and nearly collided with Win. "Oops, sorry about that," I said.

"Not a problem." She and her purple hair hurried out the front door.

CHAPTER 31

I powered up Miss M and the heat but switched off the radio. I didn't drive, though, instead sitting in the lot with my thoughts—which were many.

First, where had those tears come from? I was normally not a very emotional person, but I felt so bad for Della and Manny. It was eighty years later, and I had no connection with them, except for finding Della behind the wall. It must be the connection with my own wedding.

Plus, I had to admit, this week was a teensy bit stressful. Right now, for example, I was sure there was something wedding-related I should be doing. Like . . . centerpieces! Had we even talked about them? No, of course we had. Forrest had confirmed table flowers. I supposed, if I were an over-the-top decorator-type, I would have come up with some clever, gorgeous thing to go with or around the flowers on each table. But I wasn't, and I hadn't. And it would all be fine.

Second, was I paranoid to think Win was somehow tracking me? I didn't know why she would. It seriously had seemed like she'd sneaked up on me while I was talking with Richard. And then again as I left Al's office. Maybe she didn't like me digging into Della and Manny's past. But why not? I'd love to have seen a photograph of Sarah Winslow to see why Richard had called me by her name. I was quite sure I didn't resemble her, but Win might, her purple fade notwithstanding. Genes were funny that way.

Third, Richard had been Manny's near contemporary, and of course, Della was his big sister. Sure, they'd both disappeared a long time ago, but he hadn't shown any sadness about it. On the contrary, he'd seemed almost smug about Manny having gone missing. With dementia, though, it could be hard to tell how he felt about anything, the way memories could get mixed up.

I wasn't going to come up with any answers sitting in a parking lot. I pointed my red ride toward the Westham Public Library. If Flo also had fifteen minutes free, she could help me puzzle through at least some of this.

White flakes began to fall as I drove. Which was lovely, but a quarter inch of snow hiding ice could make for treacherous walking. Tim's family all lived in much warmer climes than here. I hoped our guests from St. John, Southern California, and Seattle all brought boots with tread. After I parked at the library, I sent him a text asking him to remind them about exactly that. The parsonage had a big basket of warm hats, scarves, and gloves in case anybody forgot—or didn't own—such items. Footwear was a different matter.

I trod the steps up to the library carefully, gripping the railing, until I was safely inside. I popped my head into busy Flo's office.

"Mac, come in. Give me a second." Her fingers flew on the keyboard.

I sat across from her. When she finished what she was doing, by some miracle, she did have a bit of time to spare.

"What's up?" Eyebrows up, eyes sparkling, she rubbed her palms together. "Nothing I like better than an information deep dive."

I leaned forward. "I want to know more about the Winslow family. You saw what I wrote about the granite company photograph. Sarah was friends with Kit Swift and presumably Della. Did Sarah have a brother or sister, or both? Also, Gin said Sarah and Kit founded the Westham Ladies' Cycling Club. Did they ride around town, or did they have other activities? And what can you find out about Richard Ruhlen? I visited him a little while ago over at Westham Village, and—"

"Whoa." Flo held up her hand. "That's a lot, Mac. Let me make a list. Winslow family, women's bike club, Richard Ruhlen."

"I texted about the boat. I also think we need to know how it sank. What kind of condition it was in, were there holes in the hull, that kind of thing."

Flo tapped away.

I kept talking. "Al Cabral said their family believed Manny scuttled the boat on purpose, but Al didn't think that made sense."

"It doesn't." She glanced up. "A seaworthy fishing

boat doesn't come cheap these days, and it wouldn't have then either."

"No." Not that I'd ever looked into the price of boats of any size.

"All right." She grinned. "I went for the low-hanging fruit. Sarah Winslow had one sibling, a brother named Eugene. Born nineteen twenty-two. Drafted into the army in nineteen forty-two but served in a remote outpost in India. Didn't do any actual fighting. Married nineteen forty-six. One son, Theo, who had two children, daughter Emily and son Lee." Her mouth rounded. "Ooh. Eugene seems to have developed a bit of an opiate problem. Claimed it was from shell shock—except he wasn't in combat. Squandered the family fortune on drugs."

"Wow," I said. "That's a lot of fruit."

"How the high and mighty do fall, right?"

"Exactly." What had Orrin said about the Swifts? Something about how fortunes rose and fell. Not only for the Swifts, apparently. "The Winslows were one of Westham's elite families. Eugene was born in nineteen twenty-two. So he would have been a pal of Richard Ruhlen's, I expect."

"And could have helped him do away with Manny and his boat," Flo added.

"Exactly."

"Unless the ladies did the deed."

"Possible. Is Eugene still alive?" Unlikely, but Richard was hanging in there, after a fashion. Eugene might be, too.

Flo kept hunting. "No. He died in a single-car accident back in the eighties. Wrapped his Chevy around a tree in Mashpee. His wife passed away in nineteen ninety-five. And Theo and his wife retired to Florida."

"So we're left with Emily Winslow Swift; her brother, Lee; and Win herself," I said. "Speaking of Win, she came to visit Richard when I was there. He called her Sarah. His reality is fuzzy."

"Hey, he's a hundred years old, and she is related to Sarah," Flo said. "Maybe the genes skipped a couple of generations when they were passed on. I'm sure glad Mom is still clear of mind."

"You're lucky." I was, too, with Reba's mental acuity.

"I know."

"I wonder where Lee is now," I mused.

"We'll have to postpone that search." Flo rose. "Sorry, off to the next meeting. Listen, want me to set you up with the modern version of microfiche so you can keep looking?"

"Sure." I followed her into a room with a dozen computer stations and paid attention to her clear instructions. "Thanks. Get off to your meeting, now."

"I have your list, and I'll chip away at it as I can."

"Perfect." I sat at one of the stations. "I'll add what you dug up to the group thread, plus whatever else I might unearth."

She gave a little wave and bustled off. I sat there, thinking about 1940. About the young elite of Westham partying together at the Swift cottage. Kit, Della, and Sarah. Richard and Eugene. And the not-so-elite, like Manny, presumably not invited to the carousing. Did Della participate, or had she used those moments to sneak away with her beloved, her secretly betrothed? Her secret got out somehow, or she wouldn't have ended up how she did.

I also didn't know if there were other Swift siblings. I hadn't heard of any. Nor did I know if Manny had brothers or sisters besides Al's father. I also didn't know Forrest's mother's name, the one who was friends with Della.

Nothing like a little research to answer those questions. I dug into the digitized society pages of the *Westham Daily News* for the early months of 1940. Miss Katherine Swift had hosted a sledding party followed by refreshments and entertainment at the Swift family guesthouse. Sarah, Eugene, and Richard were all mentioned as attending. Della was not.

I perked up at the mention of George Swift, apparently Kit's older brother, who was also at the gathering. Could he be Della's crypt carpenter? I dug into his name. No, he couldn't. He'd left town in February to attend officers' training school for the United States Army Air Corps. The last mention of George Swift, heir to the Swift fortune, was that he'd been killed over France. His body had been recovered and would be buried with full military honors.

All the rest of my hunting led to dead ends. I was starving. And I figured I should get home to Tim. Thank goodness Mom and Gin had all the wedding tasks in hand so I could focus on this. The clock was ticking if I wanted to clear up these questions before my big day.

CHAPTER 32

I left my car in the municipal parking lot behind the library and walked—carefully—down to Salty Taffy's. As it was hours since my breakfast granola, my stomach was telling me I needed lunch, but my taste buds wanted something sweet, so I decided to take a detour. Because nobody provided heavenly sweets like Gin.

She had also taken down her shop's Christmas decorations. The front windows had a display of Hanukkah cookies, albeit more expertly decorated than Norland's had been, on one side, and plain candy and fudge on the other. I was glad she hadn't launched into full Valentine's Day décor yet. The world felt more orderly to me when each holiday had a circumscribed start and end to its season. Unfortunately, I knew I was in the minority, at least among retailers.

I pulled open the door and was greeted, as always, with scents of the divine. That is, every aroma on the sweetness spectrum. Dark chocolate. Butterscotch. Taffy. Mint, peppermint, licorice, plus roasted hazelnuts and creamy pistachios.

Perfect. Emily Winslow Swift was handing a credit card to Gin. Gin caught sight of me and gave me a knowing look. Emily swiveled her head. I smiled and raised a hand in greeting. I turned away, pretending to be interested in the rainbow array of wrapped saltwater taffy flavors in open jars along the side.

Then I thought of what Gin had told me last night about the cycling club and approached the counter where Gin was handing Emily's card back to her.

"Emily, you might know I own Mac's Bikes here in town."

"Yes, I do."

"I recently heard about your aunt Sarah founding the Westham Ladies' Cycling Club. This spring I'd love to do a display about it in my store. Would you happen to have any photographs of her and the group?"

She had been giving me a head-cocked look as I talked, an expression with "dubious" written all over it, but she brightened when I asked about pictures.

"Oh, yes, I have a few lovely ones. I'd be happy to let you use them."

"Thanks," I said. "That would be great. Kit Swift was a co-founder, wasn't she?"

"She was." She accepted the bag from Gin.

I dug in my bag for one of my business cards and handed it to her. "If you text me here, I'll know how to reach you."

"Or you can always ask me," Gin said.

"You ladies have a lovely day." Emily made for the door.

I waited to speak until she was safely out. "I was going to ask if you got any dirt on the family, but Flo might have preempted you." I picked out a new toothpick from the little cup on the counter to spear one of the fudge samples and pop it into my mouth.

"Oh?"

"I didn't get a chance to text the group yet." I finished my fudge and rattled off the family tree. "Sarah's younger brother by two years was Eugene, which made him the same age as Richard Ruhlen. Eugene, later an opioid addict, had a son, Theo, who had Emily and Lee."

"Good work."

"It's good background information, but it sure doesn't solve our mystery. Have you ever run into a Lee Winslow around town?"

"No," she said. "I couldn't figure out how to ask Emily about a grandfather or great-uncle, but I mentioned to her that I'd run into a man who reminded me of her. She got a little huffy, frankly. She said she has a brother, but they are estranged. That seems like such an archaic word."

"For me it's a strange concept, too. Being strangers with your own family? I can't imagine."

Gin smiled gently. "That's because you're from a functional family. Do you know how rare that is?"

"I guess I don't." I helped myself to another sample. "I also don't know how you make this taste like heaven, but you do."

She laughed.

"Anyway," I said, "Flo had to run, but she has a list

of research topics to work on. If I ever stop eating fudge, I'll add it all to the thread."

"You'd better stop, or your dress won't fit."

I stared at her. "You think so?"

"Well, you have your last fitting today." She checked a wall clock with lollipops for hands. "In half an hour, in fact. It'll be fine."

"I do?" *I did?* So that was what my phone had dinged about, the ding I had ignored.

"Mac, where has your obsessively organized mind gone? Yes, you and the dress are due at Cape Bridal at twelve thirty."

"I have one word. Goodbye." I headed for the door. "No, three. Thank you!"

CHAPTER 33

I raced back to my car, nearly losing my balance on the ice, and dashed back to the house in Miss M. I clattered upstairs to grab the garment bag holding the dress. Tim, looking quizzical, stood at the bottom of the stairs when I ran back down.

"Where's the fire?" he asked.

I kissed him. "Dress fitting. Twelve thirty. I'll be back."

"I'll do dinner," he called after me. "Be careful."

"Love you." Careful was not exactly how I would describe how I drove back through town, but I wasn't reckless, either. The bridal shop was fairly new and had opened at the far end of town beyond the main drag of shops, municipal buildings, and churches.

I hit the directional signal to turn left into the small parking lot behind the shop. And then slammed on the brakes.

The lot was blocked with yellow police tape. The sidewalk was blocked off on either side of the bridal shop, too. A WPD cruiser with lights flashing was parked in front. Officer Nikki Kimuri stood in front of the open door to the store as if guarding it.

I angled Miss M into a curbside space on the other side of the street and switched her off. What had happened here? The big, plate-glass windows in front were intact. I hoped no one was hurt, or worse.

Glancing over at the garment bag in the passenger seat, I was selfishly grateful my wedding dress had been in my possession instead of here at the shop where I'd bought it. I'd hooked the hanger into the headrest so the dress wouldn't crumple as I drove.

Right now I could drive off. Keep accomplishing the dual tracks of wedding tasks and cold case investigation. I could call my grandmother and see what she knew. Instead, I slid out of the driver's seat and locked the door. I left the dress inside. I expected I wouldn't get a fitting today. If the dress wasn't an exactly perfect fit on Saturday, so be it. I knew Tim wouldn't care, and the last fitting had gone really well.

I stepped around the cruiser and sidled up to Nikki. "Hey, Nikki. What happened here? Is the owner okay?"

She let out the deep sigh of the long-suffering. "The owner is fine. What are you doing here, Mac?"

"I'm getting married Saturday." Finally, I had a plausible excuse to be at the scene of a crime. "I have—had—an appointment for a dress fitting five minutes ago."

"In that case, congratulations." She glanced around, then back at me. "The store was broken into from the back. All the most expensive garments were stolen, along with several jeweled accessories. Apparently, there's quite the black market for that kind of thing."

"I'm not surprised, given the cost of some of those dresses. The owner wasn't on the premises?"

"No. She doesn't open until eleven. The back-door lock had been jimmied. Not sure why she didn't have a better security system with that kind of inventory on hand."

It seemed strange to me, too. "The shop is at the end of the line out here, too." To the left of the shop was the parking lot for a garden store. After the flurry of selling trees, wreaths, and garlands for Christmas, it was now closed for the winter. A patch of woods sat behind and to the right of the shop. Across the street was the busy Coastal Grocery, a small grocery store. Still, with the thief breaking into the back, he or she would have been well shielded from view.

Penelope appeared in the doorway wearing purple nitrile gloves. "It's exactly like the other break-ins." She seemed to register that I was there. "Mac?"

"She has a valid reason for being here." Nikki saved me from explaining again. "Mac came for a fitting for her own wedding dress."

"It's in the car," I added in a hurry, pointing to Miss M.

"That's fine, then," Penelope said.

"There have been other break-ins in Westham?" I frowned. I'd better stop by my shop and make sure it was secure. That must have been what Penelope had meant the other day by crimes all over town this week.

"Yes."

"I ask because I'm a shop owner, and my business—Mac's Bikes—is closed for three weeks. My fiancé, Tim Brunelle, owns Greta's Grains, which is also closed. They're both right in the middle of town, but . . ."

"Do you have security cameras and lights in the back?" Penelope asked.

"I have lights but no camera. I'm not sure about the bakery."

"I would advise installing both on both establishments."

Nikki nodded her agreement, then stepped out into the street and waved on a few rubbernecking drivers.

"You have no idea who has been carrying out these burglaries?" I asked.

"We're starting to get an idea," Penelope admitted. "Nabbing him isn't going to be pretty."

"You know it's a male?"

"Maybe."

"Well, thanks." This was starting to resemble tooth pulling, although I was surprised they'd told me as much as they had. "Good luck."

"Thank you." Penelope bobbed her head once.

Nikki extended palms in both directions to stop traffic so I could cross. At least a burglary couldn't have any connection to Della's murder. Could it?

CHAPTER 34

Pulling into the lot next to Mac's Bikes, I felt my livelihood reel me in. I stepped out of Miss M and gazed at the building. I missed it, plain and simple. I missed my opening routine every day. I liked helping customers find the right bike, whether new or a rental, a perfect fit of helmet, a new colorful wicking shirt, the correct replacement tube kit. I enjoyed fostering the repair and maintenance part. I was well-versed in the how-to, but I hired a couple of mechanics to do the actual work. And I'd made a success out of Mac's Bikes.

I'd never been closed for so long. Theoretically, I knew it was a good idea to take time off this week and then go on a long, tropical vacation with my beloved. Still, I itched to unlock the door and hang out the *Open* flag.

Instead, I checked the front-door locks—two, ever

since the last time someone tried to break in—and wandered around to the side and back. Both doors were secure, but the back did face a similar situation as the bridal shop. No alley, no street, no other shops. My tiny house had been parked behind the shop, with access through a low hedge, but it was gone now. Beyond the site were marshes. I definitely needed a security cam back here.

Who could have been breaking into local shops? Our town certainly had its share of people down on their luck who might be desperate enough to try to rob a business or two. Gin and I were both active volunteers at the free-groceries days—that is, food pantry—and free dinners offered in the basement of Pa's church, all of which were well attended by the local hungry.

Whoever was robbing Main Street businesses, though, was savvy enough to break in at night, as they had with the bridal shop. That didn't seem like the action of a desperate person, and Penelope hadn't arrested anyone yet. She'd said an arrest wouldn't be "pretty." I had no idea what she meant by that, unless the culprit was an elected official or a bank president. In that case, why steal?

I left Miss M where she was and walked along the sidewalk past the bank to Tim's bakery. He had stashed his wrought-iron sidewalk tables inside for the duration, and the storefront looked lonely. He normally opened at six every morning and would have sold out of baguettes, boules, and beignets by about now. The coffee patrons had to go elsewhere after one o'clock in the afternoon. His popular business was successful, too.

Peering up at the eaves, I couldn't tell whether he

had a camera or not. Anyway, it was more important in the back. I made my way along the side of the building. This row of shops had an alley that served them as well as the houses behind. Garages and back fences were all I could see on the other side of the alley. I knew the fronts of the homes were on the street running parallel to Main Street.

I could see neither light nor camera over the bakery's back door. I swore to myself. This was the last thing either Tim or I needed to add to our to-do lists before Saturday. I cast around in my brain for who could accomplish such a thing in short order. I came up empty-handed. I could do it, of course, but I was totally out of time and energy for such a task. Did I have to search out a security company?

Wait. Forrest had said his grandchild Kim was a whiz with everything tech. Maybe Kim would like to pick up some extra money over the winter break. I didn't have Kim's contact info, but Forrest would. Or I could drop by the pub. I had once again missed lunch. A few fudge samples were not doing it for my metabolism. Except I should go home and tackle the vows I hadn't yet written, not to mention not practiced. I knew in my heart how I felt, but capturing it in words was harder than I had expected.

I headed back toward the street and my car, thumbing out a text to Tim.

Bridal shop broken into before I arrived, owner fine. Cop recommended security cams and lights in back of both our places. Am looking to hire person for both. Want in?

I wrinkled my nose as I walked. Tim himself was a techie when he wasn't baking. What was I thinking? Then again, his week was as busy as mine. Busier, even, since he was dealing with the contractor.

I looked up after I passed the bank. A man leaned over Miss M.

"Hey!" I yelled, moving toward him at a slow run so I didn't slip on the ice. "What do you think you're doing?"

His head jerked up. He dropped something, then took off in a sprint toward the small lot where my tiny house had been. A path leading to the Shining Sea Trail ran alongside the lot.

Out loud, I uttered a string of expletives that would have made a longshoreman blush. I stopped short. Should I call the police? But maybe he hadn't done anything wrong. I couldn't follow him, having done more running in the last three seconds than I had in four years. I wasn't a runner, plus I'd blown out my knee biking the mountains of New Zealand a few years ago.

I focused my brain on what the man had looked like. Tall. Black overcoat. Greasy hair? The guy from outside the flower shop at the start of the week. Before we'd even known who Bridey was. And the man upset about the Winslow Granite Company photograph. Maybe he was the bridal shop burglar. He could have been casing the joint—a phrase that always sent me back to Della's day—to see if it was worth robbing. Except he'd been examining my vehicle, not my shop.

Now I was worried about my car. Hurrying to Miss M, I checked her over. *Whew*. All intact. No scratches. No damage that I could see. Still locked. Wedding dress bag still there. *Whew*. So why had the guy taken off running?

I scanned the pavement to see what he'd dropped but couldn't spy a thing. Squatting, I checked under the car in case the thing had bounced or slid. There it was, behind the front wheel. Before I reached for it, I fished a tissue out of my pocket and used that to pull out a small metal object. I stood to examine it, turning it this way and that. Was it a crochet hook? No, it wasn't rounded enough at the tip. It was about six inches long. About half the length was a flat handle.

I whistled. I knew exactly what this was. Earlier in the fall someone had tried to break into my tiny house during a massive storm. This thing was a lock pick. And I thought Penelope might be interested. I could walk over to the police station and relinquish it. But no. I wasn't leaving Miss M alone again. The dude might come back.

CHAPTER 35

Behind the police station, I parked in a spot labeled *Fifteen Minutes Only* and carried the object inside. I didn't recognize the guy behind the glass.

"Is Penelope Johnson here?" I asked.

"No, ma'am. How can I help you?"

"How about Nikki Kimuri?"

"No, ma'am."

They must still be at the bridal shop. I sighed. "I came across a man trying to break into my car a minute ago. When I yelled at him, he dropped this object." I held up the tissue. "Not the tissue, but what's inside. I believe it's a lock pick."

"Where was your car parked, and was it damaged?" He swiveled toward a screen and started typing my answers.

"I own Mac's Bikes here in town, and I had parked

in its lot while I ran an errand." I gave him the number on Main Street. "The car seems to be fine."

"I'm glad to hear that. What kind of vehicle is it?"

"A Miata MX-5 convertible. Red."

He whistled. "Nice wheels."

I merely smiled. She was a good ride, my Miss M.

"Where did the suspect go?" he asked.

"He took off running toward the Shining Sea Trail."

"Please slide the object through the slot there," he directed.

I pushed it into the wide, metal opening under the thick, darkened glass separating us.

"Thank you." He took my name, phone number, and home address. "Can you describe the man?"

"Tall. Maybe nearly six feet. Black overcoat. Hair to his collar. Greasy-looking hair." I thought about when I'd seen him up close. "I saw him in town earlier this week. His eyes are a kind of purplish-blue."

"Anything else?"

"I don't think so. I know there have been break-ins this week, so I thought I should report what happened."

"Thank you. I'll let Detective Johnson know you were here."

"I appreciate that. Oh, one more thing. I know the bridal shop was broken into. I had my wedding dress in the car in a garment bag from them. Maybe this was the man who broke in there. I don't know." Why would the guy want my wedding dress? It hadn't been a super-expensive one. Still, he could have spied the bag and thought whatever it contained could be valuable.

"Duly noted."

When I got back to Miss M, Tim had texted his okay to hire someone for a security installation at the bakery. The snow had stopped. The temperature had risen enough that footing was no longer treacherous. And my stomach signaled me I still hadn't eaten lunch. The Rusty Anchor was only two doors down, but I couldn't leave Miss M here. My fifteen minutes were almost up. It seemed silly to drive a thousand yards down the road to the municipal parking lot across from the pub. I wasn't used to driving downtown. I usually walked everywhere. Still, one does what one has to do.

Even at two o'clock, the pub still buzzed with the late lunch crowd. After I told the hostess I was eating alone, she seated me at a small table. I would have perched at the bar, except I wanted to talk with Kim.

I scanned the place for an orange-haired server, who at that moment pushed sideways through the swinging doors to the kitchen carrying two armfuls of loaded lunch plates. Kim showed up at my table next.

"How are you?" I asked.

"Good, thanks. What can I get you?"

"I'd like the fish and chips." I was about to order a beer but changed my mind. Probably not a good idea. I wanted to stay sharp to think about my vows and the mystery man and everything else.

"Anything to drink?"

"I'll just drink water. Kind of ridiculous at a pub, I know."

Kim smiled. "The customer's always right. I'll go put this in."

"Thanks. I want to ask you about something when you come back."

"You got it."

A few minutes later, I had it, that is, my much-delayed lunch, which Kim had delivered. A heaping platter sat in front of me, filled with perfectly deep-fried flaky white fish coated in a glistening batter surrounded by crispy, salty fries with their skins on, exactly how I liked them, all of it.

"Thank you. I'm in heaven," I said to Kim. "Or will be."

"You wanted to ask me about something?"

"Yes." I wanted to ask about what was up with Win, but the matter of a security camera was way more important. "Forrest said you're good with tech stuff."

"Maybe." The server lifted a shoulder, casting a glance toward the ceiling. "Depends."

"Westham has had a series of businesses broken into this week. Both my shop and my fiancé's—Mac's Bikes and Greta's Grains—are closed for three weeks. Would you be able to set us up with security cameras at the back entrance? For pay, of course."

"Like, soon?" Kim asked.

"Preferably."

"I guess. I have tomorrow off. I'll check both places out on my break today. You want the cams app-controlled?"

I held my hand in front of my mouth, since I hadn't been able to resist popping in a ketchup-laden fry. "That'd be great." I swallowed. "Can you install them, too?"

"Sure. Granddad has a tall ladder, and I have tools."

The frown Kim's face had taken on when I mentioned the break-ins continued.

"Are you sure this is cool?" I asked.

"Yes." The server whipped out a phone. "What's your number?"

I rattled it off.

"Thanks. I'll text you in the morning when I'm there. You're going to want to sign off on the placement, and I'll have to show you how to use the app. You can sign up for their service and pay for it yourself, so I don't have to get involved in that."

"I appreciate it. I'll stop by when I hear from you." I'd check tomorrow if Kim wanted to be paid under the table or with a check. The camera and labor to install it were business expenses. The cost of the app was also an expense, and one I could put on the books. I didn't mind sliding a few tax-free dollars in the direction of a hardworking young person for their time and as reimbursement for a security device I needed.

Kim laid down my check and hurried away, still frowning. Something was up with her, but I had no idea what. Meanwhile, I did know what I needed, and it was right in front of me. Had I ever tasted such delicious fish, such light, sweet, crunchy fried batter?

I had laid my phone on the table. It was a challenge to tear myself away from my lunch to read the text that dinged in. But it was from my grandma, so I figured I'd better. I wiped off my hands and swiped to the message.

Can you stop by my place?

I texted back.

Sure. See you in half an hour.

Her reply came back instantly.

K.

I smiled, shaking my head at my favorite octogenarian texting a shorthand for "okay" and then adding a period at the end. Once an English teacher, always an English teacher.

CHAPTER 36

I gazed fondly around my grandmother's second-floor senior apartment. I'd been coming here since she'd moved to Westham. After my grandfather died, Abo Reba had retired from her teaching job in a mostly minority suburb of Boston. She'd lived with us for only a couple of months before this apartment opened up almost across the street from the parsonage.

It wasn't the kind of fancy retirement place with a pool and graduated levels of care. So far, Reba Almeida didn't need any of that. She went to aqua aerobics at the Y, was active in the Westham Garden Club, rode her adult tricycle with my mom when weather permitted, and was more engaged with life at eighty-one than a lot of people half her age. She ate dinner in the community room here with her pals, and, while an elevator was available, she still took the stairs up and down, claiming it kept her young.

The walls in her living room were covered with framed photographs. I hadn't known my grandfather super well, but one of my favorite pictures of my two abos had place of honor. It was of the tall and short of them in their silver-haired days, with bare feet and cuffs rolled up, walking hand in hand away from the camera on Chapoquoit Beach. Reba had adored him, but she hadn't let grieving for him stop her life.

A small telescope stood on its tripod and pointed out the window. With its help, Abo Reba tracked everything that went on here at the east end of town. And by everything, I mean including criminal activity. She had reported several cases of wrongdoing to the police in the past. Once they realized she wasn't a dotty old lady, they took her reports seriously.

After we had a good, strong hug, she said, "Mackie, honey. Sit yourself down." She pointed a knobby, age-spotted finger at the sofa, the back of which was covered by a rainbow-colored afghan she'd crocheted. "We're going to taste-test your wedding cocktail."

I sat. "We are?"

"Yes. I got the recipe from the caterer. We need to be sure it's perfect for your big day."

"Okay, then." I was helpless in the face of this diminutive force of nature, one who was fond of her cocktails. It was a good thing I hadn't had that beer.

She busied herself in the kitchen while I texted Tim where I was, and that Reba was fixing drinks.

He messaged back that he'd finished a run with Eli, and they were going for beers. He added,

Cottage rendezvous at six for dinner?

I texted back my agreement, glad that Tim was taking time for fun. He'd been working so hard on the bathroom renovation, he deserved it. I glanced up at Abo Reba, who approached holding Manhattan glasses full of a lovely pink drink, each garnished with a sprig of fresh mint leaves.

"That's so pretty." I accepted mine.

"Isn't it?" She set hers on the side table next to her easy chair by the window. The one with the telescope on the other side. "Cheers, *querida*."

I held up my glass, too, then took a sip and tried to deconstruct it. "I know we wanted cranberry juice, because Cape Cod. This also has, what, bourbon? And lime juice."

"And Grand Marnier. I think it will be a big success." She took another sip, then set down the glass.

I sipped my drink. "I think this could use a little Grenadine."

She took another sip. "Or maybe a touch of Cointreau? But no, that's just another orange-flavored liqueur."

"Maybe sweet vermouth. A bit more sweetness."

"Yes. Now, I want to tell you I've seen Lee Winslow around town this week." Reba gestured toward her telescope.

"You have?" It was a classic non sequitur from my grandmother, not that it mattered.

"At least, I think it was him." She tapped her finger on her glass.

"What does he look like?"

"Years ago, when I moved down here, he wasn't bad-looking at all. Tall fellow with those strange pretty eyes."

Purplish-blue eyes.

"But now he seems to have gone to seed." She made a *tsk*ing sound. "I haven't seen him up close, but his hair's greasy, and he moves rather furtively."

It had to be him. "I think I've seen Lee, too. Outside the bookstore the other day, and in the Sand Dollar on Tuesday he was angry they were selling a photograph of Winslow Granite. But today, Abo Ree, he was trying to break into my car." I related the details.

"I hope you reported it to the police, *querida*."

"I did. I guess he doesn't live around here."

"I don't think so." She shook her head. "I believe he resides in Fall River, New Bedford, one of those places."

Both were working-class southern Massachusetts cities on the water not far from Providence, Rhode Island. New Bedford had been largely populated by Portuguese and Cape Verdean immigrants during the heyday of the whaling industry.

"I wonder where he's staying while he's in town," I said. "It wouldn't be with his sister."

"Emily Winslow Swift."

"Emily told Gin she was estranged from her brother."

"Maybe because he's been burglarizing our local establishments." Abo Reba took a sip. Of course she would know about that.

"Do you have any proof of that we could turn over to the police?" I asked.

"No, honey. It was just a thought."

"The question is, why would he be skulking about, so to speak, and breaking into places?"

"I've heard tell that his grandfather Eugene had an addiction problem. Perhaps Lee does, too, and he's looking for objects to steal and sell to fund his habit."

"Maybe." I didn't think Lee Winslow could have any connection to my skeleton and her sweetheart. He was a contemporary, not anyone who had been alive eighty years ago. Still, that Winslow name kept cropping up. I gave my head a little shake. "Enough about mysterious thieves. Tell me again about your wedding."

"My, my, *querida*. That was a long time ago. I will say, your grandfather Alcindo was one handsome drink of water back then." A dreamy look came into her eyes as she began telling me of their courtship.

CHAPTER 37

After I left my grandma and opened the door to Miss M, my gaze fell on the garment bag. Despite making excuses to myself earlier about how the dress would be fine, it occurred to me that I'd just left the apartment of a master seamstress. My grandmother would be able to make any last-minute adjustments to my gown if it needed them. I grabbed the bag, locked the car again, and made my way back upstairs.

"I'm back, and—" I began after she opened the door.

"You'd like me to do your last fitting."

I smiled, casting my eyes at the ceiling. "And how did you know that?"

"One, you're holding your dress in a wedding shop garment bag." She held up a second bony finger. "Two, you didn't have the fitting where you bought the dress because of the break-in. Three—I'm brilliant and clairvoyant and I've known you since you were a bump in Astra's belly."

"All true."

"Go on into my room to change and let's see what's new."

I obeyed, of course. I had left the wedding heels in the bottom of the bag and slipped those on over bare feet after I peeled off my winter socks. She didn't have a full-length mirror in the bedroom, so I smoothed the satin down over my hips and took a deep breath.

I processed back into the living room whistling "Here Comes the Bride."

Abo Reba brought her hand to her mouth, her eyes filling. "Gracious, girl." She extracted a hankie from the cuff of her sleeve, where she had kept one for as long as I'd known her, and wiped her eyes. "You sure clean up nice."

A laugh eased my nerves. "Thank you, Abo Ree."

While I had changed, she'd set out what looked like a fishing tackle box on the table. After she opened it, I saw it was a well-equipped sewing kit.

"Stand there." She pointed, then sat on a swivel chair at her desk, rotating to face me. "Very nice. You're slender, but you're not a toothpick. A man likes a girl with curves, even if they're subtle ones."

I blushed but kept my mouth shut. I knew Tim very much enjoyed my figure, subtle as it was.

"Turn in a circle, as slowly as you can."

I turned.

"Extend your arms straight out in front of you and turn again."

"Like I'm slow dancing?" I began another rotation.

"Kind of. Hmm. Stop." She stood and fussed with the back of the dress. "Stay there but put your arms down. Okay. Back up, but higher?"

I obliged.

"Hang on while I get my pins." Reba strapped a pincushion with a Velcro strap around her left wrist.

I felt her adjust the fabric.

"Now sit on that chair." She pointed to a straight-backed chair.

I sat, trying to keep my shoulders down, my spine straight, my knees together.

Reba laid a hand on my shoulder. "Mackenzie, look at me. Remember what I told you about my dreamy groom, my lovely, small wedding?"

"Sure." How could I not? I scrunched up my nose. "You just told the story half an hour ago."

"You can relax, hear me?" She fixed her gaze on my face. "You're going to your own party, to celebrate your official union with that handsome fellow you adore. That's all it is."

I nodded. Was that all it was? Maybe.

"Just sit there," she went on. "Pretend you're at dinner, laughing and talking and accepting congratulations as you sip champagne. Like you will be in two days' time."

I let my spine soften. My shoulders did what they wanted to. I hadn't realized how much tension I'd been holding in my body.

"That's better, sweetheart. Now, stand up and turn around." She unbuttoned the train. "Walk into the other room, turn, and walk back. But relax into your hips. You're going to your darling, not to your execution."

I couldn't help but snort.

"Very nice," she declared. "Now, are you all set with your something old, something new, something borrowed, something blue?"

Was I? "Well, the dress and shoes are new, obviously. Gin loaned me a pair of gold earrings that have Victorian knots like my ring, so that's the borrowed part. But I'm out of luck with the old and the blue." Why hadn't Team Bride reminded me of that tradition?

"I'll be right back." Reba headed into her bedroom. She returned holding a gold chain from which a blue stone hung. "My Alcindo gave this to me when we married. It's lapis lazuli, and I've been saving it for you."

My throat thickened as my eyes filled. I held a hand to my mouth.

She tutted. "No crying, silly," she said. "I want you to have it, and you can knock off old and blue with the same piece. Now, sit down."

I sat. She came around behind me and fastened the necklace around my neck. The stone nestled in exactly the right spot at the top of my sternum. I reached up behind me with two hands and gently pulled her head down next to mine.

"Thank you," I whispered, then sniffed.

"Let me go. You'll give this old lady a crick in the neck."

I laughed and released her.

"Go take a look in the bathroom mirror," she instructed.

I gazed at a delicate gold chain and a teardrop-shaped blue stone sprinkled with flecks of starlight. Grandpa Alcindo, whom I still missed, had had good taste. I'd thought to leave my neck bare for the wedding. Instead, wearing this would be perfect.

After I came back out, I kissed Reba's cheek. "Thank you, again."

"Go change so I can get to my fixing."

In the bedroom, I slipped off the dress, pulled on my sensible winter jeans, sweater, and socks, and brought the garment back out to her. I kept the necklace on.

"It doesn't need much, but there's a little pooching in the back." She turned the dress inside out, holding a needle under a bright lamp and squinting as she threaded it. "I'll take a few tiny stitches and be done with it. Now, about Della and Manny."

"Way to pivot, Abo Ree." I gave her a quizzical look. "What about them?"

"Have you figured it all out yet?"

"Not exactly. But it seems like the Swifts and Winslows of the time had to be involved. And maybe Della's own family, too."

"The Ruhlens." Reba inclined her head with a sage look.

"Right. Did you know Richard before he started getting confused?"

"I met him a few times. He's not a kind man, Mac. I didn't care to be around him."

"That jives with what Ursula said about Richard being mean as a young person," I said.

Reba's doorbell chimed.

"That'll be the girls, picking me up for dinner. We

old ladies like to eat early." She bit off the thread, turned the dress right-side out, and handed it to me.

"Thank you." I gave her a quick hug. "For everything."

"Gotta run, darling. See you tomorrow." She grabbed her purse and headed for the door. "Lock up on your way out."

I just smiled at my dynamite grandma, who packed a world full of energy, wisdom, and love in one small package.

CHAPTER 38

"I don't know how you come up with such delicious dinners on the fly, Tim," I said at seven that night, sitting back from the kitchen table where we tended to eat when it was only the two of us. A few forlorn pieces of rotini and an errant inch of asparagus—which I now speared with my fork and popped into my mouth—were all that remained on my plate. And even though it was a casual dinner, Tim had lit two tapers and laid a pretty table with place mats and cloth napkins.

He flipped open his hands. "Hey, one makes do. We had pasta in the pantry, chicken sausages in the freezer, some asparagus nearly past its prime in the vegetable drawer, and a rosemary plant overwintering in the breezeway. A pot of boiling water and olive oil in a skillet? Voilà, it's dinner, plus some Parmesan on top."

"A skillet skill I simply don't have." I took a sip of wine. "But I'm awfully glad you do."

"One cook in the family is enough." He smiled at me. "But if you ever want to learn, you only have to ask."

"Unlikely, but it could happen." I returned his smile.

"Any late-breaking news on the wedding front?"

My smile slipped off. "I'm meeting your parents tomorrow night for the first time." And I also hadn't worked on my vows. After dinner I would, I promised myself.

"Sounds like you're nervous about that."

"I am, a little." I swallowed. "What if they don't like me?"

"Mac." He grabbed my hand and pressed it to his lips. "They are going to adore you. Seriously. And vice versa."

"All right." It wasn't, but I'd deal with that tomorrow.

"Did you get the security camera thing all arranged?"

"Yes. Forrest Ruhlen's granddaughter is going to install them. I'll meet her at either the bakery or my shop in the morning and confirm the placement. She'll give me a link to the software, so we can sign up ourselves and arrange billing. She'll show me how to use the app, too."

"Thanks for handling that. I told Joseph I'd be available all day to help with the dinner. I mean, when I'm not getting my parents settled."

"Aren't you picking them up at Logan?"

"No. Mom wanted to rent a car. Her flight and

Dad's are getting in close to the same time, and she said she'd bring him down."

"Not late afternoon, I hope." It was more than a two-hour drive from the Boston airport to here, but it could take much longer during rush hour, especially on a Friday.

"No," Tim said. "They should arrive in Westham by three. Dad's on a red-eye to New York, and then he'll hop on a shuttle up here."

"He'll be tired when he gets in."

"Maybe not." Tim laughed. "He's like me. He can sleep anywhere."

"It's a gift." I could no more sleep on an airplane than on a bed of nails, points up. I was wound too tight for that. "Remind me where they're staying?"

"They grabbed an Airbnb right here in town."

I peered at him. "They're sharing a bed?"

Tim laughed. "They're friendly, but not that friendly. No, it's a cottage with four bedrooms. Jamie and the kids will stay there, too." He pulled his mouth to the side. "She hasn't answered my text from earlier. I hope everything is okay out there."

His sister had a troubled past. Her two older children had a different father from the baby's. Neither man had stuck around. Jamie had tried to die by drug overdose in the fall. Tim had flown out to Seattle in a hurry to watch the kids until his father could drive up from California to take over. I loved that the men in the family were nurturers and hoped Jamie could get it together—and keep it together—for the sake of her kids.

"She must be busy packing for her and the kids." I stroked his hand. "The older ones have to be super excited to take a plane trip and to see you again. They're probably bouncing off the walls and not helping at all."

"You're right. That's gotta be it." He blew out a breath and mustered a smile. "Now, tell me what's happening in the case. I bet that's probably more on your mind than the wedding is."

"You know me too well." He truly did. I knew I was out of the mainstream, not being more excited about my wedding than about an eighty-year-old corpse. But that was who I was and at this age, there was nothing I could do about it. "I seriously don't think the police are paying any attention to who killed poor Della and Manny."

"But you have thoughts about it."

"I do." I sipped my pinot gris. "I think Richard Ruhlen was involved, Forrest's father. And Kit Swift."

"Related to Win?"

"Her great-grandmother. Plus Sarah Winslow— Win's great-aunt—and maybe Eugene Winslow, Sarah's brother."

"But why kill their friends?" Tim asked. "And in Ruhlen's case, it would have been his own sister."

"Awful, isn't it? I'm not sure they were all that friendly, when it came right down to it. Kit Swift had imagined Della was her rival. The Ruhlen family didn't want Della to marry Manny. I don't know why the Winslows would have been involved unless it was peer pressure."

"They were all in their teens, right? I remember what that was like. But a double murder? Gives you the creeps, doesn't it?"

"I'll say. High school peer pressure might have

made me say I wanted to kill somebody." Somebody like my archrival, Victoria. "But it was only a phrase. Nobody I knew would actually act on it."

"Same here." He drained his wineglass. "Eli said something about a Lee Winslow today. Related?"

"He did?"

"Yes."

"It's the same family. Lee is Win's uncle, her mother's brother. What did Eli say about him?"

Tim frowned. "He said he heard a noise outside last night. He went down to check, and this dude was poking around Gin's shop."

"Salty Taffy's." Gin and Eli lived upstairs.

"Yes. Eli asked him what he was doing, and the guy claimed he was interested in buying property in town."

"At night? During the last week in December? What time was it?" I asked.

"Around ten. Eli said Gin was already asleep. The man seemed harmless and possibly high on something."

"Gin didn't say anything about it."

"Eli might not have had a chance to tell her yet. He goes into work super early sometimes."

"With the break-ins around town this week, Eli should tell the police about Lee."

"Right. That's why we're putting up security cameras. I'll make sure he knows." Tim gazed at me. "You said the bridal shop was burglarized. Where else has been broken into?"

Huh. "I don't know. But Eli needs to call the cops, in case this Lee isn't actually harmless. Plus, now they would have a name for him. That could change everything."

"You're right. Mind if I call him now?"

"Of course not. I'll clean up."

Tim went into the living room to make the call. As I carried the plates to the sink, I thought about the purple-eyed, greasy-haired man snooping around a candy shop at ten o'clock on a cold night. He had to be the Westham burglar. Didn't he?

CHAPTER 39

At eight thirty that evening, Tim was on a long call with his sister in the living room, speaking in low, serious tones. I sat reading the coloring book mystery in the kitchen, avoiding my nuptial obligations. When a call came for me from Gin, I headed upstairs to talk with her. The spare room doubled as an office, with a kind of Murphy bed tucked away in a cabinet. I plopped onto the desk chair.

"I'm calling to check in with you, Ms. Bride." Her voice sounded like she was smiling.

"I am here, Ms. First and Only Attendant."

"Everything under control?"

I cleared my throat. "I might not have paid sufficient attention to my vows yet."

"Mac! You have to."

"Ugh. I know, Gin. And I will, as soon as we're finished talking. I mean, it's not like I haven't thought about them."

"But it's a really big step, right?" She gave a low laugh. "To say in front of your family and close friends how you feel about Tim and what you, well, vow to do to keep the marriage healthy and alive."

I swallowed. "It's a huge step. What if I freak out during the ceremony? What if I, like, chicken out or freeze?"

"Listen, hon." Gin's voice was low, reassuring. "You like things under control, right?"

"You know I do."

"So the best way to control this particular situation is to write down your vows. Practice saying them out loud. Don't look in a mirror, but pace around and memorize them."

"As if I was going to be in a play?"

"That's a good way to look at it. You need to learn your lines. That way you'll know what's going to happen. You'll be confident in what you're going to say. And you won't freak out, I promise. Plus I'll be right next to you with your cue cards, so to speak."

I'd never acted, but this could be a good plan to get me through the formal part of the ceremony, which for some reason I was finding terrifying.

"All right. Thank you."

"Now." Ice clinked before she spoke again. "Apparently you and Tim knew about this Lee Winslow character before I did. Snooping around my shop, indeed. Eli called the police about him. They seemed glad to have a name for the guy."

"I'm glad he called. Tim mentioned it at dinner." I told her about coming across the bridal shop break-in. "You can only imagine how happy I was to have my dress in my car instead of out somewhere as stolen property." I swiveled to gaze at the garment bag I'd hung on the outside of the closet door. "Oh, and my grandmother did the fitting this afternoon."

"Reba did? That's perfect. You're going to look stunning in that dress, Mac. You are so not a girly girl. It's simple and elegant. Just right."

I couldn't help but smile. How I looked when I married Tim wasn't one of my worries. He would love me, regardless. But it couldn't hurt to feel confident in my appearance on our special day, and the photographs of us would be around for a very long time.

"I think so, too. And wait until you see the necklace Abo Reba gave me to wear. It's old and has blue. Best of all, it was a gift from my grandfather to her, and she's been saving it for me. It's perfect."

"That's awesome, Mac. But listen to this," Gin went on. "I spoke with Emily Swift at Shearlock Combs today."

"Which is the best name for a hair salon, ever."

"Agreed. Anyway, we happened to be both waiting at the same time for our dye jobs to set up. She was focused on her phone, and then she started swearing under her breath."

"Being you, you asked her what was wrong."

"You bet. Turns out she's not that happy with either her husband or Win."

"About Orrin starting a yoga studio?" I asked.

"She mentioned that, but it seemed like they might have other conflicts, too."

"The twenty-five-year itch?" I asked.

"Could be. Then she said something about her 'damn daughter'."

"Seriously?"

"Yes. Emily and I aren't exactly buddies. She buys a lot of candy from me, but that's about it. Something must be bothering her, big-time, for her to open up like that."

So Emily was upset with Win and with Orrin. Plus, she'd said she was estranged from her brother. Was Emily a difficult character, or did she have reasons for these discontents with the people closest to her?

Gin said something away from the phone. "I have to go, Mac."

"Okay. Have you shared what you learned about Emily on the thread yet?"

"It's not much, but I will. And you have your homework to do."

"Yes, ma'am." I gave a salute, even though she couldn't see it. "Oh, you and Eli are good for the rehearsal tomorrow at five?"

"At the church, right?"

"Yes. And Gin?"

"Yeah?"

"Thanks for the pep talk," I said. "I needed it."

She laughed. "Any time, my friend."

I swiveled back to the desk, where a yellow legal pad and a pen awaited. Except . . . the lines were already filled with wedding vows. Tim had clearly been working on his. I averted my eyes and flipped the paper over the top and behind the pad. We'd agreed not to consult each other on the wording. I didn't want him to think I'd been peeking.

I sat back, thinking. Why was this so hard for me?

What happened to the old standard lines that both members of the couple recited? "In sickness and in health, for richer and for poorer, for better and for worse." Were there more of those pairs? They captured it so well, I didn't see why I had to reinvent the wheel.

Maybe I could go with something über-simple like, "I want to spend my life with you, no matter what happens." I twirled the pen and laughed to myself. I would need to add, "As long as you keep me supplied with freshly baked cinnamon rolls and blueberry scones." Humor was good, wasn't it?

This wasn't that hard, after all. I sat forward, about to put pen to paper, when Tim trudged up the stairs. I whirled and held up both hands.

"I didn't read a word, I promise." I took a second look at him. "What's wrong?"

He sank onto the small armchair in the corner of the room. The only time I'd seen him look so dejected was last summer, when I hadn't felt I could commit to our relationship. More specifically, I hadn't been ready to commit to having children with this bighearted man. I stood and went over to him, laying my hand on his shoulder.

"Is Jamie okay?" I asked.

"She and the kids aren't coming."

Oh. I leaned down, wrapping my arms around his disappointment. "I'm sorry," I murmured.

"I wanted to have the whole family together, just this once." He took one of my hands and laid it against his cheek.

"Of course you did. Did she say why she's canceling?"

"Not exactly. She claimed the kids all have colds and she was worried about taking them on the plane." He fell silent.

He didn't sound like he believed her. I waited. Gin had been right. We didn't have much dysfunction in my family, and I was lucky for that.

"I think she made up an excuse, Mac. I'm worried about her. If she's starting another slide, she might lose custody of the children. They are such sweet kids, despite their crazy family life, and they adore her. My heart breaks into little pieces thinking of them being split up."

I slid in to sit on his lap. He wrapped his arms around me and held on tight, as if he could keep Jamie's family together with his embrace.

CHAPTER 40

The next morning—the day before my wedding, I realized with a gulp—I sat at my laptop upstairs and carefully crafted my few lines of vows as Tim puttered in the kitchen. I hadn't gotten anything down on paper last night, because I'd spent the rest of the evening comforting him. He'd been so disappointed about Jamie being a no-show at our wedding. This morning he seemed in better spirits, and we'd sat sipping coffee together for the first half hour after our rather leisurely and delightful sleep-in.

Now I emailed a copy of my vows to Gin, who gave me a thumbs-up. I also checked the group thread, glad Gin had updated it about Eli talking with Lee Winslow, and about Emily being unhappy with her family. Too bad nobody else in the group had news, though. Oh, well. *Que será, será.* I added my own about Lee bothering my car yesterday.

I sat back, thinking about Lee and Emily and Win and Orrin and Barlow, the current-day incarnations of the Winslows and the Swifts. Did they have secrets they were desperate to keep? If their ancestors had killed Della and Manny, would any or all of them be trying to cover it up now that Della's bones had surfaced?

Barlow had a criminal record, or at least criminal wrongdoings in his past. Perhaps his willingness to venture outside the law had extended to protecting past family secrets.

Had his twin brother stayed out of trouble? Orrin had said he'd done well trading stocks, so they'd both been in the financial sector. I ran a search on Orrin Swift but couldn't unearth anything nefarious.

What about Emily? Did she hold down a day job? I poked around until I found a feature article about her in the *Cape Cod Times* published three years ago. The headline read, "Heiress to Winslow Granite Fortune Uses Artistic Talents to Etch Headstones." I paged through it. I'd never thought about how gravestones were inscribed. According to the article, names and dates could be chiseled or sandblasted, but the finest detail came from etching. Emily was quoted as saying that laser etching was becoming popular and was less expensive, but the best images came from hand etching.

I tapped the desk. Interesting that only Emily was described as the heir to the fortune, not both her and Lee. I searched on Winslow Granite, but the company didn't seem to be in business anymore, as evidenced by the lack of a website. Emily had kept granite in her life. Did she also have secrets she was keeping?

Lee Winslow seemed like a sketchy character, but did he have an actual criminal background? A search yielded mention of a Hard Knocks gym in New Bedford owned by him. But when I clicked the link to the website, it wasn't active. I didn't unearth an arrest record for him, though.

Of course, Della's own family members, Forrest and Kim Ruhlen, also still lived in town, as did Al Cabral, Manny's nephew. I realized I didn't know if Al had a family, or Lee or Barlow. Did Win have Swift or Winslow cousins? Did it matter?

I sniffed. Something was starting to smell fantastic. As my stomach let off a hungry growl, Tim called up from the bottom of the stairs.

"Omelets are ready."

I checked the time. *Oops.* I had to meet Kim at my bike shop at nine thirty, which meant I would have to get dressed fast and possibly bolt my breakfast.

"Be right down."

CHAPTER 41

"How's this?" Kim's breath came out in visible puffs. She stood on a ladder holding the small camera up above the back door to my bike shop. She'd already installed the camera above the bakery's back door and then hauled her ladder to Mac's Bikes. The camera lens was less than three inches across. A long power cable dangled down.

"Looks good to me." I shivered inside my jacket and tugged my cap farther down on my head. It was frigid out here. I'd walked into town, but as soon as I stopped moving, the cold hit me.

"It has a wide angle, and I'll leave it pointed down," Kim said. "In combo with your motion detector light, you should be all set." She drilled two starter holes, then pulled a glove off with her teeth to position the screws.

"I assume the camera is weatherproof?" More snow was forecast for tomorrow. Whether it evolved into a major storm or not depended on how it tracked. I had fingers crossed for it not materializing at all. Who wanted to go to an evening wedding in a snowstorm?

"Definitely weatherproof." She climbed down and lowered the ladder. "I need to run the wire inside to plug it in. That way you never have to worry about the batteries running low. Okay if I drill a hole here?"

"Sure." I unlocked the door. She quickly attached the wire to a plug and plugged in the camera. "Buy you a hot drink?"

She cocked her head as if thinking. "Sure. Thanks."

"Daisy's Doughnuts good?" With Tim's place closed, it was the nearest coffee shop. Blessedly we didn't have any chain stores in town, and the old-style donut shop with the old-style spelling made great old-style pastries, including a chocolate eclair to die for. They also had better coffee than either of the big-name coffee places in the next town.

"I'll meet you in ten," she said. "I have to return the ladder first."

I headed down Main Street toward the far end beyond the Quaker meetinghouse. Now that my vows were done, I was determined to spend the rest of the daylight hours figuring out what had happened to Della and Manny. But first a warm-up drink with Forrest's granddaughter. Followed by a visit to him, perhaps.

A few minutes later, I had my hands wrapped around a thick mug of steaming dark roast. Kim's long fingers similarly embraced a tall cup filled with hot chocolate, topped with whipped cream. I hadn't been able to resist an eclair, now half consumed, but she hadn't wanted anything to eat.

"Cold out there," she said.

"I know. And snow tomorrow, maybe." I shook my head.

She shifted in her seat and looked away, as if feeling awkward.

"I really appreciate you doing this work for Tim and me," I said. "Do you want to show me the app?"

That seemed to put her on more comfortable ground. She pulled out her phone. We spent a few minutes going over how the camera software worked, and she sent me the link I needed to set it up. She also handed me the packaging for the two cameras. "That has the serial numbers."

"Thank you. Kim, I'm happy to pay you in cash for your labor, but Tim and I both need invoices for the hardware for our records."

"No worries. I'll send a bill. Well, two bills, for the whole amount for each of you. I don't make enough money to pay taxes, so I don't care if I'm paid under the table or not."

"Sounds good." I took a sip of my rapidly cooling coffee. "You already know I found your great-great-aunt's skeleton, right?"

"Della." Her mouth pulled down at the edges. "That's gotta be, like, the saddest story ever."

"I know. I noticed the other day that you and Win Swift seemed to know each other."

"Kind of hard not to when you went to the same high school." She tossed her head. "We weren't BFFs, believe me. Didn't exactly hang with the same crowd."

My phone dinged with a text. I glanced at the

name of the bridal shop owner and tapped open the message.

So sorry about yesterday. Do you want your fitting today?

"Excuse me a minute," I said to Kim. I texted back.

That's thoughtful of you to reach out. I'm sure the break-in threw off your schedule, and your losses must hurt. I'm all set with my dress, thanks. I hope you're okay.

Another ding.

I am. Insurance claim is in. Police have detained suspect. Fingers crossed.

I thanked her, adding that my fingers were crossed too, and slipped the phone back into my pocket. I looked up at Kim.

"That text was from the bridal shop owner, who was broken into yesterday. She said the police have a suspect in custody."

Kim raised her eyebrows. "Lee Winslow?"

I blinked. "I don't know. Maybe. What makes you think he's the bad guy?" And how did Kim know of him?

"Win—Winslow—is his niece. I saw them together a couple of nights ago. They were looking kind of, I don't know, furtive."

"Where were they?"

She gestured with her thumb. "Down the street. Pretty near the candy shop. I had worked last shift that night and was driving home, so it was after ten."

The night Eli spoke to Lee outside Salty Taffy's.

"I think Win has been helping him rob stores," she said.

Whoa. That was news to me.

Kim shook her head. "Lee's a total loser, and he's

her uncle. I get that. Helping family. I'd do just about anything to help Granddad. But I know he'd never ask me to do something illegal."

"I'm glad to hear it."

"I don't like Win, but she's smart," Kim continued. "She could be the brains behind his operation." She gave a low laugh. "Isn't that how they put it in books and cop shows?"

"I think you need to tell the police you saw them together."

"Seriously, Mac? Like I said, he's her uncle. Why wouldn't they be out on a walk together? Even on a cold night. I mean, they're related. I can't quantify what 'furtive' looks like." She used finger quotes around the word. "The cops wouldn't listen to me."

"You're probably right. I'm sure they'll question the family, anyway."

And Kim hadn't witnessed them actually breaking in anywhere. Still, the whole thing made me uneasy. What was a young woman like Win—with everything going for her—doing assisting in a burglary, or even directing it, if Kim was right? And maybe more than one. People were hard to figure out sometimes.

CHAPTER 42

After Kim left Daisy's, I got another cup of coffee and sat perusing the world via my phone. What would Della have thought of this futuristic device? More than a telephone with no cord, it packed in moving pictures, newspapers, reference volumes, novels, games, a typewriter, and more, all instantly available from a thing slimmer than a deck of cards.

And what might fisherman Manny have said about cigar boats, GPS navigation, sonar tracking, and lightweight fiberglass hulls? Surely other modernizations had come to the fishing industry that I didn't even know about.

Moot questions, all. Neither of the star-crossed lovers ever experienced a hint of those inventions. I sipped the warming brew, gearing up to brave the cold again and track down more information. Where, I wasn't quite sure.

"May I?" a man's voice asked.

I jerked my head up to see Norland smiling, cup in hand, across the table.

"Please." I returned the smile.

He sat. "You looked deep in thought."

"I was. Imagine what our two victims from nineteen forty would have thought of all the tech stuff we now take for granted." I held up my phone. "This, for starters."

"So true. Your father and I both remember when all telephones were tethered by a cord. A computer was a big, boxy thing most people didn't have at home, and cybercommunication was typing gray letters into a dark screen surrounded by DOS commands."

"Disk Operating System." I nodded. "I wrote a research paper on it in college."

He nearly spit out his coffee. "A research paper on MS-DOS. Don't make me feel older than I am, okay?"

I laughed. "Sorry, Norland."

"Any news about who did away with Della and Manny?"

"Not really." My smile went bye-bye. "I'm not sure where to look next. I don't understand why the state police aren't doing more. Or are they, and I'm not hearing about it?" Did our former police chief know something but hadn't let the group know? Too many questions. "I know these are old, cold cases bordering on frozen, but still."

He made a single head bob. "I hear you, Mac. Listen, I went to chorale practice last night. I happened to snag a minute to speak with Hope Ruhlen afterward."

Ooh. "You did, did you?"

"Uh-huh."

"I hope you happened to steer the conversation around to her aunt Della's skeleton," I said.

"I know you'll be shocked to hear that I actually did."

"Shocked." I waited. "And?"

"She said she never thought Della had eloped."

"Hope told me that, too," I said. "I never got a chance to ask her why."

"She said her father—Richard—had always seemed way too satisfied with that story. Her mother alluded to some fishy business but never said what it was before she died."

"I wonder if the mother suspected her husband of having had a hand in the couple's disappearance."

"I think she must have." He sipped his coffee.

"Forrest said he was going to look for letters his mother might have exchanged with Della," I said. "Or maybe a diary she kept."

"Good. I also picked up some intel about the *Boa Sorte.*"

"Manny's boat." I leaned forward.

"Yes. Sergeant Johnson dug into police reports from the era."

So Penelope was working on the old murders, after all.

"In fact, its hull had been shattered," Norland continued. "Possibly by an explosive. That's why it sank. When the submerged wreck was found, though, Manny Cabral's remains were not aboard."

"Gin and I had talked about dynamite being a possibility."

He sipped his coffee. "You might not know that the Winslow fortune was made by quarrying."

"I know there was a business called Winslow Granite. I didn't know they made a fortune on it."

"The family business quarried a much-sought-after blue granite and shipped it all over the country." He looked at me over the top of his glasses.

"Let me take a stab at it. Sarah Winslow worked for her father's firm and knew all about dynamite."

"I think that would be a fair guess."

"Do you know if she was good with boats?" I asked.

"I don't, sorry. Although I believe her namesake is."

"Win?"

"Yes. She won a sailing regatta last year, if memory serves."

"I was thinking of having a chat with her, anyway. Thanks, Norland. She might know about Sarah." I tapped the table. "I wonder if Winslow Granite is still in operation. I looked this morning but didn't find a website for them."

"No, the Winslows shut down operations some time ago. The blue granite ran out in the quarry they owned, but they'd made a pretty penny, and it went to Emily and her brother."

"Emily is a headstone etcher, did you know?"

"She's quite talented. You must have seen that write-up in the *Times*," he said.

"Yes, this morning. It described her as the heiress instead of one of the heirs."

"As far as I know, they both inherited. But Lee squandered his half, while Emily and Orrin invested hers. They're sitting on a nice nest egg, I believe."

It seemed Lee must have been the man upset about the photo of Winslow Granite. If he had spent his half of the inheritance, that could explain his anger and resentment.

"What else do you know about Lee Winslow?" I asked. "He seems to be in town."

"He's a troubled soul. Or was."

"In what way?"

"He had anger management issues. I don't know if mental illness played a part or not, or what the cause was. He never seemed to fit into society the way the rest of the family did—and still does. But I have not encountered him in many years."

"I think I saw him trying to break into my car yesterday," I said.

"You mentioned that in the group thread."

"Do you think he's the one who has been breaking into stores this week?"

Norland smiled. "You know that's not my job anymore, right, Mac?" He drained his coffee and stood. "I have to run. Now that I'm fortified, I'm taking the grands out to lunch and a kiddie movie. Pray for me." He rolled his eyes, then chuckled. "Not really. I love it."

"Good luck." Even though his afternoon sounded a bit nightmarish, I'd be there in a few years, if all went according to plan, taking my own little ones to the afternoon matinee during a school vacation week. Heaven help me.

"See you tomorrow, right?" I was pretty sure he'd confirmed his attendance at the wedding.

He whistled the opening notes from "Here Comes the Bride" and gave me a little salute before heading out.

CHAPTER 43

As I passed the bookstore, I decided to stop in. Maybe I could see if Barlow knew anything about Lee Winslow. The Swifts and the Winslows seemed inextricably intertwined. Would he know about Lee breaking into stores? What about Kim's claim that Win was helping him? The most important question was whether he would talk to me about those people. I had only one way to find out.

I pushed through the door to find Emily Swift speaking in low tones to Barlow, her brother-in-law. She whipped her head to look at me. Oh, to have been the proverbial fly on the wall.

Barlow raised a hand in greeting. "Come in, Mac."

"Good morning, Barlow, Emily."

"Hello, Mac." Emily didn't smile.

"What can I help you with?" Barlow asked.

"I'm only looking. Don't let me interrupt you." I

headed toward the mystery section at the back. I wanted to ask Emily about Sarah, about Lee, about Win, but couldn't figure out how.

The voices resumed, too low for me to make out the words, despite how much I'd like to know what they were talking about. I pulled the hardcover of *Hid from Our Eyes* off the shelf, Julia Spencer-Fleming's latest mystery. While not a cozy, her characters and storytelling were so compelling I would read anything she wrote. This would be a good long read to take on vacation, along with the Krista Davis cozy, and it had a *Signed by Author* sticker on the front.

Before I could get back to the counter and maybe eavesdrop a little, the door opened with a whoosh of cold air and then shut. The air fell quiet. I emerged from the shelves to see Barlow staring at the door, his brow knit.

"Is everything okay?" I laid the book on the counter. "It looked like Emily was concerned about something." I winced inwardly. That question was way too personal. *Oh, well.* Too late now.

"What?" He focused on me. "Sure, um, yeah. It sounds like you know Emily."

"We've met a few times."

"She's worried about her girl."

"About Win?" I asked.

"Yes." He gazed at the door again, as if seeing Emily. "Win's a good girl, and as smart as they come, but she can get a little fanatical about things."

Things. What things? "I don't really know Win, either. But maybe it's because she's young." I laughed. "I was a bit more of an extremist when I was her age than I am now. I've heard Win is a good sailor. Is that what you're talking about?"

"She is, at that. We were all so proud of her last year. She was the youngest person to win the Bourne Regatta."

"When I went to the Historical Society earlier this week, she was showing me pictures of Kit Swift. She seemed to know a lot about her ancestor. And yours."

"Win really has a thing about Kit." He frowned again.

"What do you mean by 'a thing'?" I asked.

"She's way too focused on her. Thinks Kit was some kind of goddess. I mean, she was my grand-mother, but she was human and could be difficult. Demanding. Win never saw that side of her."

"It seems like Win really values family," I ventured.

"She does." He straightened a display of lami-nated bookmarks. "It's hard to explain. The reputa-tion, the standing of the two families seems more important to Winslow than the actual people." He flipped his palms open. "What can you do?"

A man and two children pushed through the door. Barlow gave himself a little shake and welcomed them. I pushed the Spencer-Fleming book closer to him on the counter.

"I'd like to buy this." I dug out my credit card.

"She's a great writer," he said as he rang up the book. "Such a nice lady. She came by and signed stock for us in the fall when she was on her way to Nantucket to write."

"That would be a good place to get away, at least during the off-season." I thanked him, took my paper bag, and left.

Had I learned anything of use? Not really. Except that Emily was worried about Win. It sounded like her uncle was, too. That might bear more thought.

CHAPTER 44

I popped into the tropical, scented air of the flower
shop. "Hi, Forrest," I called.

He faced the front. "Mac, I'm glad you stopped by.
I was going to call you when I finished this arrange-
ment. I don't want you to worry at all. Everything's
under control for tomorrow."

"I'm seriously not worried. Or maybe I should be
concerned that everything's going too smoothly."
Well, not everything. "Actually, there is one glitch.
Tim's sister can't make it, so we need one fewer wrist
corsage, unless you've already made them."

"No, we'll do up everything in the morning so it's
all as fresh as it can be." He grabbed a pen and made
a note. "Any other changes?"

"No, I don't think so."

"That's a shame about the sister," he said.

"It is." I kept it at that. Now I was glad I hadn't

planned on Tim's niece being a second flower girl. "Hey, Kim was a big help to Tim and me this morning."

"Oh?"

"Yes, after you said she was a whiz with tech stuff, I hired her to mount security cameras at the back of my store and the bakery. Tim and I have closed our businesses for three weeks."

"And with the break-ins, you can't be too careful," Forrest said.

"Exactly."

"I have a camera out back myself, thanks to Kimmie." He plucked a yellowing leaf off a houseplant on the counter.

"Good. So, I was wondering if you—"

"If I found anything of my mother's? You bet I did. Hang on a minute. It's in the back."

Cool. What had he discovered? And would it be useful to the case of the abandoned bride and her lost-at-sea groom? I couldn't wait to find out.

Before he could head back to grab whatever it was, though, a couple came in from the street. Forrest helped them find exactly the right flowering plant for their ill friend. Another customer blew in and wanted to order two table arrangements for her sister's sixtieth birthday party. Then a man said he needed a long-stemmed bouquet for his daughter's dance recital.

I kept waiting and kept getting hungrier. That sweet, puffy eclair hadn't been much of a snack, and it was now after noon. I grew too warm and unzipped my jacket, tucking gloves and hat in the pockets. I was dying to know what Forrest had found. He mouthed an apology.

While I waited, I considered what Barlow had said. He barely knew me. Still, he had told me he was worried about Win, and that Emily was, as well. Barlow had done something dishonest in his recent past. What if he was up to something else and trying to deflect suspicion onto his niece? That would be a rotten thing for an uncle to do. I probably should ask Flo to do some research on him. Maybe he had other crimes in his closet.

As I considered whether I should leave and come back later, the last customer walked out. *Whew*. Forrest disappeared into the back and reappeared holding a slim book bound in a faded red. I met him at the counter.

"I'm glad I was able to find this, Mac. I went through Mother's diaries, and I found this one." He folded back the cover, smoothing down the frontispiece with as much care as he would have used touching his mother's cheek. He ran his finger along the first line of writing on the facing page. "See? It's from nineteen forty."

Under the January first date was written, "Private property of Iris Colby." And Iris was Della's good friend. This could be the breakthrough I'd been looking for.

"It looks like your mom wasn't already married," I said.

"No. She was two years older than Dad, and he was only sixteen that year. I haven't had a chance to read through the diary, but you can take it if you'd like."

"I can?" I gazed at him.

"Yes. I'm not sure what to do with the book, now that I've found it. But I don't have time to peruse it.

So, please give it a read and let me know what you learn."

"I will, and I'll be infinitely careful with it."

He drew out a sheet of butcher paper from under the counter and wrapped the book. "Keep it as long as you need it, but I'd like it back eventually."

His store phone rang. A customer pushed through the door. Forrest slapped on a piece of tape and handed me the diary.

"Thank you so much." I slipped the parcel into my bag. "See you tomorrow."

"You certainly will."

I suited up for the cold again and slipped out. I couldn't wait to get home and start reading. I supposed I might be expecting too much from this journal written by eighteen-year-old Iris. She might not have written anything about Della. There was only one way to find out.

CHAPTER 45

My feet slowed as I passed the Historical Society building. Win had seemed to know everything about Kit Swift. Chances were she also knew the details of Sarah Winslow's life.

My hungry stomach and the diary were pulling me homeward. I told them to wait a few minutes and made my way up the stairs. Inside, I greeted a woman sitting at a desk near the door.

"Is Win Swift here?"

"She's cataloging in the back room." She gestured toward the rear. "You can go on in."

"Thank you." The door stood open to the back room, where Win sat bent over a stack of slender books. I knocked on the door frame.

She glanced up. "Hey, Mac."

"I was walking by and thought I'd see if you were here."

"I'm here half of the time until I go back to school, when I'm not helping my uncle." She set down her pen. "Any news about our skeleton?"

"No. I wondered if the police had told you anything."

"Nope. And they're still hanging on to the suitcase and its contents, too."

I gazed around the room, which was much more of a workspace than the showcase of the front rooms. It smelled of old paper and leather bindings. I couldn't figure out how to steer the conversation to Sarah Winslow and her possible facility with dynamite. I didn't think asking directly would go over well.

"I heard about the bicycling club Sarah Winslow started with Kit," I began.

Win perked up. "My mom told me you want to do a display at your shop."

"Yes."

"That's wicked cool. I'll help her pull some stuff together for you."

"I'd appreciate that. Tell me more about Sarah."

She tilted her head, narrowing her eyes. "Why do you want to know?"

"She was part of an influential family in Westham." I lifted a shoulder. "I'm curious."

"All right." Win bobbed her head as if convinced. "Have a seat. She was an excellent sailor, for one. I sail, too, and I like to think about her when I'm out on the water."

I sat across from her at the wide table. "And she worked alongside her brother at Winslow Granite, I understand." That was a complete shot in the dark. I waited for her reply.

She blinked. "She did, at least until Eugene was drafted."

"Did Sarah ever marry?"

"No. The story is that she was in love with a man who was killed in the war. Nobody else was ever good enough for her."

"So she probably stayed working at the family company," I ventured. "Did she have a desk job, do secretarial work?"

"She did stay, but her father wanted her to learn all the parts of the business. My mom says Sarah even worked in the quarry one summer when she was starting out."

Thus acquiring an expert knowledge of explosives.

"Interesting," I said. "You know, it was funny that Richard Ruhlen called me Sarah Winslow when I was there, and then he thought you were Sarah when he caught sight of you."

"He's a really old dude, Mac. The memories are in there." She pointed at her head. "But he gets mixed up a lot."

I looked around the room. "Someone I know recently uncovered an old diary. He's wondering what to do with it. Does the society here accept donations like that?"

"Of course. That's what these are, in fact. I found them a little while ago. The top two were Sarah's, and the rest are Kit's." She patted the top book on the stack in front of her.

"Cool." Extremely cool. Did they have the answers to all the remaining questions about what really happened in late spring in 1940? My fingers itched to page through those slim volumes. "Where did you find them?"

"In an old trunk."

"What are you going to do with them?" I asked.

She rolled her eyes. "I'm going to read them. What do you think?"

"I'd love to see them when you're done."

"Maybe. So who has the diary you're asking about?"

"A friend." A diary burning a hole in my bag at this very minute. I stood. "Thanks for letting me pick your brain. I'm going to have to run."

"Any time."

At the door I turned back. "Do you know if Sarah was friendly with Della?"

Win's suspicious look returned. "Why do you want to know?"

"Anything that might shed light on how Della died would help." I tried to keep my tone casual. "I mean, the police need to know. But she died in my house. I feel responsible."

"Well, a Winslow certainly didn't trap her in there, that's for sure." She folded her arms over her chest and lifted her chin as if challenging me to say otherwise.

Maybe. Maybe not.

CHAPTER 46

It was one thirty already by the time I sank into a chair at the kitchen table at home. I'd fixed a fat ham and cheddar sandwich, which now sat on a plate in front of me, with a dill spear on the side and a full glass of milk. The diary, still in its paper wrapping, I placed on the chair next to mine, in case of spills, and set my phone on the table.

I took an enormous bite. I usually read when I ate alone, but I didn't want to risk losing a bit of Dijon mustard or a drop of pickle juice on the antique diary or smear a greasy fingerprint on a page.

Instead, I thought about young Sarah Winslow, adept with boats, savvy about explosives. Still, what reason would she have to have a hand in killing Manny? Was it peer pressure from her upper-class friend, Kit? Or maybe handsome Manny had rebuffed her affections? Win had said Sarah had loved a man who'd been killed in the war, but that might not be true. It might have been Manny, and Sarah had been jealous of Della for capturing his heart.

A text pinged in. I took another big bite and read the message from Tim.

Mom's flight delayed. They'll prob get stuck in Friday traffic, late to dinner.

I texted back.

Too bad. XXOO

It was too bad. It would be nice if Greta were there for the rehearsal. She'd asked if she could read a few poems from Mary Oliver's *Felicity*, her late-in-life collection of poems about love. Of course we'd said yes. We could fill her in after she arrived about when in the program she would come forward.

Otherwise, because Pa was officiating, my mother was going to walk me down the aisle. Tim had said he didn't need such ceremony and would be waiting for me at the front. The only people we really had to have in the church at five o'clock today were Tim and me, my folks, Gin and Eli, and Cokey, of course.

I checked the group thread, scrolling down as I ate. Norland had added the bit about the *Boa Sorte* being destroyed by an explosive. I tapped in what I'd learned from Win.

Sarah Winslow was an excellent sailor and worked in family quarry one summer. Knew dynamite?

I drained my milk and popped in the last bite of pickle as I tapped.

I have Forrest Ruhlen's mother's diary. Iris friend of Della's. Am about to start reading.

Flo almost immediately texted back.

OOH!

That made me smile.

Will report back.

I pushed away my plate and glass and wiped my hands. To be safe, I unwrapped the book and left it atop the paper before I opened it. I'd seen the inside, which bore only the date and Iris's assertion of property. Private property.

I paged slowly through, scanning for Della's name. The handwriting was smooth and legible. At the end of January, the two had gone to see *His Girl Friday* at the Westham Rialto Movie Theater. On February sixth, they went skating with "the gang." On the tenth, Della spent the night at Iris's, with lots of girl talk, according to the author, and the swapping of lipsticks.

At the next line, I stared.

Della is besotted with MC. I don't blame her a bit. But she predicts trouble from her father. I can understand. He's a stormy type of man. By her reports he's angry more often than adoring. I wouldn't want to be in her shoes.

This man ended up being Iris's father-in-law. I wondered how that had gone, if she had kept her distance from him or if he'd mellowed with age. Or maybe she had a high tolerance for difficult men. She ended up marrying Richard, after all.

There was nothing more about Della on that page or the next few. I kept flipping pages. Iris was apparently working at a clothing store in town. I didn't see mention of what Della was doing. These girls were out of high school. Had they thought about college?

I spied Della's name again toward the end of February.

Met Della when she got off work at her daddy's office.

That explained what she'd been doing with her time.

She was so upset. We went for frappes at the soda foun-

tain to talk it through. She said her father blew his stack when he saw she had a picture of her sweetheart. She wants to run away with him. I told her that was rash, and she should wait.

I sat back. Poor Della. Even her best friend was discouraging her to act on her love. I didn't blame Iris, but still. I paged through until I reached March third. My eyes bugged out.

Saw Kit and Eugene going into the Swift cottage tonight with dear Della. Eugene had his camera, and Della wore a white dress. Was he going to photograph her in her wedding dress? But what about Manny? I was driving by with my parents and couldn't stop. I'll give her a buzz tomorrow.

Oh my gosh. It sure looked like Kit Swift and Eugene Winslow were Della's imprisoners. She must have been delighted to think she would have a wedding photo to keep. I flashed back to what Lee had said about his grandfather taking the photograph of Winslow Granite. That wasn't the only thing he'd used his camera for.

The next day Iris couldn't reach her.

I went by her work at the end of the day, but her brother, Richard, said she hadn't come in. When I asked where she was, he shrugged.

The next page was filled with Iris calling Della's home, but she kept getting a busy signal. Two days later she went to the house.

Her mother finally answered the door. She told me she didn't know where Della was. Her face looked terrible, like she'd been crying. Then Mr. Ruhlen came up behind her and told me to leave. He hadn't been crying that I could tell. My heart is broken. Della left without telling me, without a note or a last hug. Will I ever see her again? Will she at least write?

She didn't make any entries for a week.

The newspaper says Della and Manny eloped. Manny's boat is gone. I guess that's it.

All the rest of the pages were blank. I sat back. This was really big. Had Kit and Eugene told Della that Manny would be along in a minute? But he wasn't, of course, and Della was never seen alive again. Did it mean Sarah and Richard were Manny's murderers? Richard could have asked Manny to take him fishing. Sarah might have followed them. Had Richard knocked Manny out before moving to the other boat, before Sarah had lit the dynamite and tossed it onto the *Boa Sorte*? Or had it happened an entirely different way with different culprits?

What a twisted story. The diary didn't prove a thing, although the police should have a look at it. What could I do with the information? It wasn't like I could interview any of the people involved. All the criminals were dead—except Richard. I frowned. What happened to Manny was still imagining on my part. Kit's and Eugene's roles were the ones confirmed by Iris's words on the page. Except, even then, they could have taken pictures and then left. They might have had nothing to do with Della's death.

I flipped back to the page dated the third of March and took a picture of it, then tore off a piece of paper from a notepad to mark the place. I also took a photo of the first page, which Iris had dated and signed. Now, where had I stuck that business card Penelope had given me? Tim had a bulletin board on the wall behind me. Which blessedly held the card. Tim must have found it wherever I'd carelessly left it and pinned it up. Me being careless about things was a clear sign of stress.

I tapped out a short text to accompany the pictures.

Page from Forrest Ruhlen's mother's diary, 1940, which I have here. Looks like a Swift and a Winslow might be our villains—Della's killers. Do you need to see the original?

I sent it. I sent the two pictures to the group, too, with a short note.

Looks like we could have our bad guys, or two of them. Was Della ever seen again?

I rewrapped the diary with care. Then I sighed and pulled up my vows on my phone. Gin had told me to be an actor learning my lines. Learn them I would.

CHAPTER 47

By two thirty I was feeling antsy. I'd practiced my lines. I kept checking the thread, but the only message was from Flo telling me to hang on to that diary until she could take a look at it. Nothing from Detective Johnson, not even an acknowledgment of my message.

I heard the cover of the mail slot in the front door go *whap*, and then the postal carrier let the screen door bang. I picked up the mail from the entryway floor. Although it was usually ninety percent catalogs I didn't want and charity solicitations, today's delivery brought several hand-addressed envelopes. I smiled to see the careful lettering on a card from my Thai host family, where I'd lived for part of my Peace Corps service. I was glad we'd put Tim's address on all our wedding correspondence.

My host mother wished me *khor-hai-me-kwaum-suk-*

mark-mark-na-ka. That is, congratulations on my wedding, written in Thai script, which I could still read. A college friend currently living in Idaho also sent congratulations, as did the man who had taught me how to repair bikes, now retired in Florida.

I cleaned up and applied a bit of makeup and lipstick. My short loose curls, as usual, took care of themselves. I donned my new dress, a thin-wool turtleneck that fit me like a glove. With a hem that fell above the knees, it was like wearing a pretty maroon sweater, cozy and comfortable. With tights and my knee-high boots, I would be presentable and warm for tonight.

That thought brought me back to Della. The first days of March were usually still quite cold around here, but Iris had seen Della's white dress. She hadn't worn a coat over it? That wasn't a puzzle that would ever get solved. Della could have been carrying her coat, or maybe Kit toted it for her. Or it could have been an odd warm day.

I still had more than two hours before the rehearsal. I could walk over to the parsonage and visit with Belle, but I'd probably get in the way of the dinner preparations. I paced the downstairs of the cottage and ended up gazing into our bathroom-to-be, otherwise known as Della's prison cell. Had Kit and Eugene worked all night to board her in? Maybe they had drugged her so she wouldn't scream as they chained her to the wall. Were there close neighbors who would have heard sawing and hammering during the wee hours?

I peered out the bedroom window to the house next door. It was a newer home than this one, a ranch house, probably built in the 1960s. I was pretty sure the house on the other side was the same. Noise from walling in Della wouldn't have attracted much attention if nobody lived close by on either side. Kit not coming home would have, but she could have told her parents she was spending the night with Sarah. A timeless teen ruse as long as you had a friend to cover for you.

Kit. I froze. Win said she'd recently discovered Kit's diaries. And Sarah's. Had she read them yet? If they incriminated any of her relatives in the long-ago murders, would Win share them with the police? Somehow, I didn't think so. I would kill—figuratively speaking—to get my hands on those volumes.

The facts about Manny's demise remained a mystery that Sarah's diary could solve. I could imagine all I wanted, but not having that part of the story cleared up was messy. I didn't like mess. Maybe Richard Ruhlen would be having a mentally clear afternoon. Also, Al deserved to know that it was possible dynamite had destroyed his uncle's boat.

I could zip by Westham Village and pay Richard and Al a visit. If all the loose ends on this cold, sad case were wrapped up before my wedding, I would finally be able to relax.

CHAPTER 48

Before I could get ready to leave, the doorbell rang, followed by a series of knocks. I peeked through the side window and took a second look. Orrin Swift stood on the landing. I unlocked the door and pulled it open.

"Hello, Orrin," I said.

A messenger bag was slung across his chest. He clutched the bag's strap so tightly his knuckles were white. "Mac. I found something." His face was drawn, his eyes intense under the bike helmet he wore.

I stepped back. "Come in, please." Was he afraid? Horrified? I couldn't tell.

He hesitated but finally seemed to decide to move in out of the cold.

"Would you like to sit down?" I asked.

"I don't think I should."

"It looks like you rode here. Cold weather for cycling."

"My daughter has my car." He unclipped the flap of the bag and with a gloved hand drew out a purse. The slim handbag, with a curved bottom, featured pleats in a light-colored leather with a small strap. The initials *DLR* were stamped on the side in bold serif capitals.

I brought my hand to my mouth. *DLR*. Della's initials. "You found it in your attic?"

"It has Della's name inside. I found it in Grandmother Kit's trunk," he whispered. "Way at the bottom under stacks of clothing and books."

"You need to take it to the police station."

"Of course, but I thought you deserved to see it first."

"I appreciate that." My fingers itched to search it, but I didn't want to taint the evidence, if any was there. I hoped he'd been careful not to handle the contents, either. "You said her name is inside?"

"Yes. I used a flashlight to look inside without touching anything, and I found what you might expect in a young woman's handbag."

Good. He'd left the stuff in the purse alone.

"Lipstick, a folded handkerchief, and one of those little round things with a mirror inside that my wife uses to freshen up her makeup," Orrin continued.

"A compact?" It didn't surprise me a guy wouldn't know what it was called.

"I guess. But there was also a travel itinerary with Della's name on it, and two sets of train tickets, first to Boston and then all the way to San Diego."

"Do you realize this probably means your grand-mother was involved in Della's murder?" *Wow*. And as the diary had alleged. The Quohog Queen, a cold-blooded killer.

"Yes." His expression turned grim.

"Orrin, earlier today I saw Win at the historical so-ciety. She had several diaries she said were Kit's and Sarah Winslow's. Did she find them in that same trunk?"

"Yes. She was so excited by her discovery she stopped digging into the trunk and ran off to her internship with the society."

"I think she'll need to relinquish those to the po-lice, too," I said.

"She won't want to, but I'll make sure she does."

The Winslow name was everywhere in this case. "Your brother-in-law, Lee." I watched Orrin. I had no idea if he was also estranged from his wife's brother, or if she actually was. I also didn't know if Orrin would tell me anything about the strange man. At this late date, it was worth an ask.

Orrin rubbed his forehead as if he could wipe off something bothersome. "What about him?"

"He's been seen around town this week. And I nearly caught him trying to break into my car. Does he have issues of some kind?"

"You could say that." He made a sound in his throat and shook his head. "How much time do you have? He struggled in school, according to my wife, with a learning disability. Of course, there's plenty of expert help for that kind of thing, but he didn't want anything to do with it. He enlisted in the Army, but after boot camp he couldn't get through the school part of the training. All that made him angry. He got into fights, was in jail a few times. Then he opened a boxing and fitness gym."

"The Hard Knocks in New Bedford."

He cocked his head, frowning. "I'm not even going to ask how you knew that, But yes. The Hard Knocks was a success for him for a while."

"And he could take out his aggressions on a punching bag as part of his job."

"Exactly. But he didn't handle the financial side of it very well, and it folded a couple of years ago. Now he's back to being angry at people who have more than he does."

Like Orrin and his wife, I guessed. What a tough family situation.

"Thank you for sharing that," I said. "It must be so hard for your wife."

"It is. She had to cut off ties with him. But somehow our Winnie doesn't care. She loves family. Uncle Lee was doing fine as she was growing up, and they still have a close relationship."

Close enough for her to engage in burglary with him? I hoped not, for everybody's sake. Should I ask him about Barlow's past? His own twin brother? Maybe not. He'd just shared enough family news.

Orrin blew out a heavy breath. "I'd better get this handbag handed over to the police before I lose my nerve."

"Ask for Penelope Johnson," I said. "If she's not there, make sure they know it's for her."

"I will." He stuck the purse back into his messenger bag and turned to go.

"Thank you for showing me," I called after him.

He hadn't kept the purse a secret. He easily could have, and I was grateful he hadn't.

He faced me. "Nobody should have to discover the remains of a murdered girl. It was the least I could do." He trudged down the steps toward the Cannondale he'd leaned against the post at the bottom, the same bike Win had ridden earlier in the week.

I locked the door. And stood there. It looked like Della and Manny had been planning to relocate to San Diego. They wanted to be happy in a warm place on the ocean, where he could fish and she could live free of oppressive family and friends trying to run her life. I didn't think I'd ever heard a sadder story. Did the purse in Kit's trunk mean she was Della's murderer? Probably.

Win wasn't going to be happy that her beloved great-grandmother was a killer. But she was going to have to get used to the idea.

Me, I still had questions, and now I had even less time to get them answered. I grabbed keys, bag, and coat, and hurried out to Miss M, pulling on my beret and gloves as I went. In anyone else's eyes, it was nuts for a bride to be rushing around barely twenty-four hours before her wedding to solve two eighty-year-old murders. I knew that. And I couldn't help myself.

"Let's go, Miss M," I told my pretty red car, even though she wasn't voice-controlled. "Destination, Westham Village. I have some unresolved bits I need to resolve."

CHAPTER 49

"**I**'m pretty sure I know who killed Della Ruhlen," I murmured to Al Cabral in his office a few minutes later. I perched on a chair across from him.

He stared at me. "The same awful specimens of humanity who murdered my uncle?"

"Possibly not." I relayed what Iris had written in her diary. "And nobody ever saw poor Della again until Tim and I uncovered her bones."

"That Swift family has never been up to any good." He gave a quick glance at the open door. "My family had owned this business, but we leased the property from them. They raised the price higher and higher until we had to sell to them. Why a family like that wants an old folks' home, I can't guess."

That must be what he'd alluded to the first time I'd come by, when he'd said his family didn't own the residence anymore.

"I don't know about the rest of them," I said. "Kit certainly appears to have been a murderer."

"Poor Della. That is sadder than sad."

"I know. I learned something else a little while ago. Orrin Swift is cleaning out the attic of the old mansion, and he came across Della's purse in an old trunk of Kit's."

"Are you serious?" he asked.

"Yes. She had train tickets to San Diego in her bag, among other items."

"For their honeymoon." Al's voice cracked.

"Or because they were eloping to there." I tapped my own bag, thinking. "Both Della and Manny seem to have disappeared at the same time."

"It's what my father always said," Al confirmed.

"If that's so, then others must have killed your uncle. Did you know the hull of Manny's boat had been shattered, possibly by an explosive?"

"I didn't. Where did you hear that?"

"A man in my book group has access to old police reports. I've learned a few things about Sarah Winslow, too," I said. "For one thing, she had worked in a quarry."

"The Winslow family company."

"Right. She didn't stay in the office. She would have known where to get dynamite and how to use it."

He whistled.

"And she was good with boats," I added. "Here's what I think happened." I lowered my voice. "I think your resident Richard Ruhlen convinced Manny to take him out on his boat. Sarah followed them in a different boat. Richard might have attacked Manny or knocked him out so he could throw him overboard. Then Richard transferred to Sarah's boat, she lit the dynamite and threw it onto Manny's craft, and they sped away."

"Why, though? Why would these four young people conspire to kill two of their friends, their classmates?"

"I know Kit Swift was in an imagined rivalry with Della. Kit and Sarah were good friends. The Ruhlen family didn't want Della to marry Manny. Richard's father could have persuaded Richard to get rid of Manny. Maybe Sarah was sweet on Manny, but he wouldn't have her. Maybe Eugene wanted to impress Kit and did anything she asked him to. It's all horrible—not to mention all conjecture."

He sat back, tapping a pencil on the desk. "And you can't prove any of it."

"Alas, no. The only person still alive is Richard." I thought for a moment. "And Ursula, but she was much younger than the others. Maybe I'll go talk with her again."

"Good idea. You could try Richard once more, too. I'm not sure what kind of day he's having today."

"I will. Thanks, Al. I'll let you know if I learn anything new."

I found Ursula again in the plant-filled room in the back. Richard sat in his wheelchair on the other side, looking sound asleep. Ursula held a digital tablet and glanced up from it when I approached.

"Hello, Mac. How lovely to see you again."

I smiled and sat next to her. "What are you reading?"

"It's a mystery set in Key West, the latest in the series. I love dreaming about being down there again, especially at this time of year. I used to spend my winters on that key."

"Is it the food critic series by Lucy Burdette?"

"Why, yes. Have you read them?"

"I have. I love all of them. You know I'm in the cozy mystery book group with Flo, don't you?"

She laughed and shook her head. "Of course I do. Forgive me for forgetting. It was Florence who recommended these books."

"You should join our group, Ursula."

"No, I'm too old for that. I don't drive anymore, so Florence would have to pick me up and bring me home. You young kids have fun with it."

At over sixty, Flo was hardly a young kid. On the other hand, she wasn't ninety-two.

"Do you like reading on the Kindle?" I asked.

"Land sakes, yes, dear. I can make the print as big as I want for these tired old eyes." She gave a little smile. "Now, I expect you came by to talk about the two disappearances from long ago."

"I would like to, if you don't mind."

"Please ask away."

"Did you know Sarah Winslow?" I asked.

"I did. I mean, as much as a girl can know somebody older. I know she ran with that gang. She and Kit Swift were particularly tight. And just between us girls, I think Sarah had set her cap for Manny Cabral."

"Did he return her affections?"

"Absolutely not. He only had eyes for Della. I think it infuriated Sarah."

Enough to kill him? Possibly.

"Do you remember hearing about Manny's boat being found the following year?"

"No."

Rats. "How about Eugene Winslow? Did you know him?"

"Yes, from a distance. He was *his* friend." She gestured toward the snoozing Richard with her chin. "Eugene was besotted with Kit, who barely gave him the time of day. He did have quite the knack for photography, though. Always going around snapping pictures."

Or using his camera as a ruse to lure an unsuspecting young woman to her death.

"Thank you for letting me pester you." I smiled.

"I love talking about the past. Sometimes it seems so much more colorful than the present."

"I'd better get going." I stood. "I have a wedding rehearsal pretty soon."

"You'll be a lovely bride, Mac."

"Thanks, Ursula."

"I'm going to make Florence give me every detail about the wedding on Sunday when she's here for dinner. You come back and see me after your honeymoon, you hear?"

"I promise." I glanced at Richard before I left the room, but he hadn't roused.

I poked my head into Al's office.

"Did you learn anything?" he asked.

"Not really. I spoke with Ursula, but Richard was sleeping the whole time."

"Ethics be damned." His hands clenched into fists atop the desk. "I'm going to talk with Ruhlen later. If he was involved in murdering my uncle, he needs to pay."

I said goodbye and stepped out of the office. Smelling a faint scent of coconut, I glanced around. Win's purple hair was disappearing down the hall toward the back.

Had she read a diary entry telling of Sarah and Kit's parts in the murders? Maybe she wanted to talk with Richard about what happened with the boats. If so, she was out of luck, unless she woke him up. Or . . . could he be in danger from her? No, not with care providers everywhere. At least I hoped not. Anyway, she was a talented young woman with her future ahead of her. Why risk it by committing a crime? But what if I was right about what had happened all those years ago? Richard being the last person alive who was involved could feel like a threat to the reputation of Win's family, something she seemed to value highly.

I looked back at Al, but he had his back to me and was on the phone. I made for the exit, hoping only that Richard would not be clear of mind with Win— but would with Al.

CHAPTER 50

I parked Miss M in the parking lot behind the church at a couple of minutes before five. I doubted the UUs had installed a surveillance camera back here, but Lee Winslow wouldn't dare try to break into my car again, especially at a place of worship. At least, I hoped he wouldn't.

Making my way around to the front of the church, I had my hand on the big front door when my cell vibrated in my bag. I'd already switched off the volume but left it on vibrate. Was it Tim saying his parents had made good time and had already arrived? More likely the call was Gin asking where I was. But it was from a number I didn't recognize. I answered anyway. A wedding tomorrow with people coming from all around? I would answer anything.

"Mac?" the voice asked. "This is Penelope Johnson."

Not wedding-related at all. "Detective. Did you get my text with the pictures?"

"Yes, that's why I'm calling. You sent an intriguing snippet. Where did you obtain the diary?"

"Forrest Ruhlen lent it to me."

"I'd like to see the original. Will Mr. Ruhlen permit that?"

"I doubt he would object. But you can ask him. He owns Beach Plum Florist."

"Given that he grants permission, may I stop by your house to pick it up in a few minutes, or can you drop it off at the station?"

Ugh. "Neither. I'm sorry, but I'm about to be late to my own wedding rehearsal, which is followed directly by a dinner. I can bring in the diary tomorrow. The wedding isn't until the evening."

"I apologize for intruding. Go ahead with your events."

"Thanks."

"Della Ruhlen has been dead for eighty years," Penelope added with a little laugh. "Another few hours don't matter."

I spoke quickly so she didn't disconnect. "I learned earlier today that Win Swift has diaries that belonged to Katherine Swift, who went by Kit, and to Sarah Winslow. Both are ancestors of Win's, and the two women were apparently close friends."

"Are the diaries from this same era, around 1940?"

"I have no idea, but they might be. I'm not sure if Win had read them yet when I spoke to her a few hours ago. She was cataloging them in the Historical Society." I cleared my throat, spying Gin and Eli hurrying toward me, pink-cheeked from the cold. "I have to go now. But I hope you'll check out those other diaries and ask Win what she knows."

"Asking people what they know is one of my superpowers, Mac. Thanks again for the intel."

I ended the call and immediately wished I'd also told her about the purse Orrin found. With any luck, she already had it in hand.

"I'm glad I'm not the last one to arrive," I said to Gin and Eli.

"You're never late, Mac." Gin smiled, then said to Eli, "She likes things orderly."

I rolled my eyes, even though it was true. I had been described as chronically early, and I liked it that way. I hated arriving anywhere late.

Eli pulled open the door. "After you, ladies."

"There you are." In the foyer, Tim hurried toward me. "Did you hear?"

"Hear what?" I asked. "Are your parents all right?"

"They're fine, still on the road. But Cokey broke her arm."

I brought my hand to my mouth. "The poor thing."

"Derrick's at the hospital with her."

Gin stepped forward. "How did she do it?"

"She and a little friend were playing with an older brother's skateboard." Tim shook his head. "It slipped out from under her."

"I hope she didn't hit her head," I said. "She probably wasn't wearing a helmet."

"I don't think she did." Tim threw an arm around my shoulders and squeezed. "She'll be okay, Mac. Kids are resilient."

Mom approached from the sanctuary. "Derrick just called. They're still waiting to have the arm set."

I shook my head, picturing my favorite girl in pain.

"He said the worst part is Cokey's beside herself that she won't be able to be in the wedding."

"I can only imagine," I said. "Of course she can still do it, as long as she's not hurting too much. Do you think her dress will go over a cast?"

"If it doesn't, Reba will enlarge the sleeve so it does," Mom pointed out.

Of course. As I had just witnessed, my grandmother was a whiz with a needle and thread. "I'll text Derrick and have him tell her that Titi Mac says not to worry." I only wished the problem of two cold-case murders was as easily solved as fixing a flower girl's dress.

"That will make her feel better," Mom said. "I wondered if she was going to be accident prone right now, with her Mars transiting the sun."

"Right." I drew out the word. *As if.*

"Coquille is in good hands." As he often did, Pa used Cokey's actual given name, one her French mother had insisted on. "Shall we get started?"

CHAPTER 51

After we went through the steps of the ceremony—minus actually reciting our vows, and sans Greta with her poetry or the flower girl—we six trooped over to the parsonage, where Abo Reba joined us a few minutes later.

Mom poured wine. Pa carried the pot brimming with hot *cachupa* into the dining room, and we sat to eat at the table beautifully laid for a dozen. This was to be a welcome dinner as well as a rehearsal dinner, except our only out-of-town guests were delayed, and Derrick and Cokey were getting her arm tended to. Mom and Pa's other relatives were driving in tomorrow.

"Where's Tucker?" I asked.

"At Derrick's," Pa said. "I walked him over there after Derrick took Cokey to the hospital. He thought she would appreciate having the pup to cuddle with when she got home."

And our dinner would be quieter, too, although Tucker was calming down as he matured. I went in the front room and spent some time with my parrot, who was so happy she started singing, "Happy," her favorite song to dance to. When I was summoned to the table, I told her to be good.

"Belle's a good girl. Snacks, Mac?"

I joined the rest of the humans around the extended table. Pa bowed his head and folded his hands. We all followed suit.

"May the Divine of the universe surround us with blessed light and keep us safe from harm. May She heal Cokey's arm. May He guide our guests today and tomorrow with care. And may we feel grateful for this bounty. Amen."

"Amen," Belle chimed in from her perch in the front room.

I suppressed a laugh and murmured, "Amen. What a pretty table." The white damask tablecloth had been crisply ironed. A vase of white and red carnations adorned the middle, and red cloth napkins made it look even more festive. A big cloth-lined basket of crusty bread sat next to the butter dish.

"Your groom is responsible for that, including the blooms." Pa ladled the hearty stew into a shallow bowl and passed it along.

We had clustered at one end of the table, with Pa at the head.

"It's too bad we have empty chairs." Mom gestured at the unfilled places.

"My parents feel terrible to be missing this," Tim said.

"As long as they arrive safely, that's all that matters." Pa continued to serve up stew. "If they don't arrive in time to eat with us or are too tired, I'll send a container along for them. Otherwise Astra and I will be eating nothing but *cachupa* for days."

"They'll be at our house for breakfast tomorrow," Tim offered. "You're all welcome to join us for blueberry scones."

I smiled and nodded, even though inwardly I groaned a little. I had my spoon ready to dig in when Mom lifted her wineglass.

"A toast to Mac and Tim," she began. "We couldn't be happier with you joining our family, Tim."

Pa raised his glass. "To a long and happy marriage."

We all clinked glasses and sipped, while Tim nudged my knee with his.

"A toast! A toast. Belle's a good girl. Snacks, Mac?"

"Excuse me." I rose.

"Mackenzie looks lovely tonight, doesn't she?" Reba asked.

I blushed. "Oh, stop now."

"Hey, learn how to accept a compliment, Mac," Gin said. "It's true. That's a great color on you."

After I fed Belle and covered her cage for the night so we could eat in peace, I finally dug into my favorite food. I savored the tender pork, the spice of the chorizo, the melding of vegetables and spices, with flavors that somehow made me feel I was on a tropical island.

"You outdid yourself, Pa," I said.

He beamed. "I had a good crew of men helping, at

least until Derrick had to go rescue our girl." Pa pointed at Reba. "And I had a good teacher."

"Always make sure your sons know how to cook," my grandmother said.

"You have that in common with Greta, my mom," Tim said. "She had me in the kitchen from an early age."

"But what about teaching your daughters to cook?" Gin asked, pointing her chin at me.

"Good point," my mom said.

Tim gave me an adoring look. "But Mac is good at so many other things. Who cares if she can't cook?"

I blew him a kiss. Mom sipped her wine. Gin and Eli both said how much they also liked the dish.

"Have you ever eaten Cape Verdean food before?" Pa asked Eli.

"No, sir. I have a lot to catch up on."

"What about the mystery of your skeleton and her groom, Mackie?" Abo Reba asked. "Have you solved it?"

Classic Reba. Why keep quiet when you have a question about murder to ask? "Not exactly. Well, maybe Della's death." I related to the group what I'd read in Iris's diary.

"The Swifts and the Winslows," Reba said. "Ever intertwined."

"What about the break-in artist?" Gin asked. "Didn't you think that might be a Winslow?"

"Lee," I said. "Win's uncle."

"He had me do his chart a few years back," Mom said. "He's a troubled soul, that one, with Saturn ruling half his planets."

"The whole gang of them back in 1940 seem like they were troubled, the murder victims excepted," I said. "Teenagers plotting to kill their friends, their classmates. And then actually carrying it out."

"I'm sure it was a cry for help," Pa said. "A need for love, each in their own way."

"But what about evil?" I asked my ever-forgiving father. "Doesn't that play a role?"

"I believe evil is a human concept devised to disguise human hurts and failings." Pa gave me a gentle smile.

I glanced at my mom, who rolled her eyes. And then winked at me.

"Could I trouble you for seconds, Joseph?" Tim held out his bowl. "It's truly delicious."

"Eat up, Brunelle." Pa ladled. "You have a big day ahead of you tomorrow."

As did I, but nerves were starting to get the better of my appetite.

Gin elbowed me. "Have you been practicing?" she murmured.

"Yes, ma'am. I'll be ready." I crossed my fingers under the table. Would I ever be ready?

"You mentioned a Win Winslow," Eli said. "Young woman, purple hair?"

"Yes," I said. "Except her name is Winslow Swift. Win's mother's maiden name is Winslow."

"A Win was interested in the history of the Oceanographic Institute last year," he said.

"She's a budding historian. I'm sure that was her." I took a bite of bread.

"She wanted a part-time job last summer helping with our historic archives," Eli explained. "A version of the institute was founded back in the nineteenth century. But my boss felt something was a little off about Win."

"You didn't hire her?" I asked.

"No. Plus, we had another candidate who was better qualified."

Something "off" about Win. *Interesting.* I hadn't noticed that. Or had I? She'd seemed kind of suspicious of me a few times. Well, I had been snooping into her family's history. Who could blame her? On the other hand, Barlow had said Win's mother was worried about her.

I heard a faint buzzing that sounded like my phone, but I couldn't remember where I'd dropped my bag. The doorbell chimed. Tim's cell rang. Mom stood and knocked over her wine.

"I'll wipe that up," Pa said.

Tim pulled out his phone. "They're here!"

"I'll get the door." Mom headed for the front room.

My heart started pounding. I was sure I looked panicked. I knew that was how I felt.

"Hey." Tim squeezed my hand. "I told you they're going to love you." He rose and followed Mom to the door.

CHAPTER 52

Tim had been right. William and Greta were both a hundred percent warm and welcoming to me.

Greta kissed me on both cheeks. "I've heard so much about you, Mac." She wore her hair, still dark with only a few threads of silver, in a side-part cut falling just below her chin. Her eyes, the same big baby blues as Tim's, were accentuated by a bright blue scarf wrapped European-style around her neck over a black-and-white quilted jacket. "And I've never seen my boy happier."

"I'm really happy to meet both of you," I said. "Thank you so much for letting us use your place for our honeymoon."

"It's my pleasure, honey. You two will be more comfortable there than in a hotel or even a bed-and-breakfast. I've got people to see here on the continent, including my errant daughter."

"I'm sorry Jamie couldn't make it."

"You and me both." Her smile vanished. "My girl has had a tough time in life. She's an adult and has to find her path. All a parent can do is keep sending the love." Her focus came back to me, as did a smile playing with her lips. "Speaking of being a parent, Timothy says you two plan to start a family. I'm delighted."

I blushed. "We do." I glanced at my mom and dad, at Reba. "My niece broke her arm, or she and my brother would be here, too. We're big on family around here."

"Well, I can't wait, and you have my blessings."

When my eyes welled up, I swallowed down the emotion. "Thank you." Greta's blessing, her approval, meant a lot all of a sudden.

"This must be the lovely bride." William extended his hand. A slighter version of Tim and not as tall, he was Paul-Newman-handsome, with blond hair graying at the temples and the tan of someone who enjoyed the California sunshine.

"Welcome, William." I smiled and took his hand in both of mine. "We both appreciate your coming."

"I wouldn't miss it for the world, my dear."

Greta turned away to speak with Abo Reba. Tim handed his dad a glass of wine. Joseph dished up two more bowls of *cachupa* and invited the newcomers to eat. We all sat and talked until Greta started covering her yawns at about nine o'clock.

"Please forgive me," she said. "It's been a very long day."

I was beat, too.

Tim stood and started picking up dishes.

"Nonsense," Mom said. "We'll clean up."

"Are you sure?" he asked. "I'm happy to help."

"Me, too," I added.

"Absolutely not," Mom said.

Pa made a shooing gesture. "You all get along and get a good night's rest. We'll see you tomorrow." He added to Reba, "I'll walk you home, Mai."

"It's only across the street, Joseph," my grandma protested.

"Then it won't take me long, will it?"

Everyone said their goodbyes.

"Mac, want me to walk you to your car?" Tim asked.

"No, I'll be fine, sweetheart, but thanks."

"I'll run you back to where you're staying," Tim said to his parents. "Be home in a little bit, Mac."

I gazed into his beautiful face. We were really, finally, truly going to do this thing.

"See you in a bit."

CHAPTER 53

Miss M was the only car in the church lot. The wind was making branches creak and blew my hair every which way. It suddenly felt creepier than a horror movie to be here alone in the dark. Even though I didn't see anyone lurking, I unlocked the car and slid in as fast as I could, making sure the door locked after me.

I drove home, with the wind buffeting Miss M something fierce. It had been silly of me to worry about meeting Tim's folks. Now all I had to worry about was if it would snow tomorrow. If other guests would have travel glitches. If I would remember my vows. If I would trip on my dress. And all the rest of it. It was kind of a relief to worry about nothing but normal bride stuff.

As I turned off Main Street onto Blacksmith Shop Road, the way home seemed darker than usual tonight. There were no streetlights, and the snow-bearing clouds obscured any light from the stars or the moon. A few of the houses showed the flickering blue light of televisions, and in another home a man hunched over a laptop in an upstairs window. Did anybody ever sit and read in the evenings anymore?

I hit the brakes when a branch came crashing down, barely missing my car. I was glad Pa had insisted on walking Abo Reba home. This was not a good night to be out. The house before ours was dark, with the residents away on a holiday trip to a warmer climate.

What was that? The edge of the pool of my headlights caught a movement. I could swear a person had dashed into the shrubs between our house and the one beyond, which also had darkened windows. My breath rushed in. Who would be skulking around in the dark? Maybe it was Lee Winslow looking for houses to break into, people to take his anger out on. Except the bridal shop owner had said the police had someone in custody. I'd assumed it was Lee, but they could be detaining someone other than him. I could have asked Penelope who it was when she'd called. I hadn't.

I swore out loud. I hadn't left our porch light on, or any interior lamps lit when I'd left the house this afternoon. Right now? I didn't want to risk being attacked as I hurried from car to house. I didn't even want to stay inside Miss M with the engine running until Tim came home. My heart pounded in my chest.

Wait. I knew what I could do. I could drive back to the safety of the corner of Blacksmith Shop with Main Street. Unlike here, that intersection was well lit. I would watch for Tim to drive by. Oh . . . but what if he came from a different direction? There was more than one way to get onto our street, and I didn't know where his parents were staying. I shook my head. It didn't matter. I could just call and ask him to let me know when he got home.

In fact, I could call him right now. I dug around in the detritus in my bag for my phone and hit his number. Which went to voice mail. *Fine.* I still had a plan.

I pulled into our driveway to turn around. Right when I shifted Miss M into reverse, a great crack sounded behind me. *What?* Had I been shot at? I took a split second to assess myself. No. Nothing hurt. I hadn't heard glass shatter. Still, even more reason to get out of there. I looked in the rearview mirror and slammed my foot on the brake pedal. The backup lights illuminated a window covered by branches.

I groaned. A limb had split off behind me, probably from the big old maple that shaded the front of the house in the summer. Now I was trapped. I couldn't back up unless I got out in the dark—still alone—and tried to haul the branch out of the way. In my dress.

I put the car in park and switched it off. And listened closely. The wind now roared through the treetops, a din I could hear even through the closed windows. I wasn't sure I could pick up sounds of an intruder, an attacker, even if there was one.

Trying again, I pressed Tim's speed dial. At the same moment, headlights approached from the direction of town. Had I been followed? This could be a two-pronged attack from the figure who had darted into the darkness and the one approaching on the road. I was a total sitting duck staying put inside a sports car, even though it was locked. My throat thickened. My hands inside my leather gloves grew clammy. I tried to muster my courage. I had to be able to save myself or at least fight back.

Tim didn't pick up my call. Where was he? Why didn't he answer? I didn't know whether I should grab the heaviest thing in the car—except there wasn't any object like that—and unlock the door, ready to defend myself. Or if I should crouch down, arms over my head, and hope for the best.

The headlights pulled over and parked in front of the house, shining directly at me. My heart pounded like a bass drum in a marching band. I tried to swallow away my fear. It didn't work.

Tim's face appeared at my window. I blinked, praying this wasn't an apparition. I let out a long, deep, quavery breath and pressed the window button. That wasn't going to work. The car wasn't running. I unlocked the door. He pulled it open.

"Are you all right, my darling?" He leaned down, his voice more than concerned. "You're pale."

"I guess so." I held my fist to my mouth while I got myself under control. "I'm awfully glad you're home."

"You're shaking." His eyebrows pulled together. "Something happened. Something more than this branch."

"I'll tell you once we're inside."

CHAPTER 54

As soon as we got inside with the door locked behind us, I fumbled with the front porch light but
got it flipped on. I went through the kitchen to
switch on the light in back, dropping my bag on the
table as I went. Tim followed me into the kitchen.

"Uh, Mac, we're home. Why are you turning on
the outdoor lights?"

"Give me a second." I blew out a breath as I went
to the cupboard and got down the bottle of a very
fine single-malt Scotch. "Want some?" I asked him.

"Sure, hit me."

A minute later I set two half-filled small glasses on
the table. I'd topped each with a flick of water to
open the flavors, a trick Zane had taught me.

"Cheers to my beautiful bride." Tim lifted his
glass.

"Cheers." I clinked mine with his and took a sip.

Ahh. "Here's what happened. I was almost to the house when I'm pretty sure I saw someone dart into the shrubs."

He swore. "The ones at the front between this property and the next?"

"Right. And that freaked me out. Like, a lot. I hadn't left any lights on for us, and I really, really didn't want to get attacked the night before my wedding. Or ever."

"I don't blame you." He covered my hand with his big, strong, warm one.

"I also didn't want to sit in the car and wait for you. So I decided to go back and wait down at Main Street where there's a streetlight and other people going by. I was going to park there and call you. I pulled into the driveway to turn around and—bam. The limb landed."

"Did you feel it hit the car?"

"I don't think so. I hope it didn't, although the branches might have scratched the back. I sat there, listening for more noises. My imagination has never been all that active, but it sure was tonight." I shivered.

He jumped up and grabbed the fleecy vest I often wore around the house in the winter for a little extra warmth.

"Thank you." I slipped it on.

"And then I drove up." Tim sat again. "Let me guess, you thought it might be someone else out to get you."

"How did you know? I was totally freaking out, and you arrived at exactly the right moment. I mean, after I saw it was you and not . . . well, somebody else."

"Who do you think the person in the bushes was?"

"I don't know. Maybe Lee Winslow?"

"They should have that dude in jail if he's been breaking into stores." He stood, taking his glass. "Are you okay?"

I assessed myself. "Yes. Thank you."

"Good." He kissed the top of my head. "I'll clear the branch away in the morning. Right now I'm going to go upstairs and take another look at my vows."

"I'll be up before too long. But I'm going to leave the outside lights on all night. And we should remember to put a light on a timer while we're away."

"A wise move." He paused, smiling down at me. "You liked Mom and Dad, didn't you?"

"Yes. Very much." I smiled back.

"It was mutual, Mac."

"I'm glad. Now go."

To the sound of his feet trudging up the stairs, I pulled out my phone. I was sure I'd heard a text come in while we'd been eating. Sure enough, there were two. One from Al Cabral, and one from the group thread. I opened Al's first.

Mac, Richard Ruhlen admitted everything. He and Sarah knocked Manny overboard without a life vest and blew up his boat.

I stared at the message.

He was almost gleeful about it. He even dared me to call the police. He's a monster.

That was incredible. For one thing, that Richard had had a clear enough few minutes to tell Al. And second, that he'd told him the story at all. He could easily have taken it to his grave. That must have been what he'd meant when he'd told me in a satisfied voice that the *Boa Sorte* hadn't brought Manny any good luck.

Richard was probably right. With no other evidence, there was no way he would be arrested for a crime committed eighty years ago. Or could they charge him? He was a monster, in fact. Expressing no remorse, even at the end of his life? I was as stunned as Al's text sounded.

I felt bad for Forrest. He would be devastated when he learned his father was a murderer.

That was the last message from Al. Had he, in fact, called the police on the centenarian? I thought of phoning him, but nine thirty seemed too late. At least now I had his cell number. I saved it under his name, then texted in return.

Shocking. Thx for telling me. Did you call the PD?

I waited a moment, but he didn't write back. Next, I swiped open the group thread. Nothing new from anybody. I sure had news to add.

Al Cabral says Richard Ruhlen admitted working with Sarah Winslow to kill Manny and explode the boat. I'm stunned. Off to write to the detective.

I sent it. Before I could contact Penelope, my phone rang with a call from Flo.

"Mac, I just saw your text. Al was attacked this evening outside the assisted living place."

My breath rushed in. "Oh, no."

"He might have died out there, but my mother saw it happen from her window and called security."

"Did she see who did it?"

"No. She said it was somebody in dark clothes," she said. "It's December. Everybody is covered up, wearing dark clothes and hats."

Like the person in the bushes here. "Is Al going to be all right?" I asked.

"Not sure. He's in the hospital in Falmouth."

"Thanks for letting me know."

"Of course. See you at the wedding."

We disconnected, but I stayed in my seat. It seemed too much of a coincidence that Al had been attacked shortly after he'd learned the facts of another long-ago attack. Would Win have come after him and then left him to die? Had she then come by here, hoping to attack me, too? Anyone knocked unconscious and left outside in this weather would be dead by morning.

I located Penelope's number, the cell number on the card she'd given me, not the police station. Should I call or text? I opted for the latter. If the detective was off-duty, she'd still see the message and could decide what, if anything, to do about it.

I tapped out a message.

Someone was lurking outside my house in the dark tonight. Don't know who, and nothing happened. Also, I'm forwarding a shocking message from Al Cabral. Did he report it to the WPD? And did you hear about the attack on him in Westham Village parking lot tonight? He's in the Falmouth hospital.

I sent it, forwarded what Al had written, and sat back. Would she respond? I thought about Orrin and the purse and added another message.

Orrin Swift showed me Della's purse on his way to relinquish it to the police. Hope you have it in hand, as well as the diaries Winslow Swift found.

I hit Send. Still no response. The detective was either on another case or was off-duty and having too much fun to respond to messages from an overly persistent amateur. More power to her, except it was frustrating in the moment.

When a text came in, I held the phone in front of me in a hurry, but it was from Mom.

Cokey's home, with a purple cast to match the wedding colors. XXOO

I smiled. My niece was determined not to miss her flower girl moment of fame. And now her cast would match the flowers and pick up the violet in her dress.

Thx. She rocks. Love you.

I waited a bit longer, sipping my whiskey, but Penelope didn't text or call.

My smile slid away. Richard and Sarah had plotted to murder Manny—and succeeded. Kit and Eugene had figured out how to kill Della—and succeeded. The well-off young people of Westham, with everything going for them, had decided to commit malicious acts with fatal consequences. And then they'd all kept it a secret for decades. Many decades.

Unless Sarah and Kit's diaries revealed what they'd done, that is. Would Win give them over to Penelope? Maybe she would refuse. With the information in Iris's diary, combined with Richard's confession, could the police get a warrant to view the diaries Win had found? I didn't know how that worked when the cases were so cold.

I yawned and drained my whiskey. I stashed the bottle in the cupboard and washed the glass. It was time for this bride to go upstairs and get her beauty sleep. My most important priority was tomorrow's wedding, although I sent up a little apology to Della and Manny for putting them second.

CHAPTER 55

The irresistible allure of coffee and baked goods awoke me the next morning at eight. I pulled on glasses, yoga pants, and a fleece hoodie and padded in slippers and glasses downstairs to an empty kitchen. The coffeepot was full. Two cooling racks were covered with fat, glistening triangles of blueberry delights.

A note from Tim sat on the table. *Gone for a long run, back by nine thirty. Parents come at ten. Hands off the scones!* He'd added a winking smiley face, plus "XXXOOO."

Rats. I lowered myself to inhale their aroma close up. To. Die. For. Instead of nibbling on one, I slipped two pieces of bread into the toaster. I was glad Tim was getting a long run in, despite the weather. It always made him feel better. I poured a fat mug of coffee—which always made me feel better—and sat at the table with my phone.

Nothing had come in from Penelope. It was a holiday weekend, and I was sure she had a life outside policing. Still, she seemed to be the one authority who cared about Della and Manny. *Huh.* She'd said she would come get the diary today. Maybe she was a person who liked to sleep in on the weekends.

The Cozy Capers thread contained chatter and reactions to my text of last night. Everybody had something to say about Richard's admission.

Hard to believe he confessed to that.

He must think he's immune from prosecution.

Think he's been faking his dementia?

Young people from elite families think they can get away with anything.

That last one was from Flo. She'd written one about the attack on Al, too, after she called me last night, to which there were also plenty of responses.

Terrible!

Who would have done that?

I hope he'll be okay.

Stephen had texted, **Praying for him.**

But nobody had any new information. Too bad.

I checked the weather report and let out a big breath of relief. The snowstorm had tracked out to sea. The only precipitation we were going to get was flurries, if that. I sipped my coffee and brought up my vows. I practiced saying them without looking at the screen until I was pretty sure I had my lines down. Unless I froze, and then I had Gin.

When my toast popped up, I slathered one with butter and raspberry jam and the other with peanut butter and sliced banana. I knew I'd be hungry again for the family breakfast. I ate and sipped and thought about poor Al in the hospital. It was only eight thirty. I hadn't planned to shower until this afternoon before I got dressed for the wedding. I had plenty of time to run out to the hospital, pay Al a visit, and still get back by ten.

Resolved, I cleaned up my dishes and wiped off the table. I was constitutionally incapable of leaving a kitchen messy when I left the house. I ran upstairs to accomplish some personal hygiene, contact lenses, and a foundation undergarment—otherwise known as a bra. Back in the kitchen, I added to Tim's note.

8:30. Al Cabral in Fal. Hosp. Driving to see him, home by ten. XXOO.

I also texted the second and third phrases to the group thread and sent it.

Wait. This plan would only work if Tim had cleared that windfall for me. I could do it, of course, but it might take too long, depending on the size of the limb that had fallen. I hurried to the front window—and smiled. The driveway behind my car was free of branches.

Two minutes later, garbed for the cold with my phone in my pocket, Miss M and I headed for Falmouth. The community hospital was a satellite of the main Cape facility in Hyannis. It wasn't big, but they provided excellent care.

I parked next to a black Prius. Seeing it rang a little bell in my brain, but I couldn't figure out why. I hurried in, suddenly feeling an urgency to see Al. At the hospital information desk, I asked where Al's room was.

"Are you family?" the white-haired man asked.

I thought fast. "I'm his niece."

He squinted at me. "Another one?"

Another one? "Yes." I gave him my brightest smile, but inwardly I was chilled. Who else would lie and claim to be Al's niece? Al didn't have siblings, and neither had his wife. He didn't have any nieces. Win was the only one I could think of who could be here, but why would she be visiting Al? I did not have a good feeling about this. "She's already here?"

"She is." He pulled down the corners of his mouth. "It's before visiting hours, but family's allowed. Room two-fourteen. Elevators are there." He pointed. "Turn left when you get off."

I thanked him and hurried away before he changed his mind about whether I was actually family or not. I drummed my fingers on my left thigh while I waited for the elevator, which was never coming, as far as I could see. If Win was the one who had attacked him last night, she could be trying to finish the job right now. Maybe I was rushing to judge her, but she'd been acting oddly since I met her, and others had reported the same.

Where in heck was the elevator? I glanced around. *Aha.* A door labeled *Exit* was beyond the second elevator. That door had to lead to stairs. I ran up to the second floor and hung a left in the hallway, scanning the signage for room numbers. A sign labeled 209–214 had an arrow pointing down another hall to the right. I slowed and smiled at a scrubs-clad man at the nurses' station when he glanced up. I continued with an air of knowing what I was doing, a trick that worked in all kinds of situations.

The hall smelled of cleaning solution. A tall cart was filled with breakfast trays. The doors to the patient rooms I passed were open, and televisions droned in some of them.

The door to Room 214 was shut. Why? Al could be having some kind of personal care—or he could be in danger. I pushed it open and gasped.

Tall, strong Win stood near the head of the bed. She leaned with her long, lithe arms on a pillow. A pillow she pressed with all her weight onto Al's face.

CHAPTER 56

"Help! Security!" I yelled down the hall as I raced in. I pushed Win aside as hard as I could and grabbed the pillow, throwing it across the room.

Al gulped in a huge breath. Win's nostrils flared. She pulled her fist back and swung a punch at my jaw. I ducked just in time. I rammed my head into her solar plexus. She cried out and fell backward, knocking over an electronic monitor on a stand. Alarms went off. Win kicked at my feet and connected with my left ankle.

"Ow!"

"What's going—" The nurse ran in. He stopped short.

"She was trying to smother Al." I stepped away from her toward the nurse. "I hope security is coming. I'm pretty sure she's the one who tried to kill him last night."

"Security is on the way." The nurse hurried to the other side of the bed and held Al's wrist to take his pulse. "Are you all right, Mr. Cabral?" he asked.

Al, whose head was bandaged, nodded once, slowly, and then winced. "Alive," he croaked. "Thanks to Mac here."

"She's lying." Win sat on the floor panting from me knocking the air out of her. "I found her with the pillow."

"I don't think so, miss." The nurse shook his head. "You were in here for five minutes, and she just arrived."

A burly man in a blue police-type shirt rushed in. "What do we got?"

I pointed. "Her name is Winslow Swift, and she tried to kill Al. Twice. When I arrived, she was pressing a pillow onto his face." I joined the nurse on the other side of the bed in case she tried anything else and to get out of the guard's way. "Please contact Westham Police and make sure they notify Detective Penelope Johnson."

The guard scowled at Win but spoke to me. "Yes, ma'am."

Another guard arrived, an equally burly woman.

"Possible attempted murder," the first guard explained. "We're detaining this one." He pointed to Win.

She scooted on the floor until her back was at the wall and brought her knees to her chest. "You're all trying to ruin us."

By "us" she had to mean the Swifts and the Winslows. The scent of coconut reached my nostrils.

"Your ancestors killed my uncle," Al said in a weak voice. "They ruined it for themselves." He blew out a breath and closed his eyes.

Win struggled as the guards hauled her to her feet. They managed to cuff her hands behind her back.

"I'll get you, Mac," she snarled.

"I doubt it," I said. To the guards, I added, "Detective Penelope Johnson, okay?"

"You got it," the man said.

They marched Win out the door. The nurse was now taking Al's blood pressure. Why hadn't Al pressed his call button? Every hospital bed had one. I went around to the other side. It was dangling from its cord near the floor. I picked it up and laid it near Al's hand.

Al opened his eyes. "You saved my life, Mac. She grabbed the button away from me right before she jammed that pillow onto my face."

"Did you know she was here, ma'am?" asked the nurse, whose name tag read Christopher. "You showed up in the nick of time." He attached a little clip to one of Al's fingers.

"I kind of had a feeling about it." I shrugged. "I'm Mac Almeida, by the way."

"Chris Rogers. I'm going to guess you're not actually family."

"She is now," Al said.

"Al, do you remember what happened last night?" I asked.

"The last thing I recall is going out to my car. I

thought I heard an odd noise. I smelled coconut. Then I woke up in here."

"Does Westham Village have security cameras in the parking lot?" I asked.

"We sure do." His eyes drifted shut again.

Chris motioned for me to leave and followed me out. He left the door open.

"Is he going to be okay?" I asked.

He gazed at me. "HIPAA doesn't allow me to tell you. But under the circumstances, and since you're 'family,' I will." He smiled but spoke in a low voice. "The attending doctor thought Mr. Cabral will be fine. He has a contusion on his head and also has a concussion. It'll be a while before he feels normal. He's not young, but he's in otherwise good health. He should make a full recovery."

"Do you think he'll ever remember what happened?"

"It's hard to say."

If Win hit Al on the back of the head with a heavy object, he wouldn't have seen her. It might not matter what he remembered. What the security cameras showed was another matter.

CHAPTER 57

After breakfast, I helped Tim clean up. Abo Reba had volunteered to show Tim's parents around town. They had arrived by the time I got home, with my parents and grandmother right after them, so I hadn't had a chance to fill Tim in on what had gone down at the hospital.

"I saved someone's life this morning." I scrubbed at a bit of bacon stuck to the skillet.

Tim laid his hand on my shoulder. "You save my life every day simply by being in it." He kissed the back of my neck.

A delicious shiver ran through me. "But I actually did."

The doorbell rang.

"Hold that thought," Tim said. "I'll see who it is."

He returned a moment later, followed by Penelope.

"Good morning, Mac," she said.

"Please have a seat, Detective." Tim gestured at the table. "Coffee? Blueberry scone?"

She blinked. "You know, that would be fabulous. Both, thank you. Black coffee." She pulled out a chair.

I left the pan to soak in the sink and dried my hands before sitting opposite her. "You heard?"

"We have Winslow Swift in custody." She thanked Tim when he set down a mug of coffee and a plate holding the last scone. "Good save, Mac."

"I'm sure glad I showed up in time," I said.

Tim tilted his head and gave me a quizzical look.

"I was about to tell you," I said to him. "I caught Win trying to smother Al with a pillow at the hospital."

"Wow," he said. "Attempting to murder him?"

"That was what it looked like." I blew out a breath. "I called for help, pushed her out of the way, and got rid of the pillow."

"Of course you did." He smiled at me, then turned to the sink and took up my scrubbing job. "Is he going to be all right?"

"It looks like it," I said.

"You didn't know Win was going to see Al, did you?" Penelope asked.

"No, but I had a feeling I wanted to see him. Needed to see him."

"Your timing was impeccable." She broke off a piece of scone and popped it into her mouth.

"Has Win told you anything?" I asked Penelope.

"She went on a rant about the need to preserve her family's reputation." She sipped her coffee and sighed, as if she'd needed it. "You know, that girl presents well. But who tries to kill someone so the truth about her ancestors being murderers doesn't come out? I think she has a couple screws loose." She tapped her head.

"She must have been listening when Richard told Al about killing Manny."

"I believe so," Penelope said. "One of the aides saw her near Richard's room while Al was in there but didn't think anything of it. Win was always visiting him."

"This morning Al said he didn't see who hit him, but he smelled coconut." I smoothed the napkin at my place. "Win always smells faintly of it. Can that be used as evidence?"

"Maybe. We also have our video enhancement guy looking at the security footage from the parking lot. Even though it was dark, he can do magic with the software, lightening and sharpening an image."

"Cool. You wanted to see Forrest's diary. I'll go get it." I came back and set it in front of her. "That slip of paper marks where she talks about seeing Kit and Eugene taking Della into the house. This house. The Swift guest cottage."

She wiped off her fingers and pushed back her mug before opening the old book with care. She paged through to my bookmark and read, shaking her head.

"Were you able to get the other diaries from Win yesterday?" I asked. "She didn't know about this passage, I'm sure. But Kit's or Sarah's diaries could have told about what they did."

Penelope shook her head. "She never returned my call. Believe me, we have cause to get them now."

"Will anything happen to Richard? He's a hundred years old and mostly has dementia, but he did confess his crime to Al. Will he be charged?"

"That depends on what's in the other diaries. He might be charged and given a suspended sentence. Nobody's going to send a man like that to prison for a crime he committed when he was a minor. As far as I know, he never committed another infraction. Not one he was arrested for, that is." Penelope closed the book and bit into her scone.

I straightened the salt and pepper shakers in the middle of the table. Tim dried the skillet and put it away, then joined us at the table.

"We'll probably never know if Win was the person lurking around here last night, right?" I asked.

She swallowed. "Unless you have a security camera outside, or if she says she was, no."

"No camera, but it doesn't matter. Nothing happened." I tapped the table. "Win usually rides a bike, but yesterday Orrin told me she'd borrowed his car. If she was driving, she easily could have driven out to Westham Village and then hung around here, as well." She must have driven to the hospital this morning, too. "Oh!" I exclaimed.

"Oh?" Penelope asked.

"When I spoke to Orrin at their home, a new-looking black Prius was in the driveway. I saw one in the hospital parking lot this morning. I recognized it without realizing whose it was."

"So noted," Penelope said. "We'll be checking with hospital security, believe me, and with Westham Village's."

"I wonder if Win's mother knows she's gone off the deep end," Tim murmured.

"If Emily's been helping, you mean?" Penelope took another bite.

"Yes, or trying to stop her and being unable to," Tim said. "We all know how well some young adults listen to their parents."

"Or maybe she was surprised to hear about her daughter attacking Al," I added. "Except . . . yesterday Barlow Swift told me Emily was worried about Win, that she was becoming fanatical, I think was the word he used."

"I'll be interviewing Emily Winslow later today," Penelope said. "For her sake, she'd better not have been aiding and abetting. I have a daughter. I'd say mothers usually know their daughters pretty well. I'll bet Emily at least had a sense of Win's propensities."

"You got Della's purse from Orrin Swift, didn't you?" I asked.

"Yes," she said. "It's another nail in the coffin, so to speak, for Katherine Swift. Orrin showed a lot of guts by bringing it to us. The woman was his relative, after all."

"He seems like a good guy," I said. "It's going to be tough for both of Win's parents, going forward." I felt especially bad for Orrin. Maybe he and Emily had enabled Win's behavior. Or maybe the young woman had acted with murderous intent all on her own. Either way, she was legally an adult and responsible for her own actions. Barlow now had a murderer for an ancestor, too.

"What about Lee Winslow, Emily's brother?" I asked. "Was he the person breaking into stores? Yesterday the bridal shop owner said the police had a suspect in custody."

The detective swallowed a bite of scone. "As a matter of fact, he was. We finally got some decent footage showing it was unmistakably him."

"Was Win assisting him?"

"She was," Penelope said. "He informed on her."

On his own niece. *Wow.*

"What a family," Tim said.

"That's for sure." Penelope gave a nod. "By the way, our printing of your secret closet back there yielded a definite match with Eugene Winslow. The army still had his fingerprints on record."

"That's amazing," Tim said. "Finding something like that after eighty years."

It was amazing.

"Stranger things have happened." Penelope drained her coffee and stood. "Thank you for the refreshment. The scone was excellent." She gazed from me to Tim. "Let me guess. He made them."

"Correct," I said. "We don't need two bakers in the family."

"Aren't you getting married today?" Penelope pulled a watch cap out of her pocket. "You both seem awfully calm for such a big day."

I laughed. "He's always calm. And I've been a little distracted. Which is a good thing."

CHAPTER 58

At three o'clock, Gin and my mom arrived together to help me get ready. I took their coats.

"You ladies look lovely," Tim said.

They did. Gin wore a deep purple tea-length
sheath dress in a shimmery fabric. Mom had found a
pale yellow dress with a swirly skirt that fell below the
knees. It came with a short lace sweater in the same
color. The shade was perfect with her pale skin. I wasn't
lovely, in my glasses and my sweats, but I was clean.
My turn would come soon enough.

"Off with you, now," Mom said to Tim.

He was going to Gin's to get dressed with Eli.

"Yes, ma'am." He lifted the garment bag holding
his wedding clothes in one hand and his new dress
shoes in the other.

I reached up to kiss him. "See you at the church."

"Mmm. I can't wait."

The door clicked shut behind him.

"First things first." Gin lifted a tote bag. "Come with me."

We followed her to the kitchen, where she drew out a bottle of chilled rosé. "Zane's finest."

"But firster, and yes, I know that isn't a word." I picked up the gifts I'd gotten them, which I'd set out on the kitchen table. "These are the tiniest of tokens of my thanks." I handed each of them a box.

Gin unwrapped hers and read the inscription aloud. "'Team Bride Rocks!' I love it, Mac."

I'd had the store add today's date below that. "It'll keep your cold wine cold, too."

"You didn't need to give us a gift, honey," Mom said. "But thank you. I love mine, too. And look, they're sippy cups as well."

"I already washed them out. You don't have to use the lid, of course." I grabbed mine off the shelf. "And I have a matching one. Now you can pour," I told Gin.

Mom lifted hers when it was filled. "To the loveliest of blushing brides."

"I wasn't blushing before, but I am now." I clinked my tumbler with each of theirs. "I sure am lucky to have both of you."

"We love you," Gin said. "Sounds like Al Cabral was awfully lucky to have you this morning."

"I'm so glad I got there in time."

As Tim had this morning, Mom looked puzzled. I had told the group what had transpired but not my parents.

"Why was Al lucky?" Mom sipped the wine. "My, this is good."

I tasted it and agreed, then briefly explained

about Win, Al, and a nearly fatal pillow. "Don't worry, Win is in jail."

"That old scoundrel Ruhlen." Mom shook her head. "Never liked the man. I'm not surprised he was a teenage murderer."

"What a crew of entitled young people they all were," Gin said.

"That sense seems to have persisted over several generations to Win," I said. "It must be in their family lore or something."

"All right, ladies," Gin said. "Time to get to work."

We three trooped up the stairs, sippy cups—and bottle—in hand. I pulled off my sweatshirt and leggings and put on a light robe, so nothing would get messed after my makeup and hair were done.

"Hang on," I said. "Let me put my contacts in." I popped into the bathroom. It would be a disaster to push apart my eyelids after eye makeup went on.

Gin opened a fat makeup bag. I sat in the desk chair and took one more swallow of wine. I closed my eyes. And then opened them.

"Mom, I forgot to ask about Cokey. How is she today?"

"She's raring to go." Mom sat on the small, upholstered chair in the corner, her hands curled around her glass. "But I told her quite firmly she is not to skip up the aisle."

"I'm so glad she's feeling well enough," I said. "I would hate for her to miss the ceremony."

"Close your eyes," Gin ordered.

I closed them. It was actually happening. I was getting married to the sweetest, smartest, most handsome man I had ever met. I had friends, I had family,

I had a thriving business. How could one woman get so lucky?

An hour later, I was transformed into a bride. Mom brought in the full-length mirror from the bedroom. Gin pinned the headpiece on my hair, which she had somehow styled to look fancier than usual. Subtle makeup enhanced my eyes and cheekbones and lips without looking overdone. I handed her Abo Reba's necklace.

"You two somehow forgot to remind me about those four things. You know, the—"

Gin interrupted, "Old, new, borrowed, blue?" She fastened the chain around my neck.

"Yes."

"We didn't forget. Why do you think I loaned you those earrings?" Gin asked.

"And I was well aware Reba was going to give you the lapis necklace, honey," Mom added.

"I should have known everything was taken care of." I should have. "You two have been on top of every single detail. Thank you." I stood, shedding the robe, and stepped carefully into the dress Mom held out, then rotated so she could fasten it up to the vee in the back.

Facing the mirror, I smoothed the satin over my hips once again. Had I ever looked so good in my life? I didn't think so. I pictured Tim seeing me like this, as he would in an hour. I'd bet the house he would tear up. He was sentimental enough for both of us, and I loved that part of him.

"Perfection," Gin said.

"You know, honey, I wasn't sure you were ever going to find someone," Mom said, her eyes shining.

"You and me both, Mom." Another person might think that was a horrible thing to say to a daughter on her wedding day. I didn't. I knew it came from my mom's love. Besides, it was true. I hadn't been sure I would ever find someone, either—until I did.

"And now look at you, a happy woman and a beautiful bride," Mom added.

I studied my reflection. I thought about the bride who had been entombed downstairs for so many years. *This is for you, Della.*

CHAPTER 59

"May life amaze you and bring you great joy together," Pa ended in his deep, sonorant voice.

He paused, gazing out beyond Tim and me at the friends and family gathered. Greta's reading had been lovely and meaningful. I had made it through my vows—including *"I want to spend my life with you, no matter what happens"*—and Tim had, too, although he'd choked up a little during his and had to swipe a tear from his eye. He was model-handsome in his new gray suit and violet silk tie. Someone had pulled his hair into a French braid, which looked perfectly masculine on Tim. And our left hands now sported matching gold bands, with mine snuggled against my engagement ring.

Pa focused on us again. "We have all witnessed and affirmed your union of love. And now, by the power vested in me by the Commonwealth of Massachusetts, I pronounce you married. You may seal your vows with a kiss."

We held that kiss for possibly a few seconds longer than we should have. We broke apart and clasped hands, turning to face our dearest ones.

"Yay!" Cokey cried out, followed by the sound of tiny hands clapping.

Everybody stood and joined in, laughing and clapping, with a few adult shouts of, "Yay!" Mom, sitting in the front pew with Reba, Derrick, and Cokey, wiped her eyes with a handkerchief. On the other side, Tim's father did the same. Sentimentality apparently ran deep in the Brunelle men.

Gin handed me my bouquet. "You were perfect," she whispered.

"Thank you," I mouthed in return.

Cokey now stood on the pew, holding her purple cast–clad forearm with the other arm. I shot her a thumbs-up, which she returned with her biggest smile. Reba stood next to her, also beaming, but with her hand clasping her great-granddaughter's sash to make sure she didn't fall off the bench.

"Shall we, dear wife?" Tim murmured.

"We shall, darling husband." I hooked my arm through his, and we walked slowly down the aisle. Amid friends of my parents and other guests, the entire rest of the Cozy Capers book group sat together, minus Tulia, who hadn't made it back from her trip because of weather delays.

I did a little double take when I saw Detective Lincoln Haskins sitting alone in the back row. I'd invited him but hadn't ever gotten a response. He must have returned from his vacation or wherever he'd been. I was glad he'd made it.

He smiled and lifted his chin. Tim and I stepped into the foyer, where the caterer had set up drinks. After an hour, everyone would transfer to the reception hall in the Westham Hotel, a lovely space a few miles away, for dinner and dancing and ringing in the new year. We'd hired a bus to transport people to the church and then to the hotel, if they wished. Tim and I would stay in the bridal suite at the Westham for the night.

I stood with Tim—with my husband—as people started filing in from the sanctuary. Gin and Eli and our families first, and then everyone. I'd decided to postpone a cranberry-based cocktail until I was finished hugging people. A spilled splash of pink on this dress would not be a pretty sight. And the heck with Namaste hands. I planned to hug every single person there.

Greta gave me a strong embrace. "Welcome to our family, Mac."

"Thank you, Greta. And likewise."

Cokey rushed me, wrapping her uncasted arm around my legs. "Titi Mac, how did I do?"

I squatted to get to her level. "You were perfect, Cokester." I'd watched as she'd preceded Gin up the aisle with the basket slung over her cast, carefully strewing rose petals right and left.

"I didn't skip because Abo Astra told me not to," she lisped.

"Always do what Abo Astra tells you."

Reba came next. She stood on the tiptoes of her sparkly purple sneakers and held up her arms to Tim. He leaned way down to embrace her.

"You take care of our girl now," she told him.

"You know I will, Abo Ree." He cast me a mock frown. "If she'll let me."

Reba guffawed. "That's our Mac. Come on, Coquille, let's get you a Shirley Temple."

Lincoln hung back until everyone else had greeted us. "Many congratulations to both of you." He held out his big hand first to Tim and then to me.

The detective and I had gotten friendly but hadn't moved on to a hugging basis.

"Thank you, Lincoln," I said. "You're back from your vacation?"

"Yes."

"Mac, I'm going to go introduce my dad to someone." Tim squeezed my hand and turned away.

"Johnson briefed me on your week." Lincoln's expression became serious behind his dark-rimmed glasses as he gazed down at me. "Good work, Mac."

"Tim and I found poor Della's remains. She never got to have all this." I gestured around the room. "I felt I had to find out what happened."

"You did, and stayed safe in the bargain." He smiled again.

"You'll join us for a drink and the reception, I hope."

"I'm afraid I can't. But I didn't want to miss the most important part."

"Thank you so much for coming. It means a lot to me." I threw caution to the wind and held out my arms for a hug.

He looked surprised, but leaned over for the briefest of embraces, carefully leaving space between our bodies. "Take care, and have a good party." He headed for the door.

Zane walked up carrying two cocktails. "You look like a bride in need of a drink."

"I thought you'd never ask. Thanks, Zane." I sipped. That addition of Grenadine made all the difference to the drink.

Stephen materialized at Zane's side, followed by Gin, Norland, and Flo.

"That was Lincoln, wasn't it?" Flo pointed her chin at the door.

"Yes," I said. "He apparently just got back and didn't want to miss the wedding, but he said he can't stay for the rest of the festivities."

"Had he heard about the murders and about Win?" Norland asked.

"He had." I sipped more of the drink. "He actually said, 'Good work' to me. It was good work by the whole group, really."

Gin pointed at me. "But you're the sleuth-in-chief."

I laughed. "Whatever."

"I loved that you managed to work baked goods into your wedding vows," Zane said. "Way to go."

"Thanks." I let out a happy breath. "A little levity seemed like the way to go."

"I don't suppose you've gotten any more information from Penelope Johnson about the other diaries?" Flo asked.

"No." I frowned. "I don't even know where my phone is. Gin?"

"It's safe with your stuff, Mac," she said. "Don't worry."

"Well," Flo began, "I found a diary of Katherine Swift's that the library owns. I had no idea we had it.

It's not catalogued. But I was going through our archive room looking for something else this afternoon, and there it was."

Kit's. "From winter, 1940?" I asked.

"Yep." Flo bobbed her head.

"That's a crazy coincidence," Gin murmured.

"I know," Flo said. "If it took place in a book, we would never believe it. But coincidences do happen. Anyway, Kit doesn't talk about her plans, but on March fourth she wrote a stunning entry. '*It's done. E and I duped her. We built the wall. I won't ever have to see DR again.*' Or something to that effect," Flo added.

"That's incredible," I said.

"Incredibly stupid," Gin added.

"She actually put it in writing." Zane looked sorrowful. "I suppose she didn't worry about someone finding it."

"She should have," Stephen chimed in.

"You'll give the diary to Penelope, right, Flo?" I asked.

"I already dropped it off at the station for her attention."

"Good." The words *We built the wall* kept echoing in my head. A wall around a living would-be bride. A tomb for Della.

"Hey, Mac," Gin said. "Cheer up. It's the end of the chapter. You have a wedding to celebrate."

Zane lifted his glass. "Here's to Mac and Tim!"

The rest of them followed suit. Tim caught my eye from across the room and blew me a kiss. I smiled at him and turned back to my friends, lifting my own glass.

"And to Della and Manny." I gazed at the faces of these friends, who always had my back.

"To Della and Manny," Gin murmured as the others echoed her.

"Thank you, dear ones." I sipped and lifted my glass again. "Here's to future crimes staying strictly on the page."

Recipes

Blueberry Scones

Tim makes tasty blueberry scones for the wedding morning family breakfast.

Ingredients

2 cups all-purpose flour (spooned and leveled), plus more for hands and work surface
½ cup granulated sugar
2½ teaspoons baking powder
1 teaspoon ground cinnamon
½ teaspoon salt
½ cup (1 stick) cold butter
½ cup sour cream
1 large egg
1½ teaspoons pure vanilla extract
1 heaping cup fresh or frozen blueberries (do not thaw)
2 tablespoons whole milk, as needed
Coarse sugar

Directions

Line a dinner plate with parchment paper.

Whisk flour, sugar, baking powder, cinnamon, and salt together in a food processor. Cut the butter into inch cubes. Add it to the food processor and pulse until the mixture comes together in pea-sized crumbs. Place in the refrigerator or freezer as you mix the wet ingredients together.

Whisk sour cream, egg, and vanilla extract together in a small bowl. Drizzle into chilled mixture in food processor and mix for only a few seconds until it starts to clump.

Turn onto a floured counter and, with floured hands, mix in the blueberries, forming a ball. Dough will be sticky. If it's too sticky, add a little more flour. If it seems too dry, add 1–2 tablespoons milk. Transfer to the lined dinner plate and press into an 8-inch disk.

Refrigerate for at least 15 minutes.

Preheat oven to 400°F.

Transfer disk and parchment paper to a baking sheet. With a sharp knife or bench scraper, cut into 8 wedges. Arrange chilled scones two inches apart. Brush with milk and sprinkle with coarse sugar (or regular granulated if you don't have coarse).

Bake for 22–25 minutes or until golden brown around the edges and lightly browned on top. Remove from the oven and cool for a few minutes.

Serve hot or at room temperature.

Honey-Spice Hanukkah Cookies

Norland and his grandson bake Hanukkah cookies for Zane and Stephen's party.

Ingredients
½ cup (1 stick) butter, softened
½ cup firmly packed brown sugar
½ cup honey
1 egg
2½ cups unbleached flour
2 teaspoons dry ginger
1 teaspoon baking soda
1 teaspoon cinnamon
1 teaspoon nutmeg
½ teaspoon salt
¼ teaspoon ground cloves

Directions
In a large mixing bowl, cream butter and brown sugar until well combined, and then beat in honey and egg. In a small bowl, combine flour, ginger, baking soda, cinnamon, nutmeg, salt, and cloves; add to honey mixture. Beat on low speed until well blended. Cover dough and refrigerate at least 1 hour. Line cookie sheets with parchment paper and set aside.

Working with ¼ of the dough at a time, roll out on a lightly floured surface to ¼-inch thickness. Cut into desired shapes, or for a non-holiday theme, use a round cookie cutter. Using a spatula, place on prepared cookie sheets 1 inch apart. Reroll and cut scraps. Bake in a preheated 350° F oven for 7 minutes, or until done. Transfer to wire racks to cool.

Pasta with Lobster

The caterer makes this easy and delicious dish for Mac and Tim's wedding dinner.

Ingredients
2 cups cooked lobster meat
1 pound sturdy pasta, like rotini or farfalle
4 tablespoons olive oil
½ small onion, finely diced
4 garlic cloves, minced
½ teaspoon red pepper flakes
1 cup halved mixed gold and red cherry tomatoes
½ cup pasta water
Salt and pepper
½ cup basil leaves, slivered
Parmesan cheese

Directions
Set a large pot of salted water to boil. Add pasta.

Pour olive oil in a wide skillet over medium-high heat. Add onion and cook for 1 minute, without browning. Add garlic and red pepper and cook for 1 minute. Add tomatoes and season generously with salt and pepper. Add lobster meat, stir to coat, cook 1 minute, then turn off heat and cover until pasta is ready.

When pasta is al dente, add ½ cup of the water to the skillet. Drain pasta, add to skillet, add basil, and season with salt and pepper. Toss well and transfer to a warmed wide bowl or platter.

Serve immediately with freshly grated Parmesan cheese and a green salad.

New Year's Eve Wedding Cocktail

Mac and her grandmother put the finishing touch on the special cocktail served just after the wedding.

Ingredients
For one drink:
2 ounces cranberry juice
2 ounces bourbon
1 teaspoon fresh lime juice
1 ounce Grand Marnier
Splash of Grenadine syrup
Mint leaves

Directions
Shake all ingredients except mint over ice and serve garnished with a sprig of mint.

Cape Verdean Cachupa

Pa makes his version of the Cape Verdean national dish for the Friday night welcome dinner.

Ingredients

2 tablespoons apple cider vinegar
6 cloves garlic, minced, divided
1 teaspoon smoked paprika
1 teaspoon salt
½ teaspoon black pepper
1 pound pork roast, cut into two-inch chunks
1 tablespoon olive oil
1 onion, finely chopped
1 can (14-ounce) tomatoes, with juice
2 cups chicken stock
1 small green cabbage (about 1 pound), 1 cored
    and quartered
1 sweet potato, peeled and cut into chunks (about
    1 inch/2.5 cm)
1 can (15-ounce) hominy, drained
1 can (15-ounce) red kidney beans, drained
1 8-ounce dry-cured chorizo sausage, thinly sliced

Directions

The night before, mix vinegar, two cloves minced garlic, paprika, salt, and pepper in a bowl. Add pork. Mix, cover, and refrigerate.

The day you plan to serve the meal, preheat oven to 325°F (160°C).

In a Dutch oven, heat oil over medium heat. Add onion and cook, stirring, until softened, about 3 minutes. Add pork and sauté until browned. Add garlic and cook, stirring, for 1 minute. Add tomatoes with juice and stock and bring to a boil. Reduce heat and simmer for 30 minutes.

Stir in cabbage, sweet potato, hominy, kidney beans, and chorizo. Cover and transfer to preheated oven. Stir after half an hour.

Bake until pork and vegetables are tender, about an hour.

Remove from oven. Let pan stand, covered, at room temperature for about 30 minutes before serving.

Serve with crusty bread and a green salad.

Visit us online at
KensingtonBooks.com
to read more from your favorite authors,
see books by series, view reading
group guides, and more!

BOOK   CLUB

BETWEEN THE CHAPTERS

Visit us online for sneak peeks, exclusive
giveaways, special discounts, author content,
and engaging discussions with your fellow readers.

Betweenthechapters.net

Sign up for our newsletters and be th
to get exciting news and announcem
your favorite authors!
Kensingtonbooks.com/newslett